# Two Loves

# Two Loves

## Siân James

THOMAS
DUNNE
BOOKS

ST. MARTIN'S PRESS
NEW YORK

THOMAS DUNNE BOOKS.
An imprint of St. Martin's Press.

ISBN 0-312-20037-4

First published in Great Britain by Judy Piatkus (Publishers) Ltd

First U.S. Edition: December 1999

10  9  8  7  6  5  4  3  2  1

# Chapter One

Ingrid Walsh sat on a sofa staring at the fire. The sofa was sumptuously covered with antique shawls and hand-painted cushions, but wasn't at all comfortable. There was another sofa back to back with it, facing some work in progress and a table holding paints and brushes and various plastic containers. Her hostess sat comfortable and relaxed on a dark blue modern-looking chair.

'How did you meet him?' Ingrid asked. 'Your late husband?'

'I contacted him when I was in my last year at Brighton Art College. I'd been very impressed by his poem, *Seagull.* Do you know it? The girl staring at the seagull and the poet staring at the girl. That's the painting I did of it.'

Ingrid looked up at where Rosamund Gilchrist was pointing; a large canvas, two figures in grey on a greenish-grey background, grey-whites, egg-shell whites, whites with sunshine behind, no seagull visible, but certainly wing-curves and clamour; a feel of sea and wind.

'Did he like it?' she asked.

Rosamund seemed non-committal. 'Do you?'

'Very much. It seems incredibly mature for a student's work. How old were you?'

'Twenty-one, I suppose. Almost twenty-two. What are you writing?'

'Only what you've just told me. If you like I'll show you the article before it's published.'

'Really? No one else has ever done that.'

'You've had a bad time from journalists?'

'No, not really. The only things I've ever sold have been as a result of their soppy articles – *Poet's muse finds consolation in her painting.*'

They smiled at each other.

'Did you illustrate any other of his poems?'

'No. For a while I didn't paint at all.'

'Simply a poet's muse?'

'Simply an art teacher. I needed to earn a living.'

'Where did you teach?'

'Liverpool. St Bartholomew's Comprehensive in Toxteth.'

For a moment they were both struck by visions of that different world. Here, the wide green valley lay silent beneath them, the only sounds the bleating of sheep and lambs in the distance.

'How long had Mr Gilchrist lived here?'

'He bought it in the late Sixties. It was once the village school, of course. It closed during some reorganisation; there were only eleven pupils here in the last few years – too few to be viable, I suppose. He had several visits from the last headmistress when he first came. She's dead now. I never met her. Her name was Dorothy Mason. She used to bring him home-made wine.'

'It's made a wonderful studio.'

'Yes. I feel guilty having it all to myself. I've advertised – had one or two artists come to view, but they felt it was too remote.'

'You must feel that too, don't you? From time to time?'

'Not really. We get bad weather up here, but I've got a van with four-wheel drive; I can generally get about.'

'Isn't it very lonely for your son?'

'He has friends living quite near. My mother's moved to one of the new houses in the village, so he stays with her occasionally. I suppose he will start complaining, but he hasn't yet. He's only nine.'

'Will he go away to school?'

'No, I'd be lonely without him . . . I expect I'll have to drive him into town on a Saturday night when he's a bit older, but I'm sure it won't be too much of a problem.'

Ingrid looked at the drawings of Rosamund's son which were pinned up haphazardly on the wall between the piano

2

and the fireplace, none of them framed. 'Do you sell any of these?' she asked, surprising herself by the question, realising that she'd very much like to own one.

'No, I never have. This part of the studio is my sitting room. These are really my private things.'

'Doesn't it get very cold here in the winter?'

'Do you mean inside the house?'

'Yes.'

'Not particularly. Anthony had two central-heating systems put in, oil and calor gas – he wasn't very robust. I don't usually bother with the log fire, that's just because you were coming.'

'It looks lovely. All this was done before you moved in?'

'Years before. It's nice, isn't it? Those cupboards are the original ones, where all the schoolbooks were kept. The blackboard would have been where the piano is now. There was a piano here, but over on that wall. I wish he'd bought it. This one seems too new.'

'Do you play?'

'Not well. An old school piano would suit my playing.'

Ingrid couldn't think what else to ask. Her article was meant to be on Rosamund Gilchrist's paintings, but it was Rosamund herself who interested her. She'd speculated about her for years. All Anthony Gilchrist's obituaries had ended with two sentences summing up his third marriage. '*He leaves a wife and six month-old son. He was seventy-five.*'

She looked again at Rosamund. He had been seventy-five. Well, it happened. Artists were more attractive and perhaps more virile than ordinary men – look at Picasso, look at Casals. Anthony Gilchrist looked a pretty shrivelled-up specimen, though, tall and dignified, but stern. She'd often watched him on television, but never with a flicker of sexual interest. What had Rosamund seen in him? A good studio, perhaps, and an escape from teaching.

'Listen,' she said, 'I've got something to tell you. I've come here on false pretences. I do intend to write an article on your paintings, I think they're really good, but there is something else.'

'I thought there might be,' Rosamund said gently. 'No one's

been interested in my work since Anthony's death. So what are you after?'

Ingrid tensed. 'I'm not *after* anything. I've just got something to tell you. My boyfriend works for one of the Sundays. And they've been offered a series of your late husband's poems and letters.'

There was only a second's delay. 'Would that be from Erica Underhill?'

'That's right. You know her?'

'I know about her. I've never met her.'

'They're fairly . . . well, pornographic apparently. I thought you should know about them.'

'Why?'

'Simply so that . . . I mean, I simply wanted you to have time to prepare for the shock. It's bound to come as rather a shock, isn't it? At least now you'll have time to consider what to do about them. Perhaps you should get in touch with your solicitor or something. I didn't want you to get hurt.'

Rosamund stared at the fire and Ingrid studied the drawings of Rosamund's son and started to count them. There were twenty-two.

Rosamund got to her feet. 'Did your boyfriend know you intended to warn me about the poems?'

'No.' Ingrid started to count the drawings again.

'You thought they'd shock me? Well, it was very good of you to warn me about them. That's all I can think of to say. And now you really needn't do anything about my paintings. You've done your good deed.'

Ingrid stood up and faced her. 'I've been commissioned by *Country Homes* to write a four thousand-word article about them with five or six photographs. I'd like to examine them now. Will you tell me something about them, please?'

'Of course.'

They walked to the far end of the long room. 'Well, that's *Seagull* hung up there in the place of honour. I've already told you about that. I didn't paint another for three or four years. Not until I finished teaching and came to live here. The others are mostly of these hills and this valley.'

'This is lovely, this little one. Wonderful sky, wonderful

colours. How can I possibly describe this? "Cool greens, warm purple and gold, the gentle hills of summer," ' Ingrid wrote in her small red notebook.

'I have read the poems, you know.'

'You have? That's a relief. I needn't have mentioned it then. But I'm glad I did.'

'So am I. He was obsessed by Erica Underhill for several years, but not to the extent that he'd send her the only copies.'

'Where are yours?'

'In the bank. He wanted them to stay there for twenty years after his death. Then I'm to release them for publication.'

'Why the delay? Did he tell you?'

'His second wife was still alive and I suppose he didn't want to upset her. I suppose he felt he'd given her enough grief.'

'Is she still alive?'

'As far as I know. Yes, I'm sure she is or I'd have heard.'

'There's a son, too?'

'Yes. Alex Gilchrist. Also his wife, Selena, and two children. Teenagers now, I should think.'

'Has his son read the poems?'

'I shouldn't think so. They weren't very close. But I don't know.'

They moved towards another series of small paintings. 'My Cubist period,' Rosamund said. 'Mercifully short. You're welcome to note the influence of Cézanne. This one should be called, *After Cézanne. A Long Way After.*'

'It's good. Don't knock it. People take you at your own valuation . . . Do you ever come up to London?'

'No. Haven't been for three or four years.'

'Do you have a boyfriend?'

'No. If you'd asked me a week or so ago, I might have said yes.'

'What happened? Your secrets are safe with me.'

'I thought you were a journalist. Oh, the usual thing. His wife found out . . . This one's called *Anthony's Gate.* Not even up to my usual mediocre standard, but I thought someone might buy it because of the association.'

'Is that where he proposed to you?'

'No. Where I sometimes posed for him.'

'Did he paint?'

'No. Just looked.'

'Poet's muse. Botticelli's *Venus*.'

'Botticelli? That's a nice change. Pre-Raphaelite is the usual description.'

'Not at all. Those heavy women; all eyes and goitres. Not you at all . . . So, you used to take your clothes off and sit on this gate?'

'Or astride it. You're not writing that down, are you?'

'Definitely not. And don't give anyone else that sort of detail, please, or you'll have a most unsuitable mob of journalists after you. "The five-bar gate leading to a sheep-run with the drop of the valley behind it, was one of her late husband's favourite views and called *Anthony's Gate* in his honour." Right?'

'Right. And these are the most recent. All painted in the last twelve months.'

'These are different again, aren't they? Much darker. This one is almost a nightmare scene, isn't it? "A wickedly dark sky, a peeping moon, the gate swinging on its hinges." Is it the same gate?'

'Yes, the same gate. But I can't comment, really. I seem to be seeing the world differently now, that's all . . . You've written all that down, haven't you? I didn't mean you to.'

'You were careful not to reveal much. "I seem to be seeing the world differently now," simply implies that you're older. Or at least less young.'

'And the world does seem to be growing darker.'

'This one is very impressive. "The valley has a claustrophobic air; the trees are human arms, waving for release." How do you feel you've developed?'

'I don't know what's happened or why. I look at the landscape much more than I used to. And I suppose one gets to a point where one sees one's own life reflected in it. I don't know. I don't have any theories about anything.'

'Tell me something about your life since your husband's death.'

'Would you like to come for a walk – as far as the head of the valley? We could talk as we go. I can lend you some boots.'

6

'That would be great. Cheers.'

Rosamund led Ingrid into the kitchen which, along with an adjoining bathroom, had been converted from the second, smaller schoolroom. It looked like a normal country kitchen; an Aga, a pine table, dresser. Unlike the studio which was twenty feet high, the kitchen had a low ceiling, the open staircase behind the range leading to three bedrooms created from the roof space.

'I'm sorry I haven't offered you any tea. We'll have tea and cake when we get back.'

They went through the kitchen to a long, low cloakroom.

'This was the original school cloakroom. I often wish Anthony had left the partitions and the little pegs. Sometimes I can almost smell wet coats and hats and boxes of plimsolls. Isn't this a pretty window? Almost like a church window. If naughty children were sent out here they'd at least have a lovely view. The lavatories were over there by the rowan tree. Anthony had them taken down because they obscured the view. The children used to say, "Please can I go across the yard?" when they wanted to go to the lavatory.'

The boots Rosamund found for Ingrid were much too big for her, but she fetched her a pair of thick hand-knitted winter socks to fit inside them.

We look a strange pair, Ingrid thought as they started out. Dirty wellingtons didn't look too out of place with Rosamund's floral dress and beige cardigan; if she'd been carrying an ancient-looking pail, she'd have passed as a milkmaid in a Laura Ashley catalogue. But she, in a long-sleeved black dress, tight-skirted with side vents, and round black-framed glasses, looked ridiculous in her over-sized green boots.

For a time they didn't talk at all, Ingrid finding it more and more difficult to keep up with Rosamund who had a large stride and was used to hill country. Ingrid did very little walking.

'Here we are,' Rosamund said, slowing down at last. 'This is the highest point and the best view. I often paint from here. Shall we cross the stile and go down?'

'No. I'm out of condition; tired already. I'm going to sit here

7

for a moment. This is like looking at another of your paintings. But even more representational, I suppose.'

'I can't get away from this damned landscape. It's here, it's on my doorstep, so I feel I must try to get to grips with it, all its moods and rhythms.'

'"I feel I must get to grips with it, all its moods and rhythms",' Ingrid repeated, a hint of mockery in her voice.

'It may sound pretentious, but that's what I feel. Most of the time anyway.'

'What about the rest of the time?'

'I'd like to stop messing about and have more children. Two more at least.'

'Any chance?'

'Who knows. A handsome stranger may turn up some day.'

'What's your son called?'

'Joss. Have you got any children?'

'No. I don't think I want any. Lots of my friends, all career girls, got broody when they reached thirty, but I haven't. And I'm thirty-five now.'

'So am I. I thought you were about my age.'

'Thirty-five last month,' Ingrid said.

'And me! What date?'

'The third.'

'Oh, I'm on the nineteenth. I thought we might be twins.'

They laughed together like schoolchildren. What's your favourite colour? What's your lucky number? Can I be your best friend? was in both their minds; the questions eight-year-olds ask in order to get to know each other – and themselves. They were both silent for a few moments.

'Well, what else do you want to know?' Rosamund asked at last.

'That sounds as though you want to get rid of me.'

'Not at all. Joss is going to my mother's after school today to give us more time together.'

'What more do you want to tell me? I've got pretty well enough for my article now. I'll let you have a look at it before I send it in.'

'Why don't you bring it here and stay for the weekend?'

'Lovely idea. But . . .'

'You have better things to do.'

'No. I'd love to come again sometime. But not next weekend. I'm flattered to be asked, though. Thank you.'

'You could bring your boyfriend with you, if you'd like to.'

'No, I'd rather come on my own. Soon . . . Listen, there's a bit more than I've told you. About those letters, I mean.'

Rosamund glanced at her, but made no response.

'Ben's paper didn't feel they could publish either the poems or the letters as they stand. They're a respectable paper and it's not the sort of thing they do.'

'So she went to the other sort?'

'No. They suggested that to get the sort of money she obviously felt she should be entitled to, she'd have to get her autobiography published, which could, of course, include the poems and letters. Following that, the paper could pay her for certain extracts from the book.'

'That seems a pretty roundabout way of doing things.'

'It's the way it's done, apparently. And the thing is, Ben, as the one who first answered the phone to her, or at least the first one to take her seriously, was the person she chose to ghost her autobiography for her.'

'I see. But, no, I don't quite see what it's got to do with me.'

'It's just that I don't want to keep anything from you.'

They walked on in silence for a minute or two. 'I don't know,' Rosamund said, then, 'but I find it difficult to believe that you haven't any ulterior motive in all this.'

'Well it would help Ben if he had your good will; I suppose I'm aware of that.'

'Why? I've never even met Erica Underhill. It all happened thirty years before I got to know Anthony. I could be of no help.'

'But you must still have some of his private papers and so on.'

'Did he ask you to sound me out on all this?'

'No. It was he who suggested I should try to get a commission to write about you, but I think that was simply for my sake. Because I've been short of work lately. I don't for one minute believe he'd think me capable of being much help to him.'

'He sounds a real bighead,' Rosamund said. 'Let's go home and have some tea.'

'The thing is, you've always intrigued me,' Ingrid said, after they'd walked another few yards. 'Ever since reading your late husband's obituaries – with the inevitable photograph of the two of you with your baby son. I knew we were about the same age and I was extremely curious about you. I wanted to get in touch with you then, but I couldn't think of any excuse – I wasn't even a journalist at that time. I was obsessed by you for months, and when all this came up, I could hardly believe it and couldn't bear the thought of you being hurt by the letters.'

'And it was simply a coincidence? Your boyfriend getting involved with Erica Underhill?'

'Absolutely. He works in the newspaper's features department and by chance her call was put through to him. When he told me about it a few days later I was able to tell him something about you; that you were an artist, and so on. And that you were still young, only about my age.'

'I can't see why you were so struck by that. Lots of girls marry much older men.'

'Not these days. Not unless they're multi-millionaires, anyway. You can't have been in love with him . . . Oh, I'm sorry!'

'That's all right.'

'But I mean, you were twenty-four, twenty-five or something when you got married and he was over seventy. You were an art student when I was at University. How could you have given it all up? I mean, going to gigs and parties, trying out men, all that tremendous . . . *fun*?'

Ingrid's voice faltered. Rosamund was striding ahead; she wondered if she was even listening to her.

Was there a definite reason, Rosamund asked herself. There was certainly a man I was madly in love with in my first year. And when it didn't come to anything, I lost my confidence, I think, what little confidence I had. I suppose I really floundered after that, afraid of any commitment. And that was it really. No, I didn't have much fun.

'I'm sorry,' she said, slowing her steps. 'You asked how I could have given it all up. I'm not sure I ever had very much to give up.'

'But why?' Ingrid asked, almost aggressively. 'You're very attractive. You seem very normal. I mean, what was the matter with you? That you opted out at twenty-four? It worries me. I mean, why?'

# Chapter Two

Though Ingrid Walsh had been enthusiastic about her work – the first person for a long time – Rosamund was far from happy after she'd left. Ingrid had seemed to feel she was some sort of freak. Had she really opted out of life? 'How could you have given it all up?' she'd asked, more than once. 'All the excitement; being young and in the centre of things?' Was her life so abnormal, then? Until recently, Rosamund had thought of herself as fairly contented; she had a son whom she adored, a very supportive mother living nearby, a lovely house and almost enough money.

Her painting wasn't much more than a hobby, she'd always realised that, but it gave her a certain amount of satisfaction and enough money for treats – extravagant Christmases and holidays abroad. She exhibited twice a year with a local art society and always sold three or four paintings.

It was true she didn't have much of a social life; she was invited to certain functions, the occasional party, but had never enjoyed standing about with a drink and a plate of indigestible food, making small-talk. And none of the men who'd shown any interest in her had seemed worth pursuing. A few years ago she'd met a young doctor at a charity ball; he'd persevered in his attentions for a while, but they had little in common. Going out with him often seemed rather an effort even though her mother was always ready to babysit, and after a few months' desultory courtship he'd stopped ringing her and later phoned to say he'd got engaged to a nurse at the local hospital. She'd run into them soon afterwards. His fiancée looked about eighteen, was very glamorous and had succeeded in bringing him to life as she herself had never been able to do.

Rosamund was slightly peeved at being supplanted, but only her mother was really disappointed: 'He was so fond of you, dear.'

'Joss didn't like him,' Rosamund had said firmly. 'He had no rapport with children, so it wouldn't have done, would it?'

Joss adored Thomas, not that that made any odds, because he wasn't available; less so now than ever.

Rosamund sighed. Thomas's son, Harry, had been Joss's best friend since they were in nursery school together, so of course she and Thomas had been thrown together for years; he was always around, returning Joss from their house in the village or fetching Harry from the schoolhouse. They were comfortable together, liked each other, got on well, and three years ago had become lovers. Neither of them had planned it, but after it happened, it had seemed natural, almost inevitable.

She sighed again. He was also very nice-looking. She wished that didn't make as much difference to her as it did; it seemed the trait of a very superficial person.

Thomas's wife, Eliza, was a career woman who seemed to have little time for him; that's why Rosamund didn't feel as guilty about their relationship as she otherwise would. Occasionally she fantasised about his leaving Eliza and coming to live with her and Joss, but knew it was impossible because he was a devoted father – with three sons of his own – and a dutiful husband. He was husband material, warm and loving rather than exciting. Whenever they were able to snatch an hour together, she felt, not dazed by love, but comforted, more reconciled to life, more completely human.

It had taken her some months to realise that it was much easier for her than for him; he was the one torn between two women, two lives. She started noticing the deep frown lines between his eyes when he got out of her bed and the way he held his body as he got dressed, his elbow tight in against his ribs as though deeply uneasy by what he was involved in. He was a nicer person than she was.

And then the previous year, Eliza had become pregnant again. Rosamund was surprised and rather shocked when

14

Thomas broke the news to her; she'd somehow assumed that they didn't have sex together, though Thomas had never said so. She'd suggested at that point that they should give up their affair, but they hadn't, though their meetings had become more infrequent. And they'd hardly seen each other at all since the baby was born the previous month.

Then just over a week ago, she'd called on Eliza, taking her a present for the baby. She'd felt uncomfortable about going, but thought it might seem strange if she didn't, since they were neighbours and their children friends. Also she was longing to see the new baby.

She didn't know Eliza well, or particularly like her; she seemed to have no time for those she obviously considered lesser mortals. At one time Rosamund had felt slightly aggrieved to be so often asked to pick Harry up from school and to keep an eye on him until his father fetched him at five or five-thirty. Especially since Eliza seemed to assume that she couldn't possibly have anything more important to do, and never phoned to thank her. She'd never bothered to find out what exactly Eliza did as a business consultant, but it was probably very high-powered and certainly well-paid; the family had a large new BMW every year and the children had every conceivable gadget and a roomful of computers, which wouldn't have come from Thomas's salary as science master at the local comprehensive.

'Do you want to come in?' Eliza asked her after opening the door, almost as though she was delivering pamphlets rather than visiting a new baby.

'Please. If it's convenient, I'd love to see him. I've brought him a little sweater. I'm sure he's got dozens, but this one was so pretty. Joss thinks he's wonderful. What are you calling him?'

'We haven't decided yet.'

'May I see him? I hope he's not asleep.'

Eliza looked at her wearily and pointed to a chair. 'Sit down, won't you. Look, I don't feel like making small-talk, but now that you're here, I'd just like to ask you to lay off my husband. All right?'

'To lay off your husband,' Rosamund repeated, shocked to the bone by Eliza's attack. 'But you've always said . . . I mean,

Thomas has always said that you didn't mind his spending some time with me occasionally when you're working.' She glared at Eliza. 'And you're always working,' she said, unwilling to take all the blame. 'I mean, Thomas and I are friends. I mean, I don't see him very often, hardly at all these days. I mean . . .'

'I admit to treating him in rather a cavalier fashion, I know I cut him out of my life to some extent, I know I didn't give him enough time and attention, but—'

'A man needs time and attention.'

'All right, I've admitted to being negligent. I don't blame you for trying to take him away from me – he's an attractive man – but now I want him back. It's as simple as that.'

'Have you given up your job, then?'

'Yes.'

'I see.'

'So what's your answer?'

Rosamund took a deep breath. She wasn't prepared to accept Eliza as the wronged wife and herself as the intruder; it was far more complicated than that. 'I'll have to discuss it with Thomas – he's got a part in all this. I don't want to make you a promise I can't keep.' They looked hard at each other. 'Do you love him?' Rosamund asked.

'Of course. He's my husband.'

'That sounds a bit glib. What if I love him, too? I'm certainly very fond of him. I'm always very happy to see him.'

'You're just happy to be fucked. Because you haven't got anyone else.'

Rosamund looked straight into her eyes. 'Have you? I answer your questions. Why don't you answer mine?'

'He's my husband and the father of my children and I want to turn over a new leaf and be a good wife and mother. I want us to be a proper family again. And if you have any decent feelings you won't stand in our way.'

'Does that mean you love him? That's what I want to know. That's what I asked you.'

'I certainly don't love anyone else. Though I admit to neglecting him, it was never for another man – there's never been another man – it was only for my work.'

16

'And I expect your work will take over again quite soon.'

They were interrupted by a sudden cry from the pram standing outside the French windows, not the first shaky bleat of a new baby on waking, but a sharp wail of pain, a cry to be immediately attended to.

Eliza fetched the baby, put him over her shoulder and patted his back. He grew quiet.

Rosamund was surprised again at how small new babies were. She wasn't able to see his face; Eliza seemed determined to keep his back to her, but the little body cocooned in its white cotton blanket seemed too small to be living a separate life. She suddenly decided that if she was about to give Thomas up, she'd like to be pregnant first. 'I'd love a baby,' she said. And was surprised at how fretful she sounded.

'They're nice little things,' Eliza said, her voice milder.

And then she must have realised how lucky she was, or at least how strong her position, because she took the baby from her shoulder, loosened his shawl and showed him off to Rosamund. His face was red and stern and his hands were little trembling claws. 'Oh, he's beautiful,' Rosamund murmured, her voice hushed as though in a church.

She hadn't expected Eliza to breast-feed in front of her, especially as her breasts were rather slack and tired-looking, white with greyish veins. It made her look weak and vulnerable instead of sophisticated and powerful. Rosamund felt pains in her own breasts, almost as sharp as when Joss was newly born. 'I'd really like a baby,' she said again.

'Well, you certainly can't have Thomas's; that would be most unfair. It's bad enough for him already. He's very worried about giving you up.'

So it was already arranged? Rosamund felt she should at least have been consulted. 'Perhaps he's miserable rather than just worried. We've been . . . quite close.'

'I don't want to know. Please don't upset me. I try to clear my mind of worries when I'm breast-feeding.'

Rosamund relented. 'Do you have any other worries? Besides me, I mean?'

'Of course I do. Money.'

'Money's always a bloody problem.'

17

'We used to have oodles and now we've only got Thomas's salary. We're selling the BMW. We may have to sell the orchard. We'll certainly have to sell the—'

Eliza looked up to see that Rosamund was looking about her and yawning, so she stopped abruptly. 'Sorry to bore you,' she said.

'It's just that you used to be so genial towards me,' Rosamund said. 'That evening we were all at that parent–teacher barbecue, and you came across Thomas and me sitting on our own behind the beer tent and you seemed so complacent about it, almost as though you were giving us your blessing. "I've got to go now, Thomas," you said, "but if you want to stay longer, I'm sure Barbara and Tony can give you a lift back." To tell you the truth, I was sure you'd got someone waiting for you.'

'No, I just had some work to finish. Work was always more important than anything else. I had to keep at least one jump ahead of all the others who were scrabbling around for my job. I was the first woman to be made a director of the firm, so I had something to live up to.'

'And yet you gave it all up to have another baby?'

'That's right.'

'Aren't you going to give him the other breast?'

Eliza glanced at her sharply. 'No, he's all right now. He's dropping off.'

'But won't you feel lopsided?'

'No, he'll have the other side when he wakes up next. Though I don't know what concern it is of yours.'

'I can't help being interested in babies, that's all. Who does he look like?'

'Can we change the subject? I don't know why we should be discussing mothercraft. The thing is, I thought I could trust Thomas. I thought you and he were just friends. I wanted him to have friends because I felt guilty about neglecting him. I didn't know he was fucking you.'

'As a matter of fact, I didn't know he was fucking you.'

'Christ, I'm his wife. Haven't you got any decency?'

'We didn't for ages. He used to come to the house to fetch Harry and we'd just sit and talk and drink coffee. I was

18

pleased to have company, I don't meet many people except my mother's friends.'

'And then?'

'Well, it was the evening Harry stayed the night in that little tent Joss had. I think it was Joss's birthday. Yes, his seventh birthday.'

'That was . . . three years ago.'

'Almost three years. Yes, three years in June. And Thomas strolled up to see if they were all right – you know how they can suddenly get homesick and frightened of the dark. But they were both fine. Asleep, in fact. They were both asleep.'

Rosamund's voice had become low and meditative as she re-lived that night, but Eliza's acid look brought her back to the present. 'So we sat and talked for a while. And then there was this terrific thunderstorm; thunder, whipping lightning, rain in torrents flowing down the garden, so we simply had to get them in. We went out with torches and scooped them up, still in their sleeping-bags, and would you believe, they were still asleep as we laid them down on the floor in Joss's room. Their faces were soaking wet from the rain as we carried them in, but they were still fast asleep. Then I went to my room to get a dry shirt and Thomas followed me.' Rosamund felt herself blush and put up her hand to shield her face. 'And . . . well, that was that. Quite unpremeditated. Not that that excuses us, I know.'

Rosamund sighed as she thought of that stormy night, all the pleasure she'd be giving up.

Eliza laid the baby back in the pram.

'Don't you wind him after his feed?' Rosamund asked.

Eliza gave her another angry look, but disdained to answer. She came back to her chair and sat down rather heavily. And then, with no sort of warning, she started to cry – great shuddering sobs, one after the other as though she would never stop.

Rosamund started to tremble. 'Oh, it's terrible, I know,' she said, as soon as she could make herself heard. 'But I'll give him up, I promise you. I honestly didn't realise how much you needed him. You see, I always thought you had someone else, someone connected with your work, someone more your type, more exciting. I suppose I wanted to think that, needed to. I'm very, very sorry. Honestly.'

Eliza's sobs gradually subsided and became deep intakes of breath. 'I was sacked,' she said at last. 'We had a new boss and he must have seen me as a threat because I'd been there nine years – longer than anyone else – and had all the relevant information at my fingertips. He called me into his office one Monday morning and said he was reorganising the business and had to make some changes.'

She broke down again and there was another bout of anguished sobbing. 'I was sacked,' she said again, 'and my PA, a girl of twenty-six, with no business degree, no experience, no personality, was appointed in my place. I gave my all to that company. I built up my department from nothing and it became the power base of the whole organisation. Everyone said so.'

'You'll get another job,' Rosamund said, beginning to regret her promises. 'You'll build up another department, be a director of a firm again.'

'No, no. Things are getting tougher all the time. I'm too old to start again. I haven't the stomach for it, haven't the fight. I'm too old now, almost forty. That's why I decided to have a baby. From pique, I suppose, or to feel there was something still left to me, that I wasn't quite finished. I really need Thomas now as I've never needed him before. Oh, Rosamund, you must give him up. I'm so afraid he'll leave me and go to live with you. You're so much nicer than I am. I'm in such a state, always shouting at everyone or sobbing my heart out.'

There was a long, heavy silence. 'Don't worry, you'll be better when the baby's six weeks old. It's post-natal depression, that's all. Thomas has never even suggested coming to live with me.'

Rosamund got to her feet. 'He's never even suggested coming to live with me,' she said again, rather sadly, as she left.

Thomas came by that night; the first time he'd called since the baby was born. It was gone ten o'clock and Joss should have been in bed and asleep, but he wasn't, he was running a sudden high temperature and leaning up against Rosamund on the sofa, drinking hot lemon and honey. He was very miserable, his face flushed, his black hair lying in sweaty streaks on his forehead. 'My throat's burning,' he wailed when he saw Thomas, 'so don't tell me to go up to bed.'

'Thomas never does,' Rosamund protested. 'I'm the one who's always chasing you upstairs.'

'You and Thomas,' he insisted in a hot little voice. 'I always have to go to bed whenever he comes.'

Thomas and Rosamund regarded each other guiltily, failing to say anything in their own defence. 'Perhaps you'd better go,' she told him. 'This may be something infectious. I've heard how things are and I quite understand.' She put her arm round her son, needing the comfort of his small hot body.

'And that's it, is it?' Thomas asked, his usual calm quite gone.

They sat looking at each other miserably. Minutes ticked by.

'I think you can carry him up for me now,' she told him later. 'I think he's fast asleep.'

'I'd like to stay here with you,' he told her, when Joss had been settled in his bed. 'That's what I'd like.'

'No, you wouldn't,' Rosamund said. 'You're much too dutiful and so am I. We both know it isn't feasible. You've got to put me out of your mind and try to be happy without me.'

'And you'll be happy without me?'

'I'll try, too.'

He followed her downstairs, looking as though he'd only that minute found out about loss and pain. 'I've always dreaded partings,' he said.

'Let's cut it short then, shall we?'

She led him out to the cloakroom where generations of schoolchildren, happy and unhappy, had hung their coats, and they stood there looking at each other for a moment or two. Then she opened the door and very gently pushed him out into the mild spring night, and stood watching him walk away from her. He didn't once turn round.

'He's a lovely, gentle, sweet-natured man,' she said to herself, 'but it's over. It's over. It's over. It's over.'

She didn't cry, but found that the muscles round her mouth

21

had begun to quiver and jerk. She went to bed immediately, without locking up, without even brushing her teeth. The telephone rang, but she put the pillow over her head and let it ring.

'That's why I'm feeling so vulnerable,' she told herself that evening, a week later. 'If I were still seeing Thomas, I wouldn't be as affected by what Ingrid thinks of my life. All right, it isn't exciting. I suppose I have buried myself away. But the thing is, Thomas made up for its shortcomings.'

# Chapter Three

'Well, you've certainly made inroads into the cake,' Marian
said.

'It was very good. You must give me the recipe sometime.
Do you want another piece, Joss?'

'He's gone upstairs to watch *Neighbours*. Don't you ever
listen to what he says?'

'He seems to thrive on neglect,' Rosamund answered. 'He
knows I'm dotty about him; that's all that counts.' She didn't
at all want her mother's company that evening. She'd been on
the point of setting out to fetch her son when Marian's little
white Fiat had appeared at the front gate.

'I don't think he'll need to eat much more, dear. He had a
very good tea; mushroom and broccoli risotto, followed by
apricot flan and custard. I brought some over for you – some
of the flan and custard. Would you like it now?'

'Oh, please.'

Marian bent to get a plastic container from her bag, then
fetched a plate and spoon from the kitchen.

'I don't know what I'd do without you.'

'Neither do I.'

They were sitting outside in the old playground, still called the
yard, though Anthony had had the concrete surface replaced
with old bricks, grey and faded rose pink, worked into circular
and semi-circular patterns. There were large terracotta pots
round the slatted wooden table. Another job for me, Marian
thought, looking at the near-dead wallflowers they contained.

Luckily, she and Brian had plenty of geranium cuttings in their neat little greenhouse.

'So what did she think of your paintings?' she asked her daughter. 'What was she like? Did she take any photographs? Isn't it too cold to be sitting out here now?'

'Well, I don't think she's in any way an art critic,' Rosamund said, scraping her plate very thoroughly, 'but she enthused about the house and took lots of photographs and she's going to send me the article for my approval.'

'*Country Homes*,' Marian said. 'I'll have to order a copy. I'll tell Mrs Johnson about it and I'm sure she'll display it in her window. If only you could arrange an exhibition in Stow or Cirencester, I'm sure you'd do so well, dear.'

'My own exhibition? No, I don't think so; it would be too much of a gamble for any gallery. You're the only one who's bought one of my latest lot of paintings . . . And you don't really like it.'

'Oh, I do, dear. Now that I've had the lounge re-done in Malaga Spice, it looks much better, much less obtrusive. Even Brian says so.'

'What I'd really like is a new baby,' Rosamund said.

'Darling! Darling, that's the last thing you need. Whatever's brought this on? You couldn't possibly cope with a new baby as well as your painting. You couldn't cope with Joss, you know that. I had to leave my home, sell my business. I'm not going to leave Brian again if you have another.'

'Mum, that's not fair. I couldn't cope with Joss because Anthony was ill. I had to look after Anthony, you know that.'

She remembered nights of sitting up with Anthony, talking to him, reading to him, playing music to him; anything to make him forget that he was dying. Usually she didn't know whether he was listening or dozing, but occasionally he'd say, 'Fetch the little one. I want to see the little one.' 'He's asleep, love.' 'I want to see him.'

She'd fetch the baby and lay him down in the crook of his arm and he'd smile and fall into a deep sleep. She'd carry Joss back to his bedroom, listening to his faint murmurings, breathing in his warm sweet smell; baby soap and talc and clean nightie – Marian would have no truck with anything called a baby-gro – with sometimes a slight suggestion of ammonia. It was an effort to go back to the hospital smells of the sickroom.

'You did look after him so sweetly,' she told her mother.

'Of course I did. But we're both getting too old for another.'

'I'll make a fresh pot of tea,' Rosamund said. She'd hoped for at least a little enthusiasm.

'I didn't really want Joss,' she said then, without getting up. 'I mean, he certainly wasn't planned or anything. Well, you know that. But now I feel really broody. It's my age, I suppose, the old clock ticking away. Of course, I'd like a partner as well, if possible. Someone intelligent and helpful.'

'What's brought this on?' Marian asked again, getting up to make the tea. 'Last week you were going to save up for a walking holiday in Spain. You can't have everything, you know.'

'Last week is a lifetime ago. Everything's completely changed since last week.'

'Whatever happened, dear?' Marian sat down again.

'Oh, just an ordinary, just a quite desperately ordinary little upset. Which seems to have changed everything. Made me realise that I have to face up to things and try to make a new life for myself.'

'But not a baby, dear. I often wish you could meet a really nice man, but you never seem to hit it off with nice men. Dr Wilby, for instance, was quite smitten, anyone could see that, but you weren't at all interested, were you?'

'I suppose I might meet someone on a walking holiday in Spain, but I'd probably never see him again, you know what holiday romances are, and what I'd really like is a more per-manent arrangement. Dating agencies cost too much, and who'd come out here anyway? How did you meet Brian?'

Rosamund looked at her mother with considerable respect. Her mother had remarried, found herself an eligible, solvent, fairly presentable widower with no apparent effort. 'This is Brian, dear, who's very kindly asked me to marry him.'

Marian bridled. 'Brian is a thoroughly decent man, far more thoughtful and considerate than your father ever was, and very fond of Joshua. I won't have anything said against Brian.'

'Of course not. I wouldn't dream of it.'

'Good.'

There was a short silence. 'Do you love him?' Rosamund asked then.

'Love him?' Marian repeated, as though she'd never really thought about it. 'Well, obviously I do, or I wouldn't have married him, would I?'

The question was relegated to the very back of her mind: there were more pressing things to consider. 'You see, my feelings are that you should be satisfied with one child, as I was. You have a really beautiful and lovable little boy.'

Joss appeared as though on cue. 'I'm going over to Harry's,' he said. 'I've got my torch.'

They watched him climb over the school wall. 'Be back by nine,' Rosamund shouted. 'Don't be late.'

'I saw Harry's mother in the butcher's yesterday,' Marian said. 'She looked really washed-out. Who'd believe she'd have wanted another baby at her age! She'd got three boys already, hadn't she? She must be well over forty.'

'She's thirty-nine. Four years older than me.'

'Well, she looked really terrible. Women who have babies in their late thirties are very foolish, in my opinion. It plays havoc with their hair and skin, to say nothing of their figures. Very unwise.'

'Didn't you ever hanker for another baby? Didn't you ever get broody?'

'If I did, I'd just buy myself a very tight-fitting new dress, and that cured me. I'm going to get that pot of tea, dear.'

In a few minutes her mother was back with scrambled eggs prettily dotted with chives and two pieces of thin toast as well as tea in the best flowered teapot. 'Really, Mum, you shouldn't have. Thank you. I could have done this, you know.'

'Oh, yes, no doubt,' Marian said drily. 'Anyway, dear, I've been thinking. What you need is a boost to your career. Why don't you have a nice little break in Fulham with your father and Dora? When did you see them last? It must be almost a year. Brian and I will look after Joss and you could go round the Bond Street galleries and try to get one of them to arrange an exhibition of your work. That article in *Country Homes* will be very useful, they'll be impressed by that. But first, of course, you must get some new clothes. Dora's got good taste, though a bit *outré*, and she could certainly tell you where to find a smart outfit. Because you'll have to look the part – stylish rather than Bohemian. Something quite plain in cream or ecru.'

She looked up at Rosamund and frowned. 'The things you wear are just not right for London.'

'Ingrid Walsh had a smart outfit. Black.'

'Black needs a great deal of care, dear. Not black.' She got to her feet again. 'And now I must go home. It's my WI night, otherwise I would have kept Joss a bit longer. Some lecture on industrial architecture. Never mind, it's the gossip and the coffee and biscuits afterwards that we enjoy. Why don't you phone your father tonight and tell him about *Country Homes.* He'll be so thrilled.'

'No, he won't.'

'Well, phone him anyway. He was very fond of you, you know, when you were little.'

'All right, I may phone him later.'

'And if he's not very responsive, ask for Dora. Dora will do anything for you. Well, you know that.'

'Bye, Mum. Thanks again.'

As soon as her mother left, Rosamund started to think about Eliza again; the way she'd wronged her, and hoped she'd been able to convince her that she was truly sorry.

In her heart, she still believed that Eliza had more or less abandoned Thomas, but whatever the position between them, they were married and had children and she should have respected that.

Several times she'd wanted to phone to ask if she was feeling better, but had held back fearing that Eliza might have revealed more and pleaded more than she'd intended, so would be embarrassed. I've got to put it behind me, she thought. It's they who must find ways of making their marriage work again. My part is to keep out of it.

It was even more difficult not to contact Thomas, who'd become a close friend as well as lover. When she'd told him that they mustn't meet again, his eyes had looked into hers as though into a great darkness. It was difficult not to love someone who seemed so desperate for that love.

She was still deep in thought when the phone rang.

It was Ingrid: 'I did enjoy myself with you this afternoon, and I loved seeing your work. I hope I didn't cause you too much distress.'

Rosamund found herself floundering. 'Of course not. It was a lovely afternoon. You were so kind.'

'I meant about the poems. Your late husband's poems.'

'No distress at all. I already knew about the poems.'

'So you won't object if they're published?'

'To be honest, I haven't had time to give it much thought, but I don't think it's going to affect me much. Anthony always intended that they should be published eventually, I think I mentioned that.'

'Yes, but in twenty years' time.'

'I'd have stuck to that – that's what he wanted – but now it seems to have been taken out of my hands. I don't think it matters too much.'

Rosamund wished she could remember the poems more clearly.

Anthony had passed them to her one evening when he was already very ill. 'I know you won't object to these, Rosie,' he'd said, 'because, well, you know what I'm like and you've never objected to any of it. But I know Molly would be very hurt by them and so, perhaps, would one or two other women. Read them, will you?'

She'd read them there and then, sitting at the bedroom window, getting the last of the light. Eighteen poems, some of them quite short.

They'd made her feel very tender towards her husband, then so frail and near death. He'd loved women, loved their bodies, their intimate smells, all the things he'd been able to do to excite them, all they'd been able to do to excite him. There were several words and phrases she hadn't seen in any previous poem, but nothing that shocked or displeased her.

'I wish I'd known you when you were young,' she'd said.

She'd taken all her clothes off then, to perch on his bed. He loved to look at her, though he couldn't bear to see his old hands on her young body. Looking deeply into his eyes, she spread oil on her breasts and her belly and her thighs, while he smiled at her as gently as he did when watching a robin pecking crumbs at the windowsill.

She'd promised to safeguard the poems for twenty years.

He must have thought the originals were safe with Erica Underhill. They'd had a long, passionate relationship, perhaps she owed him some loyalty – but she was surely well over seventy by this time, everyone she knew and cared about probably dead and everything getting more and more expensive. Perhaps she'd had to pay for an urgent operation – or a face-lift – and was deeply distressed at having to have the poems published. Could his former wife, Molly, care so much after all this time? It must be over thirty years since she'd divorced Anthony. Could she still be jealous?

Anyway, Molly had inherited the large London house and the copyright of his three collections of poetry, while Erica had probably had nothing.

She sat at the window waiting for Joss to come home. The thrushes and blackbirds were still singing their passionate courting songs; pornographic perhaps, but certainly beautiful. The little wild daffodils were out in the orchard, the narcissi and tulips already in bud. Spring was making her restless, stirring her blood. She had a moment's longing for Thomas, but thrust it out of her mind again. No, what she wanted, she told herself, was the wilder love of Anthony's poems: she wanted passion. Yes, she wanted a baby before it was too late, but even more she wanted that intensity of love she'd only read about.

She watched the light fade. Evenings were sad. She had a sudden vision of becoming like her mother, a woman fulfilled by the trivia of everyday life – the trip to the supermarket in town, the chat to so-and-so at the library, the weekly visit to the hairdresser, followed by lunch at the George with Brian. She kept herself busy, ate the right health-giving foods, never drank too much, washed her underwear every day and went to church every Sunday. There was nothing wrong with her mother. She loved her, of course she did, couldn't begin to manage her life without her. But she wanted to be someone else, someone vastly different. Oh, what was it she wanted? She'd once had large ambitions of becoming an important artist; those were long gone. It wasn't that she'd matured, rather the reverse. For the first time in her life, she seemed to have the preoccupations of an adolescent: she wanted to be swept off her feet by some violent passion. 'You'll find love one day,' Anthony had promised her. 'You've got it all in front of you, all the fever and the fret.'

She'd first met Anthony when he, much to her and everyone's surprise, had visited the students' exhibition in Brighton to see her paintings. Perhaps he'd been intrigued by her phone-call, perhaps happened to be in the area. Whatever the reason, he'd asked to meet her, had been introduced to her, had congratulated her on her work. 'You needn't have asked my permission,' he'd said. 'It's a work of art in its own right.'

'It was your poem that made me paint it,' she'd said. 'I like your poetry. I don't understand it all, but it moves me.'

'I like your paintings,' he'd said. And then something had made him add, 'Come and have lunch with me next week.' He'd given her his address and she'd realised at once that he was inviting her to something more than a meal.

She'd driven up from Brighton the following week. His daily help had shown her into what was then a sitting room and study. Anthony was sitting at a table heavy with books, working on his volume of critical essays – his poetry had already dried up by that time. He'd got up from his chair, walked over to her and turned her towards the window to examine her. 'What do you want from me?' he'd asked. 'Tell me, and if I'm able to give it to you, I'll tell you what I want from you.'

'I'd like a month in Florence,' she'd said, because that was what she'd been thinking of for several months.

'I'll arrange it this afternoon. Do you have a passport? How soon do you want to go?'

'What do you want from me?'

'To look at your body and perhaps take some photographs of it.'

It seemed a fair and just exchange.

She'd started posing for him that afternoon. She hadn't

found it difficult or embarrassing. She'd attended life classes herself for three years and now it was her turn to be the model, that's all there was to it.

He'd studied her as though she was a work of art and he a collector; she never got the impression of an old man ogling her.

She wrote to him from Florence, telling him about everything she was seeing and including pen and ink sketches of churches and statues and American tourists.

She went back to visit him before going to Liverpool to start teaching. He was touched that she'd come, thinking that their bargain was over, but within minutes she'd thrown off her clothes and was showing him her tanned body with its white bikini patches, delighted at his pleasure. She'd returned to see him for some part of every holiday, before and after the foreign trips he helped finance.

He was already ill when they got married, a secret wedding at a Register Office in Cleeve. Her mother had been very upset, hardly prepared even to meet Anthony who, she kept telling Rosamund, was old enough to be, not merely her father, but her grandfather.

Her disapproval had survived Joss's birth; she hadn't even visited them in hospital, had only sent them an over-large bouquet of beetroot-coloured chrysanthemums with her best wishes.

It was only a few months afterwards when Anthony was dying that she had relented and come to stay with them, taking over the baby and the running of the house, leaving Rosamund free to nurse her husband, read to him and keep him company.

Her mother had been magnificent at the funeral, dealing with the journalists who turned up with a most kind condescension, passing them cups of tea and treating them to little homilies on poetry, poets, marriage, children and death; so that they soon left.

For weeks after Anthony's death, Rosamund had read and re-read his poetry in a kind of frenzy, as though needing a closer connection with him. She had loved him.

\*

31

Joss came over the wall flashing his new torch about like a searchlight.

'Why are you sitting in the dark?' he asked her. 'Can I have some oven chips? I had a rotten tea.'

'Gran said you had a lovely meal. Broccoli and mushrooms.'

He shuddered delicately. 'Poor Uncle Brian,' he said.

'I'm thinking of getting an Uncle Brian myself.'

'Oh, don't. We're all right as we are, aren't we?'

'Not really. You're out all the time.'

'I'll put some chips in the oven. For the two of us. And I'll stay home from school tomorrow, if you like, to keep you company.'

She heard him clattering a packet of frozen chips onto a tray and slamming it into the oven. When he came back, he looked at his mother, head on one side as though being cute for a television advert. 'I'd never marry anybody old,' he said 'because they'd only die. Didn't you think of that?'

'One can't be wise all the time.'

'Never mind. You're a jolly good painter, anyway. Did that woman come? The one who was going to write about you?'

'Yes.'

'Shall we have some baked beans with the chips?'

The next day Rosamund walked morosely round the studio. She realised that she was now only painting the same landscapes in darker colours. Ingrid had very kindly suggested a growing sense of doom and nightmare, but she was flattering her; they were simply darker.

She wondered why she had ever imagined she had the talent to become an artist. She'd always been able to draw fairly well and at school this had been played up because she wasn't particularly good at anything else.

'Rosamund should definitely go to art school,' her form mistress had told her mother on one of her visits to the small private school she attended, and Marian had seized on this as the perfect solution. Rosamund knew she was becoming a problem. Her mother complained that she was dreamy, withdrawn and lacking in ambition. Other girls at seventeen were longing to get away from home, while she talked of getting a job locally. 'But doing what?' her mother asked, over and over again. 'Couldn't I be a receptionist at a hotel? Something like that?' 'Certainly not. That's no sort of career.'

Marian had recently become friendly with her accountant, a widower called Brian Spiers, and Rosamund realised that she was in the way. Had she been sent to art school so that her mother and Brian could start living together with less embarrassment? Or was her mother determined that her father should continue to pay towards her upkeep, feeling that if she left school and found a job, he'd be getting away too lightly? Her parents had been divorced for five or six years at that time, but there was no real truce between them.

She remembered the interview she'd had at Brighton. The lecturer in charge of admissions had looked through her portfolio in a slightly bemused way. 'They're certainly different,' he'd said. 'Everyone else is showing me abstracts in grey and black.'

'Perhaps he meant that yours were more interesting,' her mother had suggested afterwards.

'I don't think so.'

She could hardly believe it when she was accepted for the following year's degree course. And throughout her four years she was the only person who'd stuck with representational art. Amanda Wright, her closest friend, had told her quite kindly that she mustn't blame herself but the way she'd been brought up.

Most people blamed the way they'd been brought up. But she, she told herself, had never been ill-treated or neglected. Her mother had always fed her nourishing meals, bought her the best Startrite shoes and sent her to bed at the proper time with a story and a goodnight kiss. If she'd been bitter about her husband's treatment of her, she'd kept it from Rosamund as much as she could. They'd certainly never fought in her presence, though she'd been aware of the undertones of tension between them. Had she adored her father and been devastated when he'd left them? Not as far as she could remember. He'd never been much more than a handsome but occasional presence. She remembered feeling pleased when he reappeared after a week's absence, and enjoying the games he played with her at bedtime, but could recall no stronger feelings.

His absences in London had gradually lasted longer, though she hadn't been aware of the actual divorce. When she was thirteen, though, her mother had let her know that her father intended to get married again. Some marriages worked, she'd said, but theirs had failed and now he'd met another woman and was going to try again. Rosamund had been appalled by this turn of events, tormented by the idea that her mother was being replaced.

'I'm certainly not going,' she said when her wedding invitation had arrived. 'You're not going, so I shan't.'

'Your father will be very disappointed, dear, and so will Dora, the woman he's going to marry. I've talked to her on the telephone and she seems very pleasant. She invited me, too, but quite understood when I said I didn't think it appropriate, so we're meeting for lunch next Monday.'

'You're meeting her for lunch?'

'Darling, we're civilised people.'

'I don't feel civilised.'

'You must, dear. She's very anxious to be liked.'

'But don't you mind that she's marrying . . . your husband?'

'She's very keen that your father should make me a generous settlement.'

'What does that mean? What is a settlement?'

'It means that I'll be able to buy a little dress shop that I've got my eye on.'

'Do you mean money? Is that what a settlement is? Do you mean that you're giving him up for money? That's horrible! Oh, that's really horrible!'

'Don't spoil things for me, dear. Money can buy a person a new way of life. You'll understand that one day.'

A few weeks later, Rosamund went to the wedding dressed in a new peacock-blue suit and long cream suede boots, and in spite of her determination to dislike her father's new wife, hadn't quite managed it.

Before that day, she'd only been to large, conventional weddings where the traditional bride, dressed like a fairy doll, walked up the aisle on the arm of a man in black fancy dress. Dora and her father were married in a Register Office, Dora dressed in a saffron-yellow suit and scarlet shoes and seeming more than capable of walking on her own.

'This can't be much fun for you,' she'd said to Rosamund after the ceremony, 'but thank you so much for coming. Paul and I did want you to be with us.'

The reception, with only twelve guests, was held in a friend's flat and Rosamund admired the way Dora took charge of everything. It was like a particularly friendly dinner party where, for the first time in her life, she was treated as an adult and not as a child or an adolescent; she drank champagne and the food was simple but delicious. There were no embarrassing speeches either, though at the end, Dora stood up and thanked everyone for coming and her father recited a short poem by Herrick in a voice she had never heard before.

> *Then Julia let me woo thee,*
> *Thus, thus to come unto me;*
> *And when I shall meet*
> *Thy silvery feet,*
> *My soul I'll pour into thee.*

On that first meeting she hadn't quite capitulated to Dora, but felt she could really like her father in this new mood.

The next thing that happened was that Dora was pregnant. And almost as soon as Rosamund had got used to that idea, they heard that she'd had the baby – a little girl – two months early, and a few days afterwards her father had phoned again to say that she had died. 'Dora wants to see you, Rosamund,' he'd said. 'I know it's a lot to ask, but do you think you could bear to visit her in hospital?'

She'd handed the phone to her mother, unable to reply, and had stood dry-eyed listening to her making arrangements for her to visit the following day.

'I'll run you up, dear,' her mother had said. 'It'll be an ordeal, but I know you'll want to do everything you can.'

Rosamund had felt no joy at the prospect of a half-brother

or sister, but was very sad to hear of the baby's death. All the same, she couldn't understand why Dora wanted to see her – her mother's explanation that she had no other relatives to visit her seeming altogether too trivial. Throughout the journey on the following day she wondered what comfort she could possibly be, but the way Dora welcomed her made her feel reconciled to being there.

While Dora had hugged her, one sob had escaped from somewhere deep down in her chest, that was the only sign of grief she'd allowed herself. After that they had eaten grapes and talked about Christmas which was imminent. Rosamund had promised to visit them on the day after Boxing Day and then Dora had kissed her and said she wanted to sleep. 'What did you call her?' Rosamund had asked as she was leaving. 'Louise.' 'I like that name. She was my little sister.'

Rosamund had tiptoed out of the ward and found her way back to the reception hall. Her father was there with her mother and they seemed more friendly than she could remember seeing them. Her father thanked them for coming and then kissed each of them.

'I'm more sorry than I can say,' her mother had whispered as they left.

'And I am,' Rosamund said.

They'd both been silent on the way home; her mother concentrating on driving as though she'd never driven before and Rosamund revising German irregular verbs for an end-of-term test as though they held the secret of salvation.

Not one of them mentioned the baby's death ever again. Sometimes it seemed to Rosamund that she'd only existed to bring her and Dora together. For several months, though, she used to write *Louise Harcourt* in fancy letters on scraps of paper with wreaths of roses or leaves around it. It was a way of grieving, she supposed.

Dora and her father had never had another baby.

# Chapter Four

The copy of Ingrid's article arrived at the end of the week.

It was entitled *Poet's Muse* and seemed to be more about Rosamund herself than about her paintings. '"Wide-set eyes, the colour of faded speedwell, hair like rippling water" – well really,' Rosamund said aloud, '"tall, shapely body, strong hands."'

After the description, the story. Ageing poet falling in love with the young beauty fate had sent his way, finally marrying her a year before his death. A mention of Joss – 'the charming pencil drawings of him are not on sale' – hinting at joyous consummation. The paintings themselves were praised rather ponderously, the word 'impressive' much used, so that they sounded worthy but dull. Prints of the five photographs the art editor had chosen were included, one of her looking rather sulky by the school-room door, one of the studio, showing the high Gothic windows and the long table with the painting paraphernalia on it, and three of the actual paintings – predictably Anthony's Gate in its two variations, one entitled *In Love's Day*, the other *In Love's Wake*; the last was the small painting Ingrid had particularly liked, entitled *Pastoral*. The whole article was bland and overwritten, but neither unkind nor indiscreet.

Ingrid had enclosed a short letter. '*I told you I wouldn't be able to do justice to your paintings. I experienced them – and you – too deeply. However this article, unless there's something you'd like altered, will find its way into* Country Homes *in one of the next issues.'* As a postscript she'd added: *'PLEASE come up to stay with me.'*

Rosamund had feared that Ingrid might have been more acerbic; once or twice she'd caught her looking at her with what seemed like pity or even scorn.

It was a delightfully warm afternoon and Rosamund, still in a restless state, decided to walk the two miles down to the village to call on her mother, realising that she ought to warn her about the possible publicity regarding Anthony's poems.

Brian was in the front garden of their new house, brushing up fallen cherry blossom as though it were lethal fall-out. Their garden could probably have won a prize for the neatest in the whole world; everything in it savagely trimmed and pruned and disciplined. Brian made her mother seem a dare-devil. 'How are you, Brian?' she called out in a chummy voice she never used except to him.

'Mustn't grumble,' he said. 'My back isn't as bad as it was last spring. Not yet, anyhow.' He straightened up with a faint but audible groan.

'Take care, now. Don't overdo it.' She waggled her fingers at him as she walked up the path.

She rang the bell, opening the door at the same time. 'Come in, dear,' Marian said. 'I was just going to stop for a cup of tea. I've been doing a spot of spring cleaning. These Swedish blinds, dear.'

'Is that a new rug?'

'Yes. Do you like it? I don't suppose so.'

'Why do you say that?'

'We never like the same things, do we? Never mind. Go and call Brian, dear, while I make the tea.'

'Can I talk to you first?'

'Good gracious, what about?'

'About Anthony.'

Marian sighed her relief. A dead husband seemed less worrying than almost anything else. She made herself comfortable on the oversized sofa.

'When Anthony was married to Molly he had a mistress called Erica Underhill and he wrote her some very private

38

poems. Anyway, she's now short of money and she's having her autobiography written, which will include the poems, and some of the papers will publish extracts from it. I think there may be a fair bit of publicity. And I thought you should know about it beforehand.'

'Good gracious. When you say private poems, do you mean pornographic, dear?'

'Erotic, anyway.'

'Good gracious. Well, I only hope I'll be able to understand them. I haven't understood much of his work so far.'

'I think there could be quite a fuss. You know, because he's considered an important poet. I suppose he'll come in for quite a bit of criticism about his private life and so on. Perhaps some of his other mistresses will discover some other poems. There may be a certain amount of mud-raking.'

'I wonder how it will affect Joss.'

'Joss? I don't suppose he'll understand much of it, will he? He's not ten yet.'

'That boy understands far too much, dear. The things he insists on watching on the television! And if I pretend not to understand something, oh, he explains it to me. I blame all this sex education they have nowadays. I didn't know anything about erections, dear, until I started nursing, but Joshua . . .'

At the same moment they both realised that Brian was standing at the open door of the lounge – in stockinged feet, of course – and listening to them with some interest.

'I came in for a cup of tea,' he said, 'but don't let me inter-rupt you.'

'Come and sit down, Brian. Rosamund's a bit worried because Anthony had been writing some rather risqué poems to one or two of his mistresses and now they're going to be published. There'll be quite a little scandal, Rosamund says.'

Brian seemed to come to life. 'Fancy that, now! That'll be something to live up to in the George, won't it? What relation is he to me, Marian? My late stepson-in-law? Yes, my late stepson-in-law. Harvey, have you read those little verses by my late stepson-in-law? All right, aren't, they? What are they like,

39

Rosamund? "There was a young man of Khartoum . . ." How does it go? That was a good one.'

'That's a limerick, dear. Not the same thing at all. And no, we don't want to hear it.'

They had tea and some home-made lemon cake, Marian and Brian seeming very lively, Brian telling them about the time he did National Service and knew a thing or two, and Marian recalling her three months on Men's Surgical when she did her nursing training.

'I must get back or Joss will be home before me,' Rosamund said after her second cup of tea. 'And by the way, Mum, I love the new rug.'

A few days later, Anthony's son Alex contacted her. Rosamund and Alex had always treated each other warily; he resented her, with the result that she was nervous of him. 'I'm ringing on my mother's behalf,' he said stiffly. 'My father's agent has been in touch with her about something rather worrying.'

'Is it to do with Erica Underhill?'

'How did you know? Did Giles contact you?'

'No, of course not. He's completely loyal to your mother, still regarding me as an interloper.'

'So how did you know? Erica Underhill's been in touch with you?'

'I've never spoken to her in my life. Nor heard from her.'

There was a long pause before Alex decided to continue.

'Giles had a phone-call from a journalist who asked whether he could have access to my father's private papers as he intended to write his biography. He was a little suspicious since there'd been two official biographies already, so he said he'd need a written application with full details of his proposal, the name of his publisher, etc. etc. And in the meantime he heard from a friend, another literary agent, that Erica Underhill had been making enquiries for a writer to ghost her autobiography. Naturally he warned my mother not to speak to anyone however plausible he might seem. And naturally she's in a state about it. You can imagine how Erica Underhill's auto-biography would upset her.'

40

Rosamund sighed. 'No, not really,' she said. 'It's all so long ago, and anyway Erica Underhill was the guilty party. Your mother would have nothing to fear.'

'She's thinking of my father's reputation.'

'His reputation seems in pretty good shape.'

'It's all very well to say that. Up to now his biographers have been very circumspect. They naturally mentioned his divorce, but not the circumstances leading to it. They've been very civilised.'

'They even made his marriage to me sound fairly innocuous.'

'You had nothing to do with the break-up of my mother's marriage. She doesn't feel any animosity towards you.'

'That's magnanimous of her.'

'She's got a proposition to make to you.'

On this occasion again Rosamund was silent so that Alex had to continue. 'She wants you to write a book about him. Your personal recollections. She knows you'd be careful of my father's reputation and she's confident you'd be fair to her, so it would be an answer to Underhill's. She also thinks you should be in a position to make money from it – as well as his mistress and some cheque-book journalist. She knows you weren't very adequately provided for.'

'She's right about that.' There was another long pause before Rosamund added, 'And it's kind of her to think of it.'

'My mother's not an ogre, whatever my father might have told you.'

'He mentioned her very little, as a matter of fact.'

'Will you think about it?'

'Yes, I'd like to. I'm at a stage of my life when I'm restless and on the lookout for some new project, though I've no idea whether I'm capable of writing a book. Anyway, will any publisher be likely to be interested in a further book after Erica Underhill's?'

'Giles thinks so. He thinks hers will have whetted the readers' imagination so that yours could be a real money spinner. My mother would let you have access to all his private papers and she'd give you permission to quote from any of his poems. She owns the copyright of all his poetry, as you probably know.'

'Though I suppose Erica Underhill would own the copyright of the poems he sent her.'

There was another pause. 'She has poems of his? Love poems, presumably?'

'Yes, love poems. And I think they'd be the reason her autobiography would be rather well received.'

'You've read them? These poems?'

'Yes. Anthony kept copies of them, but asked me not to have them published until twenty years after his death.'

'So that they shouldn't upset my mother?'

'I suppose so.'

'Perhaps you could inform Erica Underhill of that.'

'She may need the money, though. She must be quite old by this time. Well, I may go to see her. I suppose I'll have to if I take this on. But I really can't see that I can ask her not to include the poems. They're erotic but very beautiful, and they'd be the book's main attraction, wouldn't they?'

That night in bed Rosamund went over the last weeks of Anthony's life. He was very weak and frail, and unhappy, too, knowing that he was dying. Occasionally she would read aloud some of his poems, hoping they'd comfort him, remind him of his achievements, but he didn't seem to think much of them. 'I didn't read that very well,' she'd say. 'Shall I try it again?'

He'd shake his head feebly as though all his most famous lines meant nothing to him now. To Rosamund it was unbearably sad. That he had nothing to say and nothing he wanted to hear.

During the last days, though, he seemed to rouse himself and want to talk. He gripped Rosamund's hand, though she wasn't sure that he knew who she was, 'I'll tell you,' he said over and over again, but without saying anything else.

At last she guessed what he wanted. She got a pad and pencil and said, 'Right, I'm ready to take it down,' and then he dictated a few sentences to her – the beginning, she realised, of his life's story. Less than half a page it turned out to be, before he lapsed into sleep again.

Rosamund had kept that page in a cardboard box with Joss's baby clothes, and that night she got out of bed to fetch it. She hadn't looked at it for years, hadn't thought of it for years: *'When I was two or three years old, my nurse would take me past the grounds of a mansion where there were soldiers convalescing, soldiers wounded in the First World War. They would come over to the gate as we walked past. Some of them had only one leg and walked on crutches, but the ones I was really frightened of were those with bandaged heads. I was afraid the tops of their heads would fall off. I used to dream of those men.*

*'I was very fond of my nurse who was called Florence Maud. She was a large pretty girl with dark eyes. Her breasts would bob up and down when she ran downstairs. One night I woke up and went upstairs to the attic to find her and discovered my father lying on top of her and hurting her. I said, "Papa, Papa."'*

That was the last thing Anthony said. 'Papa, Papa.' He repeated it several times over.

# Chapter Five

Rosamund and Erica Underhill sat at the window looking at photographs of Anthony. He was certainly handsome when he was young, Rosamund thought. She wished she'd known him at that time.

She'd expected at least a measure of hostility when she'd first contacted Erica, but there'd been none; Erica had agreed to a meeting as though it was the most natural thing in the world. 'I expect you've heard about the book I'm planning to write,' she'd said on the phone. 'I hope you're not worrying about it. I won't have anything bitchy to say about Anthony, I promise you. You see, I loved him.'

'Do you live on your own these days?' she asked Rosamund when they met.

'Apart from my son who's almost ten now.' She described Joss; his charm, his forthright manner, his dark eyes and hair.

'I'd have liked Anthony's child,' Erica told her, 'but it wasn't possible. In my day it was one thing to have a lover, quite another to have a baby outside marriage. Anyway, I still hoped to get married at that stage. I needed to get married. I needed money. All my life I've needed money. Such a bore. I've never had a proper job, just odds and ends.'

Was she apologising for publishing the poems, Rosamund wondered. If so, there was no need for it; she already felt both pity and affection for her.

Erica had great style, even now. A grey jersey suit, a bottle-green blouse exactly matching her eyes, peacock-blue glass beads, elegant shoes. Rosamund, who had made an effort with her appearance, subduing her natural enthusiasm for too many colours, too many patterns, had only managed to look neat in a cream linen suit her mother had chosen for her.

'You see, I wasn't educated for anything,' Erica continued. 'Girls weren't in my day. I stayed on at school, a boarding school in Kent, until I was eighteen, then went abroad for ten years. It was the thing to do in those days. You got a job as companion to some American woman who was travelling to South America or India, and hoped to pick up a rich admirer while you were at it.'

'I bet you did, too.'

'Not the right sort, though. I think I was always seen as a girlfriend or mistress rather than a wife. I don't think I had that steely determination that other women seemed to have, that insistence on the wedding ring. Oh, I had a good time with one or two wonderfully handsome young men, but didn't manage to get myself a husband.'

'You were too beautiful. Men are easily frightened.'

Erica smiled. Such blatant flattery! She liked Rosamund.

'How did you meet Anthony? He wasn't the type you'd come across abroad.'

'I came home because my mother was ill. She died in a few months and left me this flat and some money which gave me the opportunity to change my lifestyle. It was time for change.'

Rosamund looked round the room with added interest. She hadn't realised that this was the flat that Anthony had visited so often. She felt rather as though she were spying on him. It was easy to imagine him here.

'Not enough money, of course,' Erica continued, 'but just sufficient to live on with some other odds and ends. Never had a proper job. Wasn't trained for anything.'

'You used to cook for parties, Anthony said.'

'Yes, I did for a time. What else did he tell you about me?'

'That you posed for several well-known artists.'

'That didn't last long. Oh, I did a bit of everything over the years, took parties of tourists round London and Oxford and Stratford-upon-Avon, translated from Italian for publishers and film companies; I'd lived in Italy for several years. That's how I got to know Anthony. He'd seen my advertisement – in the *Statesman* I think it was, and brought along some Italian poems for me to translate.'

'He was already married to Molly at that time?'

'Yes. His first wife had died, as you probably know, and he'd married again almost immediately.'

'Did you ever meet Molly?'

'No. Did you?'

'No. Of course I shall have to if I decide to go ahead with my book.'

'Tell me what she's like, won't you?'

'You must know what she's like.'

'No. You can never trust a man when he's talking about his wife; always that mixture of slavish devotion and implacable hatred. She can't be as bad as I imagined her . . . Shall we have some tea?'

'Lovely. I brought some pastries from the delicatessen by the tube.'

'Oh, darling, they're hideously expensive! What a treat though.'

Erica sat back, the thought of tea quite forgotten. 'The poems are all I have left to sell,' she said.

'They're wonderful poems. You should be very proud to have inspired them. Anthony showed them to me a few weeks before he died. He asked me not to have them published for twenty years, but I'm sure he wouldn't want you to be short of money.'

'You can't be rich yourself.'

'No, but I'm not desperate . . . Shall I make the tea?'

'That would be very kind. Are you sure you don't mind? The kitchen is an unholy mess, I'm afraid.'

'My mother says that. "What an unholy mess!" But only about my kitchen, not hers.'

Even after the warning, Rosamund was appalled by Erica's kitchen, not the untidiness, but the filth. She'd already realised that Erica was at least ten years older than she admitted to, she was nearer eighty than seventy, almost eighty, and needing someone's care. Still the remains of beauty, the deep-set eyes, the cheekbones and the wonderful jawline, but an old woman and unable to cope on her own. The sink and the working surfaces were squalid, the only tea she had was the cheapest variety, the milk in the grimy fridge old, not quite sour, but full of blue lumps, a smell of rotting swede coming from somewhere. She washed some cups and saucers, a milk jug and a plate for the pastries and carried in the tray.

Erica was leaning back in her chair, her eyes shut. 'Oh,' she said, waking with a jolt. 'It's you, Stevie.'

'No, it's Rosamund. Rosamund Gilchrist.'

'Of course it is. Such delicious cakes!'

'Who is Stevie?'

'Did I say Stevie? Oh dear: She was a maid my mother had in the old days. I haven't thought of her for years.'

The room was getting dark, shadows of the plane trees outside the window patterning the dark red carpet and the heavy furniture. Rather nice furniture, Rosamund thought, solid Edwardian mahogany, a faint smell of pot-pourri coming from somewhere, a marble fireplace fitted with a gas fire.

'Anthony would have liked this room,' she said. She could imagine him sitting in the straight-backed wing chair, spreading a napkin over his thin knees, cutting the pastry very precisely, leaning forward to avoid making crumbs, looking at the young Erica as he'd later looked at her. 'Was he a very ardent lover?' she asked.

'I'm far too old to remember,' Erica said, but looking as though she remembered very well, 'but his letters seem to sug-gest that he was fairly happy in my company.'

'I bet he was.'

'But not so happy that he was prepared to leave his wife – who didn't make him at all happy, or so he said. Men have a strange sense of reality.'

'He had a family.'

'Yes, he had a family. And the family won. And I have no children and no grandchildren . . . I'd have enjoyed grand-children, I think.'

Rosamund looked at her spearing the last piece of éclair, raising it to her mouth and chewing robustly. 'That abortion you had made a tremendous impact on Anthony,' she said. 'He told me he'd never been so unhappy as he was then.'

Erica raised her hand to steady her trembling mouth, while in her other hand her fork clattered against her plate. 'He shouldn't have told you about the abortion,' she said. 'He promised he'd never mention that to a soul.'

'He was very old when he told me. He'd obviously forgotten.'

'I won't mention that in my book and I hope you won't.'

There was a silence during which they looked hard at each other.

'Of course I won't,' Rosamund said.

'It upset him, you think?'

'It devastated him. He said you very nearly died. The poem called *The Reckoning* was written about it. You must have known.'

'I suppose I did. But you know, I hardly saw him after that. I went to Provence for a short holiday – which he paid for – and there I met Roger Kingsley whom I married the following year.'

'I didn't know you'd got married. Anthony never mentioned that. It hurt him too much, I suppose.'

'I went to America with Roger and lived there until his death three years later. I never saw Anthony again.'

'Did your husband know about the abortion?'

'Of course not. Nobody knew about it. Abortion was highly illegal in those days. Roger would certainly not have married me if he'd known about it.'

'That's why Anthony wouldn't hear of my having an abortion – because of the agony you and he had gone through. So it's you I have to thank for Joss, I suppose. My son, Joshua.'

'You weren't married, then, when he was conceived?'

'No. We'd never considered it. No, Anthony was just someone I visited in the holidays. I was teaching in Liverpool and of course used to love being able to visit the famous poet. He was always so pleased to see me, took me out to expensive restaurants, cooked for me, tried to educate me. But marriage was the last thing either of us had thought of.'

For a while they were both caught up in memories, their eyes losing focus.

49

'My inside was all messed up. Though it was done privately of course and cost plenty,' Erica said, her voice harsh.

'He was nearly fifty years older than me, almost half a century older. If he were alive now he'd be eighty-four.'

'I meant nothing to him.'

'Nonsense. He talked a great deal about you. He loved you. He never talked of anyone else.'

'He forgot about me. I wrote to tell him about Roger, about the apartment we had in New York, hoping he might visit us – he liked America – but never got a word in reply.'

'He was probably too hurt,' Rosamund said. 'He'd thought you'd always be there for him. He was like that, wasn't he? A tremendous egoist. I'm not trying to make excuses for him, but he must have had a terrible shock . . . Served him right, of course. He should have had the guts to leave Molly.'

'When I got back from America, he had someone else.'

'You were the only one he talked to me about.'

'She worked for the BBC. Beth Stallworthy. He was divorced by this time so I assumed they'd get married, but the next thing I heard, she'd married someone else and he'd left London.'

'What about you? Were you with someone else by this time?'

'Perhaps so. Yes, I was usually with someone else. It was usually better to be with someone else, I found. Being alone isn't much fun. What about you?'

'I'm on my own. You're right, not much fun.'

'But you're an artist. You have your own resources.'

Rosamund sighed. 'I haven't enough talent or energy to call myself an artist. I had enough money to indulge myself for a while, that's all. Now I've got to get cracking on something else. So I suppose I'm going to have a shot at writing this book.'

'Are we both going to betray him, then?'

Rosamund looked at the old woman for a few moments, not knowing how to reply. 'Anthony's a great poet,' she said at last. 'His reputation is assured.' She got to her feet. 'Would you like me to make another pot of tea? Or shall I wash up now? My father and my stepmother are taking me to the theatre tonight, so I can't stay long.'

50

'I really need money,' Erica said. 'Everything comes down to money in the end, doesn't it? I want to spend next winter in a luxury hotel in Madeira or Florida. For five or six days last February I was too cold to get out of bed.'

# Chapter Six

Rosamund's father, Paul Harcourt, had been an up-and-coming solicitor when her mother had married him. According to her, though, he'd been bad-tempered and moody through all the years they'd been together, forever threatening to give up his law practice to become an actor. Marian had considered this a childish self-indulgence and had always vowed to leave him if he did, adamant that she didn't intend to give up her home and security.

When Paul's father, himself a successful solicitor, had died, leaving Paul most of his money, he'd been able to support Marian and Rosamund in Surrey as well as pay for his training at drama school. During those years he'd spent more and more time at his flat in London – Rosamund had been only seven or eight when he'd first left – and gradually the rift between him and Marian had ended in divorce.

He'd never become a very successful actor, though his English good looks ensured him a certain amount of television work; the small part of the father in situation comedy being his most usual role, and as far as Rosamund could judge, he was still as impatient and bad-tempered as ever. But she supposed he was now less frustrated, able to feel that his big chance – the important lead part that was going to make his name – might finally come his way.

Rosamund realised that Dora was a much more suitable partner for him than her mother could ever have been; Dora was a busy careerwoman who idolised him but without taking him too seriously.

Rosamund arrived twenty minutes late at the restaurant where they were to have a pre-theatre supper. She'd felt in need of fresh air and a long walk after the sadness of her afternoon with Erica; the tragedy of her lonely old age. Dora and her father were already halfway through their meal. 'I knew you wouldn't want to find your father in a bad mood,' Dora said, kissing her. 'I've ordered lasagna for you. I hope that's all right.'

'Perfect,' Rosamund said. 'How lovely to see you. And you,' she added, smiling at her father who just managed to smile back. 'Don't worry,' she told him, 'I'm a very fast eater.'

'How beautiful you look,' Dora said. 'She's so lucky to have your looks, Paul, isn't she?'

Her father looked at her critically, so that she was immediately aware of her three-year-old linen suit, bought in a sale to please her mother, a good label but a poor fit and not really her colour. She ate fast and had soon caught up with them.

'Gâteau? Fruit? Cheese and biscuits?' Dora enquired.

'Cheese and biscuits,' Rosamund said rather sadly. 'I had an éclair for tea.'

'We'll all have the strawberry gâteau,' Dora told the waiter, 'and coffee and the bill.'

Dora was small with cropped black hair shot through with grey in a most attractive way. Brindled, Rosamund thought. Her mouth and her eyes were large, her face freckled; a lovely, ugly face like an intelligent pug. Exquisitely dressed, not in a careful, studied way like her mother – everything co-ordinated and of the best possible quality – but in strange exotic clothes that would probably have looked appalling on anyone else.

The three of them ate their gâteau feeling pleased with one another.

They saw a musical comedy, so undemanding that Rosamund could follow it while giving most of her attention to her afternoon with Erica, the way she'd felt so close to her.

After the play was over they went backstage to see one of the actors whom her father knew, all of them congratulating him warmly on his performance, though he'd only been on stage for five minutes, her father ridiculously over-indulgent, it seemed to her, though the actor seemed to take it as no more than his due.

After they'd spent far too long discussing his performance, he'd turned to Rosamund. 'And this is your daughter,' he said, taking her hand and gazing into her eyes, as though audition-ing for a romantic lead. 'Shall we have a drink together in the pub over the road when I've changed?' he asked her father. 'Is she on the stage too? I must get to know her.'

'No, she's an artist,' Dora said briskly. 'Yes, we'll wait for you as long as you don't take too long.'

'Oh, let's get a taxi,' her father said as soon as they got outside. 'Let's not wait. He's such a boring old fart.'

'Oh Paul,' Dora wailed when they were in the taxi. 'How selfish we are. We should have waited. He was bowled over by Rosamund, and they might have hit it off.'

'No,' Rosamund said, 'I wasn't at all interested. I thought he looked moth-eaten and a bit spiteful. I was glad to escape from him.'

'So why are you looking so gloomy?'

'I was thinking of old age, as a matter of fact.'

'It's time you had a new man,' Dora said. 'You've been on your own too long. I know several attractive young men. Just give me a few days, that's all I ask.'

'She doesn't like young men,' her father said drily. 'Surely you know that much about her.'

'Darling,' Dora said later that night when Rosamund was tucked up on their sofa. (Dora and Paul had a smart flat in a smart square in Fulham, but it was minute, with only one bed-room.) 'You must come and stay for a longer time and let me find you a boyfriend. I know exactly the sort of man you'd like, someone very handsome and very dependable and rather rich. I was thirty-five when I met your father. It's the age of discern-ment, the age when one makes the right choice. Trust me.'

'You think you made the right choice?' Rosamund asked, surprised but pleased.

'Of course. We're very happy together.'

'But isn't he rather . . . rather self-absorbed?'

'Oh yes. But you won't find a man without faults. But if he

55

gives you enough pleasure, you'll put up with him very happily. That's what it boils down to, Rosamund.'

'So why didn't that work for my mother?'

They were both silent for a moment. 'Because she was too young,' Dora said then. 'She wanted everything. It takes maturity to work things out, your own worth, how much you can justifiably expect from life. You know the score by the time you're thirty-five.'

'I don't think I've learnt much.'

'I'm sure you have. You seem very wise, eager and calm at the same time.'

'I was very timid when I was at art school, I can't quite understand why I didn't get more out of it, why I didn't make the most of being with all those dazzling young people.'

'They were probably a lot of pseuds and show-offs. That's what I was anyway, when I was young – a show-off and a predator, only after the quick thrill. Now things have settled down to a nice steady richness.'

Rosamund took Dora's hand and kissed it. It was heartening to know that people could be happy instead of unhappy, bored and discontented. 'Good night,' she said. 'I'll be back by seven tomorrow night to help you make supper. I won't be late again.'

At first Rosamund thought the woman at the door was Molly. 'Mrs Gilchrist?' she said, holding out her hand.

'No,' the woman said, 'I'm her cousin, Lorna Drew. I'll take you to Mrs Gilchrist. She's expecting you.'

Lorna Drew was about seventy with short frizzy white hair and wide hips. She scrutinised Rosamund for several unblinking seconds as though she'd been curious to see her for many years. Perhaps she had.

Rosamund followed her along a wide hall to an elegant Victorian conservatory where Molly Gilchrist was sitting. She held out her hand again. 'I'm Rosamund. Please don't get up.'

'I'll bring some coffee,' Lorna Drew said, leaving them together.

'Please sit down.'

Molly was small and frail, expensively dressed in a pleated black and cream suit, perfumed, coiffeured and carefully made-up – her face a mask, but not at all grotesque. In fact rather beautiful, Rosamund thought; rather beautiful when you got used to it.

'I'm so glad you decided to come and see me. I suppose you must be as distressed as I am.'

'I'm sorry you're distressed. You must try not to be, you know. Men aren't worth fretting about.'

What a strange thing to say, Rosamund thought. She's probably fretted about Anthony for fifty years and she's not likely to stop now.

'All his life's work,' Molly said, opening out her hands as though setting it free.

'It won't affect it,' Rosamund said. 'People expect poets to be passionate. They're judged more leniently than other people.'

'Perhaps his indiscretions, his divorce, his third marriage at the age of seventy-something, yes. But not pornography. That's not for poets. That won't be excused. Well, I'm too old to fight on his behalf, but you're not.'

Rosamund chewed her lip and looked about her, trying to think of something to say, something non-committal, non-combatitive. 'What a beautiful conservatory,' she said at last. 'What wonderful flowers.' The French doors were open to a tumult of pink and cream and the conservatory itself had groups of glazed dark blue flowerpots containing shrubs and climbing plants, many with strange, exotic, trumpet-shaped flowers.

'I water them all myself every morning,' Molly said.

'Gosh.'

'Lorna does the garden, but I have a man who comes on a Tuesday afternoon to cut the lawns. A frightful expense. Frightful.' For a second Rosamund glimpsed the hard eyes and pursed lips of a formidable woman. Then the mask was in place again. 'Are you fond of gardens?'

'Very. But mine is quite informal – a wild garden, I suppose. But it suits us.'

'How is your little son?'

Rosamund felt her heart lurching. The last thing she'd

expected was to have Molly treat her as family. 'Very well, thank you. Joshua. He's almost ten now. How old are your grandchildren?'

'Seventeen and fifteen. But I rarely see them. They live in France, you know. I suppose you heard that Alex and Selena are divorced?'

'No, I hadn't heard. I'm sorry.'

'Oh, Alex had a very bad time. A total breakdown.'

'I'm sorry,' Rosamund murmured again. There was a short silence.

'I'd like to meet your son.'

Oh my God, Rosamund thought. Just what is going on? This is the crabby and intransigent ex-wife – rich, spoilt and determined on her own way. Why is she being so bloody nice to me?

'I went to see Erica Underhill yesterday,' she said, to turn the conversation away from Joss.

'Thank you,' Molly whispered, relaxing her shoulders as though all her problems were now over.

Lorna Drew brought in the coffee, Molly managing to indicate that they shouldn't go on talking in front of her. 'Lorna is my cousin and companion,' she told Rosamund.

'Also housekeeper, cook and gardener,' Lorna said briskly, pouring out the coffee. 'But I have a little flat at the top of the house where I can escape to when things get too tough.' She gave Rosamund a bright smile, as though to mitigate the complaint in her words.

'Hers even after my death,' Molly said.

'If I live that long,' Lorna replied. There was a great deal of tension between them.

'She's twelve years younger than I am and strong as an ox.'

'Did you know Anthony?' Rosamund asked Lorna.

'Oh, yes. For many years. I used to be the secretary at a girls' boarding school in Folkestone, and Molly and Anthony would look me up on their trips back and forth from France. Sometimes during the holidays they left Alex with me. Have you met Alex?'

'Yes. But not for some years.'

'Have another scone,' Molly said.

'Thank you. They're delicious.'

The conversation flagged. Rosamund could suddenly hear the bees in the garden, traffic in the distance.

'Oh Lorna, would you phone Cécile's about my new jacket?' Molly asked, then, 'They said they'd have it in at the beginning of the week. No, you may leave the coffee here. Rosamund may want to help herself to another cup.'

Lorna left, realising she was being dismissed.

'Lovely coffee,' Rosamund told her as she went out.

'How kind of you to visit that woman,' Molly said as soon as they were on their own again. 'I do hope you managed to persuade her not to publish the poems.'

'Mrs Gilchrist, I couldn't ask her that because she's very short of money, and the book won't get half the publicity without the poems. Her flat in Earls Court has large, high rooms and the central heating is totally inadequate. She stayed in bed for a part of last winter, too cold to get up. She's over eighty, she has no help and I don't think she sees very well.'

'She's certainly got round you all right, fooled you all right. She sees well enough to drive a hard bargain. Giles says she stands to make a mint of money.'

'She's very badly off.'

'Someone has to suffer. Why should it always be me? Why should I be disturbed again in my last years? She was the one who caused all the harm. Why shouldn't she suffer?'

'Perhaps it was Anthony who harmed you both.'

There was a moment's intense stillness, as though even the flowers were holding their breath. Then the moment passed. 'She wasn't blameless. That sort of woman never is.'

'I'm sure she wasn't. But it all happened so long ago. I can understand you feeling hurt and bitter at the time, but now you've built up your own life. You have your lovely house and garden, your son and grandchildren, your own full life.'

'I've never had any life since Anthony left me.'

'But *you* divorced *him*!'

'That's how it had to be in those days. I had to divorce him

59

on grounds of adultery. He wouldn't consent to any decent settlement even for Alex unless I agreed to divorce him.'

'But if he was as cruel as that, why do you worry so much about his reputation?'

Molly considered the question very gravely. 'For my own sake, I suppose. I'm the one people will feel sorry for, and I hate being pitied. I had enough of that at the time of the divorce. "Poor Molly," people said. "Such a devoted wife." And besides, Alex and my grandchildren have always felt proud of Anthony. Now they'll despise him. I don't want that, either.'

'I don't think they will. There'll be some little publicity, but it will soon blow over. He's only written some erotic poetry, after all. He didn't blackmail or murder anyone.'

'I can't tolerate the idea of that woman benefiting from them. You seem to think of them as some sort of harmless diversion. Such harmless diversions cost me my marriage.' Molly's voice had become high and shrill. She sat very still for a moment or two, then continued in a calmer voice; 'Alex tells me you've read the poems. How could you bear to?'

'It's love poetry, nothing more. It celebrates certain parts of the body, certain love games not usually mentioned in today's more respectable poetry, but in other cultures, other times, it wouldn't be anything out of the way.'

Silence again. 'It might even enhance his reputation,' Rosamund continued. 'Anthony's poetry is often considered too cerebral, too remote, too philosophical. These poems will change all that.'

Molly seemed quite unimpressed with Rosamund's attempts to cajole her, but she spoke in a gentler voice. 'At first, we were very happy,' she said, 'though I suppose he married me on the rebound. You probably know that his first wife, Frances, had cancer and died very young. Her death left him very lonely and at first he seemed so thankful that I'd taken pity on him. For the whole of that first year he was very gentle and considerate. I thought we were happy, but perhaps not. Perhaps I never made him happy. I was never really resigned to certain parts of marriage, though I tried not to show it. I expect that was the trouble. But that was the way I'd been brought up. Was it my fault?'

She didn't seem to expect any answer, but carried straight on. 'He was the one who broke the marriage vows, anyway. I would have forgiven him – I'd forgiven him several times before – but he couldn't give that woman up. She was different from the others . . .'

'She had an abortion, you know. *Did* you know?'

Molly seemed to shrink into herself. 'No. He told me nothing. Not after I'd . . .' She failed to go on. 'Not after . . .' Her mouth trembled.

Rosamund didn't prompt her, didn't really want to hear any more. Pretending to be unaware of Molly's distress, she took her hand and patted it. 'Now try to stop worrying,' she said. 'Ignore the poems. Regard them as a little aberration. They're not important.'

'I tried to commit suicide,' Molly said, 'and he wouldn't discuss anything with me after that. It wasn't that I really wanted to die, but wanted to punish him.' Her voice became harsh again. 'I cut my wrists.'

She unbuttoned her chiffon cuffs and showed Rosamund the jagged scars, yellowish like gristle. Rosamund felt faint. 'I must go,' she said. 'You're getting tired. I'll come to see you again if I decide to write the book.'

Molly thrust out her small hand at Rosamund who was almost afraid to hold it, let alone shake it. 'Bring your son with you when you come next,' she said.

Lorna Drew followed her along the wide oak-panelled hall to the front door. Rosamund turned, waiting for her to speak.

'I suppose she showed you the scars on her wrist,' she said in honeyed tones. 'Oh yes, she'd want that in your book.'

The sun, streaming in through the coloured glass panels of the door, cast purple and vermilion patterns on her face and hands and cotton dress. "Wronged wife's suicide bid." She'd never let anyone forget that.'

Rosamund tried to speak, but couldn't. If she were at all serious about writing a book, she'd need to question Lorna Drew, but all she wanted was to get away from her.

'It's terrible to have to live with someone day after day,' Lorna said, as though to excuse her outburst. 'To do what you're asked, what you're told, day after day. With no chance of escape.'

'She's lucky to have you,' Rosamund said.

'Is she? We're cousins, but there's little love between us. We're too different. And she knows, at least I think she knows, that I too was one of Anthony's small, unimportant indiscretions. You can mention that in your book if you'd like to, Mrs Gilchrist.'

'Thank you, Miss Drew.'

Rosmund walked down the curved drive and along the quiet residential road feeling as though she were in a foreign country surrounded by enemies.

# Chapter Seven

As Rosamund was in the tube, rushing along a passage to one of the escalators, she saw a man she'd known at art school sitting there playing a violin, a cap at his side. Her stomach tightened. She was already late, but she had to make contact with him: he was the man she'd been so in love with, the one she'd broken her heart over in the first year. And now, there he was, down on his luck and looking ill and unkempt. He didn't see her staring at him; he had his eyes tightly closed as though intolerably moved by the music. She went on gazing at him.

Then she took a deep breath. 'Daniel,' she said. 'Hello, Daniel.' She could feel her heart thumping about in her chest.

He opened his eyes and recognised her at once. She was delighted to find that he looked altogether healthier and less desperate with his eyes open. 'Ah, the fair Rosamunda,' he said, with exactly the same affectation as she remembered. He got to his feet, picking up the cap and transferring the coins to his pocket in one practised movement. 'Come for a drink, Rosamund,' he said.

'Oh, I can't, Daniel. I'd love to, but I can't. I'm having supper with my father and I daren't irritate him by being late again. Can we meet another time? Tomorrow perhaps?'

'Please don't rush off. Just five minutes. Right?'

She'd forgotten how dark and deep his eyes were. He held her close to him as they went up the escalator, so close that she could feel his ribs and the warmth of his body through his denim shirt. She'd been overawed by him in the past, too nervous to respond to him. Now he seemed gentle and vulnerable.

'Where do you live?' he asked her.

'In the country – Gloucestershire. I'm only up for a few days. What about you? How are you doing?'

'Hardly surviving – as you can see. But oh Rosamund, it's lovely to see you again.'

He'd been so successful at art school – the star of his year. She remembered his huge dark canvases and his enviable self-assurance. During the first weeks of her first year – his third – he'd made a great play for her, following her about, his hand on his heart, 'Ah, the fair Rosamunda,' and quoting poetry, Byron and Keats.

She'd always been very nervous of him, though, always suspecting some underlying mockery in his gallantry. 'This is what you're working on, is it?' he'd once said when he'd come across her in front of a small, precise painting of an urban allotment. 'White railings and cabbages,' he'd said. 'How very interesting.' So that she'd immediately wanted to set it on fire.

One night in the run-up to Christmas, they'd met at a party. And he'd insisted that they were a couple. 'You're my girl,' he'd kept whispering in her ear, so that she'd almost believed it. She'd smoked pot for the first time in an effort to feel more relaxed with him, but had only become more confused and fiightened as he'd become more and more demanding. It wasn't that she didn't want to have sex with him, she did, but was afraid it would mean too much to her and too little to him. She'd always been a careful, calculating person. 'A most unattractive trait,' she told herself fifteen years later. 'You wanted him but didn't think you could hold on to him, so you were afraid to take that first step.'

After several rebuffs, he'd eventually cooled towards her. And afterwards during her entire college life, she'd avoided the extravagantly flamboyant men, keeping with the quieter, less demanding types who were satisfied with hours of talk and small favours.

On the last day of the summer term though, the end of Daniel's time at college, she'd become brave or desperate enough to go to his flat to try to make contact with him again.

'He's already left, dearie,' one of his flat-mates had said, when she'd asked for him. 'Won't I do instead? Anything he can do, I can do better.'

She'd looked at him blankly. 'Could you give him a message?'

'Perhaps.'

'Could you let him know that Rosamund was asking for him?'

She wondered if he'd ever received that message. He certainly hadn't responded. She remembered how sad, how bereft she'd felt, knowing that she'd lost the last chance of putting things right between them; that she wouldn't see him again. It was something she'd buried away and almost managed to forget.

'It must be fifteen years,' she told him as they walked across the road together. 'Or is it more? Anyway, it's lovely to see you again.'

They went to the nearest pub, huge and empty, and Daniel got them a beer each and then they sat close together and examined each other like two people finding the other still alive after an earthquake or a storm at sea.

'Are you with someone?' Daniel asked her, the back of his hand against her cheek.

Her throat tightened. 'Not now. No, I'm on my own. I had an affair with someone for almost three years, but it's over. What about you?'

'On my own. Was with someone for eight years, but she went back to America last Christmas.'

'Good. I hope she stays there.'

They smiled at each other as though something was being decided. He stroked the back of her neck. 'You're lovely,' he said. 'Oh, I was so in love with you. Thought about you for years.'

'I thought about you, too. Oh hell, I'm very late, Daniel. I really must go now. But it doesn't matter, does it? I've got nothing else planned. I hope we can meet again. Can we? Tomorrow?'

He seemed to be hesitating.

'Listen, you said things were going badly with you. Well, you could come home with me if you'd like to.' She could feel herself blushing. 'I mean, you could be my lodger, share my studio for a while . . . I mean, you said you were finding it hard to survive.'

'I'd like to. Are you quite sure about it?'

'Quite sure. If it would suit you.'

They clutched each other's hands. For a minute, perhaps two, they sat in silence, hardly breathing.

'I'm a complete failure,' Daniel said then. 'My flat's been repossessed, no one's interested in my work, and now I can't even afford a studio. To be honest, I can't even afford paints at the moment.'

'I've got a good studio and a nice house – very isolated, but you might like it, at least for a while. Just until you get on your feet again. When could you come? I've got a nine-year-old son, but I think you'd like him too.'

'When are you going back?'

'On Friday.'

'I'll come with you then, on Friday, if that's all right. Just for a trial period. I've got nothing to pack, nothing to do.' He looked hesitant again. 'Will your son like me?'

'I'm sure he will. He likes all the people I like.'

'I'm a complete failure, but I can play cricket.'

As he put his hand on her thigh, it was as much as she could do not to moan in response. She felt full of hope and very happy.

She had no worries about leaving him because they were meeting again at twelve the next day outside the National Gallery – he said that people up from the country always met outside the National Gallery.

He put her on the tube train and they kissed through the window. 'I'm a complete failure,' he said, 'but I love you, Rosamunda.'

'I'm sorry I'm late again,' Rosamund told Dora as she walked into the kitchen. 'I met an old friend and stayed to have a drink with him.'

'Why didn't you bring him along?'

'I didn't think of it. Anyway, I'm seeing him again

66

tomorrow. Is there anything I can do? I'm so glad you're not waiting for me.'

'Your father was late as well, so we've only just got started. You can help with the salad. How was Molly?'

'Not as frightening as I'd imagined. Oh, I thought I was totally on Erica's side and against Molly, but now I want to adopt both of them. They're two pathetic old dears who've had rather tragic lives.'

'Open an old people's home,' her father said. 'It's certainly a paying game. Jeremy Trevis's wife drives a Porsche these days. Old people don't eat anything, that's the beauty of it. Turn up the heating and have a few large tellys about the place and they sleep all day and have scrambled eggs instead of dinner.'

'Ignore him,' Dora said. 'He's annoyed because I've asked him to cook the chops ... You see, I think Joss should be getting a share of Anthony's estate. He was a rich man, wasn't he, quite apart from his writing, and you only had the school-house and a small annuity, so surely his son should inherit half of whatever Molly leaves?'

'That was never mentioned,' Rosamund said. 'No, whatever Molly leaves will go to her son and her grandchildren.'

'That doesn't seem fair to me, does it to you, Paul?'

'What is fair?' Paul asked, turning the chops rather fussily. 'Nothing is fair. I certainly won't have anything to leave him or anyone else. That doesn't seem fair either.'

'I think you should take Joss to visit her. Old ladies adore children. And she'd probably think he was the image of Anthony.'

'He's not Anthony's son,' Rosamund said.

Her father shook his head as though concussed. He'd recently had a small part in *Casualty*, and Rosamund had seen him doing something very similar then. 'Not Anthony's son?' he said, enunciating each word very clearly.

'Well, I never said he was. People concluded he was when we got married, but I never said so.'

'Did Anthony know?' Dora asked, brisk again.

'Oh, yes. Anthony and I didn't . . . you know. We didn't . . .'

'Not at all?'

'No. Well, we slept together sometimes, but we didn't have sex. Not exactly.'

'No penetration,' Dora suggested.

'He was impotent,' Paul said. 'Well, aren't we all, we men of a certain age.'

'Not all,' Dora said in a sweet voice. 'Tell me, does your mother know?'

'I'm not sure. I've never told her, but I sometimes think she suspects it.'

'And I suppose we mustn't ask who the father was,' Dora said.

'No. He was married and not at all interested in me. And to be honest, I was even less interested in him. It was all rather sordid. Not much more than a one-night stand.'

'Who was he?' Paul asked, ignoring the way Dora was looking at him. 'I can bloody ask, I'm her bloody father. The bastard! How old were you? Eighteen?'

'Twenty-four. Oh, I don't think you'd noticed me much since I was about eighteen, so it's an understandable mistake. Anyway, I shouldn't have told you. I was actually talking to Dora who has always been interested in me and in Joss.'

'So has your father, love. He has a very busy life, but he's most interested in you both.'

'These chops are done,' her father said. 'I do hope the potatoes are ready, Dora.'

'Can you understand any of it?' Paul asked his wife as they were getting ready for bed.

'Certainly. Marriage is a matter of barter, exactly as in primitive tribes when the woman with most cattle got the man with the biggest prick. You're handsome and urbane, I'm no beauty, but I'm ten years younger and quite terrifically smart, so we were both satisfied. Don't you understand? Now Anthony was seventy-four and dying, Rosamund was twenty-four and pregnant. So she did quite well for herself, a lovely house and a small income. Of course if he'd lived to be ninety-four, she'd have had a tough deal. Unless she'd really loved him, which she didn't.'

'For God's sake,' Paul said, putting out the light.

*

Rosamund woke very early next morning and left the flat at eight-thirty when Dora went to work.

She spent the morning having her hair done in a very expensive salon, so that it looked as curly and tousled as a child's hair washed in rainwater, and buying a dress and sandals. The dress was of a gauzy material, primrose yellow with a deep burgundy hem, and the sandals were bright green. She dropped off her cream suit at a charity shop and bought some multi-coloured glass beads while she was there. She arrived at the National Gallery half an hour early and sat on the steps to wait.

# Chapter Eight

'I've had a swine of a day,' Rosamund told Ingrid when she arrived at her flat that evening. 'I ran into a friend in the Underground last night, we arranged to meet today and he didn't turn up. He just didn't turn up.'

'What a shit,' Ingrid said. 'Bloody men. Let's have a drink. I'll phone for some Chinese as soon as Ben arrives. Get that down you and you'll feel better. How was your father?'

'My father? I don't want to talk about my father. I want to talk about this friend I met. Daniel. I knew him in my first year at art school. He used to fancy me.'

'Crisps? I think I've got some somewhere.'

'He said he was in love with me, but he didn't turn up. What can have happened to him? Oh Ingrid, he used to have such beautiful clothes and now he's really shabby and down-at-heel. And he didn't turn up. And I waited for him for almost five hours.'

'Five hours! Just someone you happened to run into. Oh Rosamund, get with it. The world is full of men who enjoy making women suffer – and he's obviously one of them.'

Rosamund gave her a long, hurt look. 'I used to be so intimidated by him, but he's gentler now, much less sure of himself.'

'For God's sake, don't turn it into a tragedy. You met someone, but he turned out to be a wrong 'un. Just forget him.'

'I stayed there for hours, trusting him, having complete faith in him.'

'Rosamund, you're an idiot, but please don't cry. Would you like a coffee?'

'I meant to visit Erica again tomorrow, but now I'm far too upset. I feel desperate, Ingrid. As though everything I've ever wanted has slipped away from me. He was so loving, so whole-hearted. I can't accept that he was only having a game with me.'

'Well, perhaps he wasn't. Perhaps he intended to meet you, but after sleeping on it, realised that he was taking on more than he could cope with. You're a very intense person, Rosamund. People just aren't used to that these days.'

'I was only intense because he was. I've always been timid. I've never made the first move towards anyone. But we were so close and happy last night. It was as if all the dreams I'd had in college had come true. I had such a feeling of well-being; he was free – I mean, he wasn't married or anything – and there seemed nothing to keep us apart. Oh Ingrid, what can I do now? How can I find him again? He's not in any of the dir-ectories. I phoned every art gallery, but no one had his address. One or two people thought they might have heard of him, but no one had his address or telephone number.'

'Has he got your address?'

'No. You see, we were meant to be meeting again today. He was going to come home with me on Friday. He said he want-ed to come to live with me – I mean, to share my studio. How could he have changed his mind overnight?'

'But how could you expect him to leave London, the life he knows, all his friends, to follow you to the country where he knows no one? After one chance meeting? Anyway, what would your son think if you suddenly brought a man home with you? Surely you'd have to consider the effect on Joss?'

'No, he'd be my lodger, that's all. I've often spoken of having someone to share my studio, Joss knows that.'

'Come on, if you were thinking of him only as a lodger, you wouldn't be this upset.'

'No, of course I wouldn't. I couldn't help hoping it would develop into something more. That Joss would warm to him, he's very well-adjusted, he'd like Daniel, I know he would. And, yes, I also hoped Daniel would want to stay. Oh Ingrid, he said he loved me. I know you think I'm exaggerating, trying to make a chance encounter seem a miracle, but that's what it seemed to me. I couldn't sleep last night for the wonder of it.'

'Have another drink. And listen to me. You wanted to meet a new boyfriend – you told me that – and you wanted another child. You met someone halfway presentable and you were ready to imagine he was the answer to all your prayers. Very dangerous.'

'How can I find him again? Let me decide the rest.'

'He'll find you if he wants to. If he doesn't, what's the point of trying to track him down? You won't be able to make him change his mind. Tell yourself it was only a dream. I've often had wonderful dreams – that someone loves me so much I know I'm going to be safe and happy for the rest of my life. And then I have to wake up and face all the rubbish again. It wasn't much more than a dream, Rosamund.'

'It was. He was real, a real person – skinny body, shabby clothes, deep loving eyes. I loved him fifteen years ago, but I lost him because I was frightened and timid. And everything I did afterwards was because of that failure . . . and I thought I was having a second chance.'

'You must put him right out of your mind.'

'Must I? I'm so tired I can't think straight. I stood around for hours waiting for him. Oh, I'll go home tomorrow and never venture to London again. How can I even think of writing this book when I don't understand the first thing about life!'

'I'll tell you the first thing about life. And I'm not even drunk yet. Love is bloody great, yes, but it's never for the right person at the right time. *Never*. But quite often work can save your sanity, OK? So go to see Erica again tomorrow. You can't let her down. You were full of plans when you rang me last night. What's the matter now?'

'I was just thinking of Joss. I didn't ring him last night. Would you mind if I phoned him now? It might cheer me up.'

'Go ahead. Oh, where the hell is Ben? Bastard! He said he'd try to be back early.'

*

73

It was Joss who answered the phone. 'Mr and Mrs Spiers,' he said. 'Who shall I say called?'

'Hello, Joss, it's me. It's Mum.'

'Oh.' He sounded disappointed.

'Who were you expecting?'

'Anyone really. It's just they've got a new pad here for jotting down messages. Do you want to leave any messages?'

'Where are Mum and Brian?'

'At the pub.'

'At the pub?' She tried to keep the surprise out of her voice.

'It's Wednesday. They always go to the George on Wednesday.'

'Well, how are you, darling?'

'Very-well-thank-you-how-are-you.'

'I'm quite well too.'

'So do you want to leave a message for them?'

'No, thank you.' How could they go to the pub and leave a nine-year-old alone?

'Not even "love from Rosamund"?'

'Not even that.'

'But the thing is, I'd rather like to write a message on the pad. It's a new one bought specially.'

'OK. Put this down; "Mum rang at nine-thirty and was surprised to find you out."'

'Is it all right if I put nine-twenty because I'm supposed to be in bed by nine-thirty?'

'Yes, that's fine.'

'Mum, are you angry about something?'

'Not really. Listen, I'll be home on Friday. I'm looking forward to that – are you?'

'Do you want to speak to Linda?'

'Who's Linda?'

'A childminder. That's something like a babysitter but much more trouble, she says.'

'Joss, will you tear that message from the pad and write, "Rosamund phoned and sent her best love and thanks."'

'"Rosamund phoned and sent her best love and thanks." Right. Lucky I'm here, isn't it, to take down all these messages.'

'And best love to you as well.'

'Shall I tell you a rhyme I learnt at school today?'

'No, thanks. I know the sort of rhymes you learn at school. Write it down on the pad for Brian.'

'He's so lovely,' she told Ingrid, 'and he'd have loved Daniel. They'd have got on so well.'

'Where the hell is Ben? He promised to be home by seven.'

'He's always been in my mind, I think, the way he used to be; so young and formidable.'

'People get older. I used to be young and formidable.'

'You still are. In your prime and glossy as a cat. If I could paint, I'd love to paint you. I'd like to paint this room, too. Your flat, it's so full and cluttered. Dora's is very elegant with hardly anything in it. You feel you have to sit in just the right place or you'll spoil the effect. '

'This is only cluttered because it's got all my things in it as well as Ben's and neither of us is willing to get rid of anything. It's a mess really. We've only been together three months and we're fighting already. He's staying out to punish me, I'm sure. He doesn't like me having friends. Oh, sod him! What was Erica's place like?'

'Very Edwardian. A lot of deep red. Very voluptuous.'

'You must see her again tomorrow.'

'Ingrid, you seem obsessed with Erica. Why are you so keen that I go again?'

There was a moment's hard silence.

'I know Ben would be thrilled if I could get some photographs of you and Erica together.'

'Why?'

'It would add weight to the book, wouldn't it? The fact that you meet would indicate that you're on her side.'

'And against Molly?'

'Not necessarily. But you must see that a picture on the jacket of an eighty-year-old mistress and a thirty-year-old wife would be a superb sales gimmick.'

'I wonder if he'd like me topless as well? Would that be an even more effective gimmick?'

'It would all be perfectly discreet, I promise you, all

perfectly circumspect. Ben isn't the sort who'd go for anything vulgar. He's a serious journalist.'

'Does he stand to make a lot of money from this book?'

'He hasn't mentioned money to me. Why?'

'If money doesn't corrupt people, it certainly seems to confuse them.'

'I'm sure he'd be prepared to pay you a percentage if you cooperated with him.'

'When you came to the schoolhouse, you told me that you had no ulterior motive in visiting me. It seems to me you had. You wrote an article about me, but you were also probing and plotting for Ben.'

'Probing and plotting, that sounds awful. I would do a lot for him, but not that. I only want to take some photographs of you and Erica Underhill in her Edwardian sitting-room. Is that so awful?'

'I don't suppose it is. I think I'm just getting hungry. I always get bad-tempered when I'm hungry.'

'I'll phone now; two Lotus House specials. No, Ben won't be home for a meal. He's drinking somewhere now.'

Ingrid phoned the restaurant while Rosamund sat very still, studying her long, thin hands as though seeing them for the first time.

'I had a manfriend until quite recently,' she told Ingrid when she came back. 'He was really nice, we got on well together, but then his wife lost her job and wanted him back—'

Ingrid cut in, 'And that's why you're desperate for someone else.'

'That's not what I meant. I was simply going to say that I'm not completely inexperienced, that I have some knowledge of love, that I do know what I want.'

'I thought I knew what I wanted. For about three weeks after meeting Ben, I couldn't sleep for excitement. We've been living together for three months and already the best is over . . . Let's have another drink.'

It was just after one-thirty when Ingrid decided that Ben didn't intend to come back that night, and if he did, he could bloody well sleep on the sofa. 'You can sleep in my bed,' she told Rosamund, 'the sofa's hideously uncomfortable.' She threw a blanket and a sheet onto the sofa and she and Rosamund got ready for bed, said goodnight and turned the lights off.

After a while, though, Ingrid turned the bedside light back on, leaned over onto her elbow and pulled back the duvet.

'I've never had any lesbian tendencies,' Rosamund said nervously. 'Not even when I was fifteen. So just go to sleep, all right?'

'Neither have I,' Ingrid said, 'but we're both miserable and we can try to comfort ourselves a bit, can't we?' She put her hand on Rosamund's breast, circling the nipple very gently with her index finger. 'Take your T-shirt off,' she said. 'What's the harm?'

Rosamund complied rather crossly. 'We'll be so embarrassed about this in the morning,' she said.

Ingrid moved up closer to her and leaning over started to lick her nipples very slowly and lazily with the tip of her tongue, first one and then the other. When she felt her begin to relax, she started to suck them, first one and then the other, as slowly and gently as before. Soon she could feel Rosamund move her belly towards her, a very slight movement, not much deeper than breathing. She lifted her head and saw her closed eyes and her slightly open mouth. At that point she raised herself and lay over her, her belly over hers, their pubic mounds together. And she kissed her, thrusting her tongue deep into her mouth while her hand stroked the soft flesh of her inner thigh.

'That's all,' Rosamund said, heaving her away. 'I just don't want this. I know you think you're comforting me, but it's not what I want.'

'What makes you imagine I was thinking about you?' Ingrid asked. She sighed and turned her back on Rosamund. 'Could you put your arm round me, please?'

Rosamund moved close to her, kissed her shoulder, put her arm tightly around her and they slept almost immediately.

When Rosamund woke she could hear Ingrid and Ben having a ferocious quarrel in the kitchen. It was nine o'clock. Ingrid should have left the flat half an hour before, she was blaming Ben for her lateness and he was blaming her for his uncomfortable night on the sofa. 'You know why she's here,' Ingrid was saying through gritted teeth. 'She's here because you wanted me to interview her.'

Rosamund had a shower and dressed, and when she joined them they were having coffee together, not yet friends but at least observing a truce of sorts.

'I'm sorry I turned you out of your bed,' Rosamund said, as soon as Ingrid had introduced them. 'Ingrid didn't expect you back last night.' She took the coffee he passed her. 'When did you get back?' she asked sweetly.

'About two, I suppose.'

'Liar,' Ingrid said. 'I was awake till after three.'

'We both were,' Rosamund added. 'Whatever were you doing till three? Not working, I hope?'

'I went back to a friend's,' Ben said, the looks he was directing at her indicating that it was certainly none of her business. 'I knew Ingrid had company, so we had a few drinks together.'

'Ingrid and I had a few drinks together, too,' she said pleasantly.

Ben was small and very good-looking, black hair cut very short and olive skin, a khaki shirt and trousers. Rosamund didn't like him, didn't trust him, and realised he felt the same about her.

'I'll be off, then,' she told Ingrid as soon as she'd finished her coffee. 'I'll be staying one more night with Dora and my father and going back home on Friday. Goodbye, Ben.'

Ingrid took her to the door, tweaking her nipples as she kissed her. 'I'll be in touch,' she said.

To Rosamund's surprise there seemed not a trace of embarrassment between them.

# Chapter Nine

'I don't think I should have come to London, Dora,' Rosamund said that evening. 'It's been lovely to see you, but on the whole it seems to have unsettled me.'

'Good. Being unsettled makes you ready to take risks and live dangerously.'

'So what should I do?'

'Phone some publishers about your book, get that sorted out. Try to meet some of them. Discuss finances. Be greedy.'

'I'm not sure about the book. I can't be hard on Erica, but Molly treated me as family, so I suppose I should take her side.'

'Balls. Molly's a devious, calculating old woman and you owe her nothing. Someone's going to make a packet out of Anthony's love-life, so why shouldn't it be you? Take a deep breath, pick up the phone and get talking.'

'I don't know. Anthony seems to have been such a shit, but he was lovely to me and Joss, so how can I judge him? His first wife died when she was only twenty-five, so that excuses him, I suppose, to some extent . . . He always implied that she was the love of his life and that everything had gone wrong as a result of her death.'

'Of course he did. If your mother had died of cancer at the age of twenty-five, your father would be thinking of her as the love of *his* life and would blame everything on her death. Henry the Eighth thought Jane Seymour was the love of his life because she died young. Even though he got his doctors to hack her to death to save his child. Men love the young wife excuse.'

'Erica had to have an abortion. An agonising time, she said.'

'You know so much, darling. Who else has your knowledge? It's a fascinating story and you'd tell it with love and sympathy. Why leave it to some journalist who'll turn it into something really sordid? Molly will certainly get someone to write it; she's not going to let Erica have the last word. And think of the money you'd make. It might even be turned into a film. Wonderful parts for two ageing actresses. Could Paul play Anthony, I wonder? He's never managed to break into films.'

'And Molly tried to commit suicide – she showed me the scars on her wrists. And the cousin who looks after her now was another of Anthony's lovers.'

'My God, you'd never have to work again. You could send Joss to a good school and go to Italy to paint, live happy ever after.'

'I'm not at all happy, Dora.'

'I know, love. What happened? You seemed so happy a couple of days ago.'

'I met someone. Someone I used to know. I bumped into him on the underground . . . but it didn't work out.'

'Come to live in London. Sell the schoolhouse and get a flat near us. Let me look after you. Do you have to go home tomorrow? Stay a few more days at least.'

'No, I can't expect Mum to cope with Joss over the weekend. In any case, I'm looking forward to seeing him now.'

Paul joined them from the kitchen where he'd been washing up.

'Doesn't he look handsome in his apron, Rosamund? Your father, you see, has to dress up for every little job, it's his stage training. He's got a boiler suit for adjusting the radiators and a navy beret for going out to buy wine . . . Don't you think your daughter should come and live near us, Paul? Instead of burying herself away in the country?'

Paul studied them both for several seconds. 'I don't know,' he said, as grave as if he'd been asked to settle the fate of nations. 'If I were writing a book, I think I'd prefer the peace of the countryside.'

'If I do decide to write a book, I think I'll call it *Anthony*

80

*Gilchrist, the Man,* making it clear that I don't consider myself able to comment on his poetry, pornographic or otherwise.'

'No, no, no,' Dora said. 'I was thinking along the lines of *Wife and Mistress*. That's got a certain . . .'

'But even in the first chapter, the first few pages, I'd have to be unkind to so many people. For instance, I'd have to be unkind to Father.'

'You make some money out of it, kiddo, and be as unkind as you please.'

'You see I'd have to infer that I was looking for a father-figure, wouldn't I? I don't know whether I was – I don't think so – but it makes some sort of sense, doesn't it? I mean, I was never in love with Anthony, so it might have been something like that – which, of course, suggests that Paul had let me down as a father.'

'That's fair enough. I had.'

'No, I never felt that. I always liked it when you were home, but I always understood that you had to go back to London to work. I never felt let down.'

'But when he married me, darling, you must have felt rather bitter at that time.'

'But only for Mother's sake. I didn't feel *I* was being badly treated. And during your wedding I made an adjustment and knew he was doing the right thing.'

Dora looked at her rather timidly, waiting for her to continue.

'You see, it was the first time I'd seen Father look like that, or heard his voice like that. I mean, when he recited that poem to you. That Herrick. That was really moving. Hair-raising, I mean. I measure love from that.'

'Oh, darling,' Dora said.

'For God's sake, Rosamund, what a twit you are. I mean, to worry about my feelings when everything's OK between us.'

'Oh, darling,' Dora said again.

'For God's sake,' Paul said, 'don't let's get bogged down. Women are so bloody sentimental.'

'And then there's Brian. Mother's bound to think I'm belittling him if I tell the truth, which was that he simply didn't want me living with them. Of course he didn't. Why should he have wanted to start married life with a spotty seventeen-year-old stepdaughter, all gloom and hormones.'

'Don't even mention him,' Dora said. 'Simply say that your mother married her accountant, Mr Brian Spiers, and settled down very happily with him. People will read between the lines, but let them. That always happens. So who else are you worried about?'

'Mother won't like any of it. If I'm truthful about our early relationship – Anthony's and mine – she'll be shocked, and I don't suppose there's much point in writing at all unless I am truthful.'

'What was the truth?' Paul asked. 'Let's see how shocked I am.'

'I posed in the nude for him and he paid me. That's how I managed to get to Florence the summer I left Brighton. I told Mother I'd won the money in a competition.'

'It doesn't seem all that shocking to me,' Dora said. 'I did far worse when I was a girl.'

'Oh yes?' Paul muttered. 'And what, pray, did *you* get up to?'

'I'm not writing a book, so I'll say nothing further.'

'What an innocent I was,' Paul said. 'I actually went to a ball, met Marian and courted her very chastely for two and a half years.'

'Men are so *decent*,' Dora replied. Then, turning to Rosamund, 'You needn't mention the money. It's only the relationship between you and Anthony which is important. When did it develop beyond the nude posing?'

'I'm not sure it did. We were very happy together. I used to make him laugh. I'm not sure how, I don't think I've ever made anyone else laugh, but we always seemed to be laughing and happy. I used to look forward to seeing him every holiday, but I don't think there was much development. I suppose I'd have to admit that if I was being truthful. Our marriage was never consummated. As I told you last night.'

'And during one holiday you arrived telling him that you were pregnant?'

'Yes. And wondering about having an abortion. And this part is really about Erica Underhill because she nearly died having an abortion, so that Anthony was absolutely adamant that I wasn't to have one.'

'You didn't consider marrying the father?'

'He was married already. But I wouldn't have considered it in any case because I didn't love him. It was an altogether sad little episode. He was unhappy in his marriage and because I was on my own, he assumed that I should be grateful for whatever came my way. He called at my flat, I invited him in for a coffee and then found that he wouldn't take no for an answer.'

'Are we talking about rape, here?' her father asked.

'No. Just the seduction of an inexperienced woman by a very experienced man. Just an old-fashioned seduction.'

There was a moment's silence before Rosamund continued. 'And I'm loath to admit to all that because of Joss. He might be very hurt by it.'

'Oh Rosie, I don't know how you've been able to keep all this to yourself all this time. You really are a very strong person, isn't she, Paul?'

'Women are very strong and very devious.'

'Of course, it would do Joss good to have a father,' Dora continued.

'But it doesn't have to be his real father does it?' Rosamund said.

'Does his real father ever visit you?'

'No.'

'A man answers your telephone from time to time, Rosamund.'

'That's Thomas – Thomas Woodison. He and I had an affair for about three years, but he's married too, and it's recently ended because his wife had another baby.'

'I think I'm going to bed,' Paul said.

'One careful little affair in the last ten years. Is that enough to turn you against me?'

'I haven't turned against you, God knows, but I really feel I want to close my eyes now and think of my own small problems. Like lack of work, lack of prospects and lack of money. OK?'

'There's not much more, anyway. Thomas was a very sweet man, but we weren't desperately in love – at least I don't think so – so neither of us was heartbroken. Just rather sad, I suppose.'

'When you came in tonight, you looked more than rather sad. But I mustn't pry,' Dora said virtuously.

'I was crying about someone quite different. I'll tell you about that another time.'

'Go to bed, Paul. I'm staying up with Rosie. Just another half-hour, love, and another gin.'

'Good night,' Paul said. 'I really can't be doing with heart-break. Not at this time of night.'

They watched him leave the room. He turned at the door shrugging his shoulders; an actor trying to make as much as possible of a small part. Both women smiled indulgently at him.

'His name's Daniel Hawkins. He was a third-year student when I was in my first year at art school. I think I've loved him ever since those days, though I thought I was over it till I met him again in the underground.'

'And he's married now?'

'No. He'd been with someone for years, he said, but she recently went back to America.'

'So that's promising.'

'That's what I thought. I was so happy, Dora. But he didn't turn up for our date yesterday. I waited and waited. I thought it meant as much to him as it did to me – but it obviously didn't. And I can't track him down. I phoned every art gallery asking if they had an address for him, but no one had. '

'This is a temporary setback,' Dora said briskly. 'He'll turn up, I'm sure. Where were you supposed to meet?'

'Outside the National Gallery.'

'So he couldn't have phoned to let you know he was unable to make it. He'll get in touch with you.'

'But how can he? I didn't give him my address or telephone number. He doesn't know where I live.'

'Darling, there aren't too many Gilchrists around. He'll get hold of you.'

'I don't think he even knows my name, doesn't even know I was married.'

'In that case he'll look up Harcourt and he's bound to get us. Did you tell him you were visiting us?'

'You're not in the directory, Dora. I'd thought of that.'

'He'll find us. I expect he knows your father's an actor. He'll contact us through Equity.'

'I don't know. We didn't have time to talk much. He said he'd like to come home with me to share my studio, and then there didn't seem much more to say. Ingrid said he'd found it too much to take and decided to back out.'

'Rubbish. He'll turn up here within the next week and I'll give him your address. No, I'll drive him straight down to the schoolhouse. It's going to be all right, I promise you.'

'Oh Dora, I can't be at all optimistic. I want him so much that I can't help fearing the worst.'

# Chapter Ten

Rosamund arrived back by four o'clock on Friday and before she'd had time to draw breath, her mother was at the gate.

'Where's Joss?' she asked, kissing her and trying to keep the panic out of her voice.

'That's what I've come to tell you, dear.'

'Oh, God. What?'

'He's all right. He's fine. He's gone away for the weekend that's all. Just sit down, dear, and try to keep calm.'

'Mum, I've never been away from him before. I was looking forward to seeing him. Where is he?'

'We had bad news, dear, on Wednesday night when we were in the George. It's Harry's mother, dear.'

'Harry's mother? Whatever's the matter with her?'

'Killed herself, dear. Yes, committed suicide. No one knows why. Took a massive overdose of something. I knew you'd be shocked. You knew her quite well, didn't you? I remember you telling me about the new baby. I suppose it could be something like post-natal depression. Well, I told you how dreadful she looked when I saw her last. So old and drained. Awful, isn't it.'

'Terrible. And Joss has gone to stay with Harry?'

'Yes. They've gone to North Wales. To their Granny. Yes, the whole family. Well, her husband couldn't cope with a new baby, could he, as well as everything else? His mother is a doctor's widow, apparently, a very capable woman no doubt, with a big house near Denbigh in North Wales, and he's taken them all there. Of course the older boys were better able to cope, but Mr Woodison felt Harry would be so much happier if he had Joss with him. He came to see me after school yesterday. I think Mrs Butler or the Headmistress must have given him our address, and I didn't feel I could refuse. He'll be bringing the boys – but not the baby, of course – back on Tuesday for the funeral on Wednesday. Cremation I think, dear, though I can't help feeling that a burial would be much easier for the children to accept. There's something very brutal about . . . What is it, dear?'

'I think I'm going to . . .'

'Put your head right down between your knees. That's it. Very disturbing, isn't it? Shall I get you a drop of brandy? Oh, you really should keep a bottle in the house, dear, for this sort of occasion. Well, I'll make you some tea. Now don't sit up too suddenly. Harry's father left you his mother's telephone number so that you can contact Joss later on. I expect they'll be there by about seven. Now would you like to come and have supper with Brian and me? I've got a piece of really fresh Scottish salmon with new potatoes, new peas and watercress sauce, and you can tell me all about your father and Dora.'

'Thank you. I have to talk to Thomas first – and to Joss, of course. But I suppose I will get hungry and I'm not feeling up to doing much for myself.'

'Of course not. Drink your tea, dear. They should be there by seven, so that you can phone and come afterwards. I'll make supper for eight. We might go to the George, later, to cheer you up.'

'Mum, I had a bit of a fling with Thomas. Which is why I feel so particularly dreadful.'

Her mother sighed dramatically. 'I had gathered something, of course. Joss used to talk so much about him. Everything was Thomas at one time. I thought you seemed . . . very good friends.'

'It was over, though, Mum. We'd broken it off because of the new baby.'

'So you must put it right out of your mind, dear.'

'She'd lost a very prestigious job. That was her main worry, I know that.'

'Quite. And having a baby at her time of life was the worst

thing she could have done. It plays havoc with the hormones. Did I tell you there was an article about it in the May *Readers Digest*? Remind me to show it to you. Do you feel better now, or would you like me to stay with you for a while? Are you quite sure? I'll be on my way then, dear, to let you get on with the unpacking and so on. By the way, I put Joss's school clothes and his games kit in the washing machine as soon as he got back this afternoon, so they'll be clean and ironed for him when he gets back.'

'Thanks, Mum. What would I do without you?'

If only she had a mind like her mother's, Rosamund thought, everything thrust neatly into its own compartment and shut away. She walked with her to the car. 'Love to Brian,' she called as Marian pulled away.

When her mother had gone, Rosamund put on some boots and climbed up Barrow Hill. It was a misty evening, the sky dove-coloured, the air still, the bleating of sheep and lambs the only sound. Eliza's face was before her, thin and finely drawn, long straight nose, fair hair fashionably sculpted, pale drooping eyes with reddened eyelids; a face often plain but occasionally beautiful. She suddenly remembered the way she'd shrugged her shoulders when she'd last seen her. A gesture, she realised now, of utter despondency, a signal that she was somewhere far, far beyond hope. Why hadn't she felt able to respond to that despair? Was it from guilt? Because women were supposed to stick together – sisters – not steal each other's husbands? But Eliza, God knows, had never made the slightest overture of friendship towards her. It was Thomas who had needed her, whereas Eliza had made it very clear that she was far too busy to have anything to do with any of her neighbours in the village. She often had evenings out – dinners with important clients, she told Thomas – though Rosamund had always suspected more intimate occasions.

She felt an immense sympathy for poor Eliza, but anger too, at what she had done. She should have considered Thomas and their children. In her agitation, Rosamund climbed the hill faster and faster until her chest began to ache with the strain, and when she sat down at last on a low stone wall, she burst out crying, her loud, terrible sobs frightening her by their suddenness and because they reminded her of the way Eliza had cried the last time they'd met.

Once she'd started she couldn't seem to stop. She was filled with a sorrow and an anger she couldn't bear. Everything had gone wrong and there seemed no comfort in the world. By this time she didn't know whether she was crying for herself because she'd lost Daniel, for Eliza, driven to despair, or for Thomas left alone with three motherless boys and a baby who didn't even have a name. What had Tess called her little son? Sorrow. She started sobbing again, even more desperately than before.

And then it was over. Nothing could get worse, she told herself, so it could only get better. And as she blew her nose and dried her eyes she saw the sunset, tenderly pink and calm in all the misty greyness. It seemed an omen; it seemed like hope.

She sat for a few more minutes, then made her way home, still gulping air and sniffing.

When she arrived, she felt more tired than she'd ever felt in her life. She wished she hadn't agreed to go to her mother's for supper; what she needed was a sandwich and an early night.

The telephone rang and she rushed to answer it, hoping it was Joss. But it was Ingrid to tell her that she and Ben had had a devastating row. Something had gone wrong concerning the autobiography. He wouldn't tell her what it was because he was convinced it was something she already knew. 'What can it be?' she asked Rosamund. 'Do you know anything about it?'

'No, nothing. Erica didn't mention any sort of hitch.'

'Will you let me know if you hear anything?'

'Of course.'

'He's moved out, Rosamund. I thought he was bluffing, but he packed all his bags and went.'

'God, I'm sorry. Whatever can be the matter with him? He seemed in a pretty bad mood when I was there.'

'He was. And afterwards he got worse and worse. He seemed to think it was you who'd persuaded Erica Underhill to change her mind about publishing the poems. And of course he knows the book would be a financial disaster without the poems.'

'I had nothing to do with it. I didn't suggest that she change her mind, because I knew how much she needed the money. Perhaps Molly or her son have tried to put pressure on her. I've no idea, but I'll let you know if I hear anything.'

'I'm really upset, Rosamund. I know he was boorish when you were here, but he isn't usually like that. I'm really desperate.'

'I'll phone you tomorrow, Ingrid. I'm expecting a call from Joss now. Things are very complicated here; too complicated to explain at the moment, but I'll ring you tomorrow.'

'You don't sound very concerned or sympathetic.'

'Of course I am, Ingrid. All the same, I've got to ring off now.'

It was almost eight before Thomas rang. He told her that everyone was all right, including Joss. He begged her not to feel guilty about anything, but he himself sounded overwhelmed with guilt and despair.

'Here's Joss,' he said suddenly, as though he couldn't manage another word without breaking down.

'I'm being a great help, Mum,' Joss assured her. 'Granny said I must try to be a great help and I am. I'm not arguing with Martin and Stephen and I'm not fighting with Harry and I'm saying thank you and please may I to their Granny and passing things at the table.'

'You're a very good boy and I miss you.'

'I knew you'd say that. Tomorrow we're going to a funfair at the seaside.'

'Be very careful, won't you, on the rides.'

'I knew you'd say that.'

'Thomas is taking the boys to a funfair tomorrow,' Rosamund told her mother and Brian over supper. 'I do hope they'll all be safe.'

'Of course they will. Harry's father is a teacher, isn't he, so he's used to looking after children.'

'He didn't look after his wife too well,' Brian said. 'Frank Dudley was telling us there was another woman involved.'

'Rubbish,' Marian retorted. 'His poor wife was suffering from post-natal depression. I saw her in the butcher's last week and she looked frightful. It's strange how people can't accept any obvious explanation but have to invent some unpleasant story. They just can't resist a bit of scandal.'

'She'd lost her job,' Rosamund added. 'She was one of the directors of some computer company. She was sacked and her PA promoted.'

'That wasn't the story, according to Frank Dudley.' Brian coughed, declining further revelations till they were more suitably impressed.

'Frank Dudley is an old woman. Don't mention him again, I beg you. Why don't you stay here tonight, dear?' Marian asked Rosamund. 'Why go back to that empty house?'

'I think I should. There may be a phone-call. I feel I should be there.'

'Anyway, you'll come to the George with us, won't you? Just for one drink? You'll feel so much better to be with a crowd. It's no use dwelling on the tragedy when you can't do anything to help. Don't you think I'm right, Brian?'

Brian looked as though he might still be offended. 'No, I don't think one drink will be much help. She's had a nasty shock so she'll need at least two or three, and we'll drive her home afterwards.'

In bed, after several gins at the George, Rosamund thought about being in love, the extraordinary force of it. Suddenly, out of the blue; there she was again, all her nerve-endings quivering. It was like being nineteen again, and all the time in between – teaching, looking after poor Anthony, taking Joss to clinic and nursery school, years of conscientiously trying to paint, times when she'd considered herself growing into a sensible, mature woman – all might never have been. She was a student again, hanging out of her window, hoping to catch a glimpse of Daniel Hawkins passing on his way to college.

She thought of Thomas with affection and pain. He was bound to blame himself for Eliza's death, but she felt convinced that he'd done all in his power to make her happy. When they'd begun their affair, it was quite apparent to her

92

that his marriage was in a state of terminal decline and that he wouldn't have embarked even on an extra-marital flirtation if that hadn't been the case. 'I'll never be able to leave Eliza,' he'd told her over and over again, 'so do you think this is fair to you?'

'Of course it is. I haven't got anything else, have I, so this is a plus. We're friends, after all, as well as occasional lovers.' She knew very well that she could never have been so fair-minded and undemanding if she'd been violently in love. As she was with Daniel.

'Violently in love,' she murmured to herself, savouring the words. 'I'm violently in love.'

So how could she have come back to bury herself in the country, when it was surely her place to stay in London until she'd found her love again!

She got out of bed and went downstairs. It was two in the morning, an empty mournful time, silent except for the ticking of the clock. She felt like ringing Dora to tell her to find her a flat as soon as possible. She needed to be in London again. She had to find Daniel again. If she had enough faith in her quest she would succeed. She found herself crying once more – not in that hard, desperate way, as before – but with a quiet litany of sobs.

She'd put the schoolhouse on the market, sell the furniture with it, because it wouldn't suit a London flat, get rid of her paints and all the painting paraphernalia, give up the thought of being an artist, perhaps take a job in a gallery. 'I'm violently in love,' she told herself over and over again, whenever the prospect seemed daunting.

She went to the kitchen and made herself a pot of tea. How had she been able to stay so long in Anthony's house, with nothing of her own surrounding her? She was sick of the country pine, the blue and white china and the yellow walls; she wanted something quite different – an elegant little flat like Dora's, with of course a large, untidy room for Joss.

'I am violently in love,' she told herself, trying to forget something she'd often suspected; that violent love usually ended in violent loss for at least one of the couple. Violent loss, disillusion and destruction.

# Chapter Eleven

The baby didn't stop crying. Once or twice when Joss held his long delicate fingers, he almost stopped, went, 'La, la, la,' his mouth quivering, which wasn't so bad. Joss liked the new baby, though the other boys said he was nothing but a nuisance. If it was his baby brother he'd call him Jim – or Jimbo – and he'd pick him up and play with him and stop him being so sad. 'La, la, little baby,' he said to himself. His hand was like a starfish.

Mrs Woodison said crying was good for a baby's lungs and that he'd be spoilt if he was picked up between feeds. She said Harry was spoilt because he wouldn't finish his boiled egg. When she went to the kitchen to put more water in the teapot, Harry said it was full of shit, and they all laughed, even Thomas.

Mrs Woodison lived in a little grey village surrounded by grey hills where it rained every day; it was a beauty spot. The name of the village was 'The Church near the Waterfall', but none of them could pronounce it. She told them that the church had a famous stained glass window and that they could go to see it if the rain stopped, and Stephen said, 'How delightful,' and they all spluttered again. But when *Saturday Morning Roundabout* was over, they put their anoraks on, deciding to go and find the waterfall to throw stones at it. Thomas had important letters to write, but he promised faithfully to take them to the funfair the next day.

First they walked down the road to the shop which had two small windows full of packets of soap powder, and bought four liquorice sticks each, which was the only thing they could get with the money Mrs Woodison had given them for crisps. Then they took the path to the church, chewing contentedly and leering at one another as their teeth became more and more discoloured. 'Look at my black spit,' Joss said, gobbing at the path.

They came to a brook and Stephen said it would be bound to lead to the waterfall if they walked back against the current, but though they walked miles and miles through soaking wet grass, they didn't come to it. They came to some cows, though, who stared at them, lifted their heads and said, 'Mmm,' but kept their distance. Stephen told them not to look back at them over their shoulders because it would make them angry, but Joss and Harry couldn't help it; they liked the way they said 'Mmm' instead of 'Moo.' They both agreed that cows were much more intelligent than sheep.

A tall, thin, grey-haired woman came down the hill towards them. She stopped dead in front of them so that they had to stop too. 'Where are you going, then?' she asked them, her thin, mild voice full of surprise.

Stephen said they were going to the waterfall.

'English visitors,' she said. 'Where are you staying? At Nant Eos?' She didn't wait for an answer. 'Anyway, you're going the wrong way for the waterfall. This track only leads to Cefn Eithin, and there's no one there but me, and I'm out. But come, I'll show you the way. Now, can one of you carry this parcel for me, I wonder? Only it's very heavy. It's a old mirror with a gold frame that I'm hoping to sell in Denbigh this afternoon. Don't drop it, will you, or it'll be seven years' bad luck. Isn't this rain terrible?'

Stephen took the mirror, but however he tried to carry it, it banged against his knees as he walked.

'You'll never do it that way, *bach.*' She looked back at Martin. 'But if your friend takes one end, you'll be able to carry it between you. See if you can manage the old thing as far as the stile and then I'll take it again. Oh, that's better. Oh, you are good, careful boys. Where are you from, then? You should go to Rhyl if the rain clears up this afternoon. I used to relish a trip to Rhyl when I was a girl. Haven't been for years

96

now, of course. I'm too old for funfairs, but I used to love them. To tell you the truth I used to be a bit of a devil on the Big Wheel. There's nothing much to the waterfall, mind, only a lot of water from the mountain falling over some old stones. The tourists seem to like it, of course, they come in droves with their shorts and their fat thighs. It's reckoned to be one of the sights around here. But you get your mammy and daddy to take you to Rhyl as soon as the rain stops.'

They walked slowly and carefully as far as the stile. 'Oh, dear God,' she said then, coming to a sudden halt, as though receiving a personal revelation from On High. 'You're Mrs Woodison's little grandsons, aren't you?' She flung her arms round Joss and Harry, giving them a long, painful hug. 'And here's me bothering you about my old mirror and you with your poor mother gone. Give it here, do.'

She took the mirror from Stephen and Martin, propped it against her hip and tried to hug them, too, but they stepped smartly out of her way, so that she hugged Joss and Harry again for an even longer time.

'Now I go to the village this way, and you go that way to the church, and when you get there, just walk straight on and you'll hear the waterfall. And perhaps you'll stop to see the rose window in the church as well. Some people say it's the most beautiful window in Wales, it's very old anyhow. Well, I'll say goodbye. And, believe me, I'm more sorry than I can say.'

'Silly old cow,' Stephen said, his voice sounding as though he was full of cold.

'She had very stiff bones,' Joss said. 'My nose was bent against her chest.'

'I wish we were at home,' Harry said.

They all wished that, as they walked along the slightly wider path leading to the church, kicking at stones as they went.

The waterfall failed to impress. They stood as close to the spray as they dared, but it was only like more rain and they were soaked already, their trainers gurgling like hot-water bottles as they walked. Martin said Niagara was the biggest waterfall in the world and Stephen said the Victoria Falls, but even that sharp disagreement didn't seem worth having a fight about. And however violently they hurled stones into the

97

waterfall, they were simply swallowed up, making no impression at all.

They walked back towards the church, sodden and dispirited, but instead of keeping to the path at the front, they climbed up the grassy bank behind it. The rain stopped and a watery sun appeared between the dingy white clouds.

'I used to be a devil in the funfair,' Martin said, imitating the woman's nasal accent. They all laughed, delighted to have something to laugh about.

'I used to be a devil on the Big Wheel,' Stephen said. 'You get your mammy and daddy to take you to the funfair this afternoon.'

'Look at that bloody church,' Martin said after a few seconds' silence. 'Look at that bloody famous window. It doesn't look very bloody much from up here, does it? All dark and bloody dismal. Let's throw some bloody stones at it.'

Stephen should have stopped them, he knew that, but they were a long way away and he didn't really think any of them would manage to hit the window, though it was, it had to be admitted, quite definitely a large one. 'Six goes each,' he said, and they scrambled back to the path to pick up stones. 'Small ones,' he added firmly, still struggling to be the responsible eldest brother.

Neither Joss nor Harry managed to hit the back of the church, let alone the window. Two of Martin's stones hit it, but bounced off. Stephen aimed five stones without success so, unwilling to be outdone by Martin, he put considerable force and effort behind his last throw, and the stone, marginally bigger than the others, went right through one of the small grey panes at the very top of the window. The sharp burst of pleasure he felt at his success was immediately followed by a sickening numbness as he saw the small round hole in the window.

'What a dumb thing to do,' he said.

'And that man saw us climbing up here,' Martin added.

'Let's go back to Granny's,' Harry said.

They walked slowly back to the village.

That evening they saw the vicar coming up the drive, battling against the wind and the rain, his large black umbrella prancing before him. They were in the breakfast room watching *Noel's House Party* and expected to be called into the sitting room and questioned, but they weren't. They were all apprehensive, laughing immoderately at antics they'd normally have groaned at.

It was at least half an hour later when they heard Mrs Woodison and the vicar in the hall again. 'An act of God,' they heard her say in her usual high-pitched bossy voice, 'but I shall, of course, pay in full for the restoration.'

'You can come in to have your cocoa now,' she said at nine o'clock, opening the door and looking at them over her glasses. 'The baby's fast asleep and I've persuaded your father to go out to the pub for an hour.'

'I'm sorry,' Stephen said as he followed the others to the kitchen.

'Whatever for? Millie Roberts was on the phone earlier telling me how kind you were to her this morning. No need to be sorry about anything.'

# Chapter Twelve

All through that Saturday, Rosamund had been striding about the house and garden, trying to decide what to do. She wanted to go to London again to find Daniel, but was afraid of failure. If he had really decided not to meet her the previous week, then she accepted that finding him wouldn't be too much help. She had thought his eyes had held all the certainty of love, but how much did she really know about him, or about love? And who could advise her? Dora was sure he would both want and manage to contact her again. Ingrid was equally sure that he'd thought better of it. They were both intelligent women and both more experienced than she was.

She went to bed on Saturday night wearied by doubt and indecision, and with no Joss to wake her, slept deeply until ten and got up feeling still tired.

Sunday was a perfect day, a slight heat haze at first and then stillness and jewel-bright colours, the sky so blue she felt she could taste it on her tongue. The day tasted of hope. Why wasn't Daniel with her? He'd seemed so certain he wanted to move in with her. 'Are you sure?' he'd asked when she suggested it, as though he thought it was too good to be true. It had seemed a new beginning – exactly when she'd needed one. So where was he? The blackbird's song filled her with longing. In the night she'd heard a she-cat calling for a mate in a voice gone harsh with lust. Whereas she could do nothing but wait and hope. She didn't even have his address.

She fetched paper and some sticks of charcoal and tried to draw him. Several times she managed a decent-enough portrait of a pleasant-looking young man, but on the eighth attempt she succeeded in capturing a likeness. *Daniel* she wrote underneath and pinned it up with her drawings of Joss. For a while it seemed to ease her pain. After all, she thought, it was what primitive tribes did when they went hunting.

Marian and Brian came up in the afternoon.

'Only a cup of tea, dear,' Marian said, filling the kettle. 'Oh, I've been thinking so much about you. What are you planning to do? Brian, would you mind putting another chair out on the patio, love?'

Rosamund had told her mother nothing about meeting Daniel and wondered whether she'd been talking to Dora that morning. 'Planning to do about what?' she asked.

'About Harry's father. About Thomas. About the whole sad situation.'

Rosamund breathed a sigh of relief. 'I don't have to do anything about Thomas. Of course I'm very sad, very sorry for him and the children, but I can't really be much help, can I? He's so guilt-ridden at the moment, I'd be the last person he'd want around. Perhaps his mother will move down here for a while.'

'As long as you don't get sucked into it, dear. Thomas seemed a very decent sort of person, but I'd hate to think of you with five boys to care for.'

'I haven't even considered such a thing – and neither has Thomas, I'm sure. In fact, I've been thinking about moving to London, selling this place and buying a flat in some fairly inexpensive area. Dora thought it might be a new start for me.'

Marian said nothing, only carried the tray into the garden.

'How much would Rosamund get for this house?' she asked Brian as she poured out the tea.

'Is she thinking of selling?' he asked, looking at each of the women in turn. 'Where would she go?'

'I thought Joss and I might move in with you two,' Rosamund said, 'so that I could invest the money I got and live on that. Even pay you some rent.'

Brian sipped his tea carefully, looking about him at the garden and then at the valley beyond. 'It seems a good idea,' he said then, 'but don't do anything in a hurry, that's my advice. It would suit Marian, of course, but you might soon feel. . .'

Rosamund got up and dropped a kiss on his head. 'You're a good, brave man, Brian,' she said, 'but I was teasing you. I wouldn't dream of imposing myself on you two.'

'It would be very nice in many ways,' he said, breathing freely again. 'Oh yes, you and Joshua keep us young, you know. Our Mrs Harlin couldn't believe that Marian was going to be sixty next birthday.'

'We'd just given her a rise, dear,' Marian explained. 'But I think Brian's right. Don't decide anything too hurriedly or you might regret it. Get temporary accommodation in London and find out whether you could settle there. Leave Joss with us for the summer. You know he'd be well looked after, and of course you could visit every weekend.'

'You could even let this place if you wanted to, I could have a word with Don Latham who runs Windrush Cottages. They take a pretty hefty percentage, of course, but they see to absolutely everything. Anything that goes wrong with the plumbing, electricity, etc, they undertake to get it sorted out. And naturally, I could potter about a bit in the garden, see to the lawns and so on.'

'Think about it, dear,' Marian said. 'I don't want you to be trapped by circumstances beyond your control. While you remain here, you're in danger.'

'What sort of danger?' Brian asked, his eyebrows displaying alarm.

'The usual sort,' Marian said snappily. 'Men and children.'

The phone rang and it was Joss. They were at the funfair and having a brilliant time. Thomas had bought a family ticket so all the rides were free and Granny Woodison had given them two pounds fifty each which they were spending on chips and cider ice-pops. And, Mum, could he please, *please* buy a white mouse?

'No,' Rosamund said, 'but if you come home in one piece, I may get you that mountain bike for your birthday.'

'I've changed my mind about a mountain bike. What I want is a baby brother.'

103

'We'll discuss that when you come home.'

His money ran out and Rosamund put the phone down.

'What was that, dear?' Marian asked.

'He was telling me what he wanted for his birthday.'

'Brian and I are getting him a mountain bike. Harry's got one, apparently, so it seems only fair that he should have one too. Yes, we've ordered the very latest model, fiesta pink and moondust silver, with alloy wheels and this and that. Well, we felt it might keep him happy and out of mischief for a year or two.'

'Sex and drugs will be the next stage, no doubt,' Brian said. 'Of course, there was none of that when I was a boy.' He sounded gloomy. 'A glass of shandy and a hurried fumble at the front door was all we had to look forward to.'

'You speak for yourself, dear,' Marian said.

The next morning Rosamund received a letter from Ambrose Lockhart, Molly's solicitor: *At Mrs Gilchrist's request, I have undertaken a fresh study of the last will and testament of your late husband, Mr Anthony Gilchrist. As you are aware, he made provisions for both Mrs Gilchrist and yourself; Mrs Marjory Gilchrist receiving the matrimonial home, 42 Albany Crescent, St John's Wood, London NW8, an annuity of twenty thousand pounds and the monies from the copyright of his three volumes of poetry; Mrs Rosamund Gilchrist receiving his second home, The Old Schoolhouse, Compton Verney, Gloucestershire, an annuity of ten thousand pounds and the copyright of all his poetry and prose written after 1964, the year of his divorce absolute from Mrs Marjorie Gilchrist.*

*'As there is no provision made in his will for any other person or persons, the copyright of any poems written for and sent to Miss Erica Underhill in or around 1965 are owned not by her but by yourself.*

*'At Mrs Gilchrist's request, I have written to apprise Miss Erica Underhill of this matter, further informing her that she therefore has no legal right to publish the aforementioned poems without permission from Mr Gilchrist's estate.*

*'Mrs Gilchrist is confident that you will abide by Mr Gilchrist's stated wish concerning the aforementioned poems i.e. that they*

*shall not be published until twenty years after his death, where-upon you will be the sole beneficiary of the copyright fees.*

*Should you wish to receive any further clarification upon this matter, I shall be pleased to discuss it with you.'*

Rosamund read the letter several times, finally becoming so angry that she could hardly swallow her toast. How dared Molly have instructed her solicitor to act on her behalf! Now she understood why Ben had been so angry. He must have thought that she was the Mrs Gilchrist behind the move to stop the poems being published.

Not that she cared about Ben. But she did care a great deal about Erica, and couldn't bear to think that she was going to be thwarted again by Molly. She had to get things sorted out, wanted to shout defiance at both Molly and her solicitor, wanted to assure Erica that she'd had nothing to do with the letter she'd received, wanted to let Ingrid know the position. And at the same time, knew she couldn't do a thing until she felt calmer.

When the phone rang she was still sitting at the breakfast table doing the breathing exercises she'd been taught before Joss's birth and still finding them as useless. 'Rosamund Gilchrist,' she said angrily.

'Good God, Rosamund, whatever's the matter?' It was Thomas, sounding weary and rather abrupt.

'Oh Thomas, I don't feel I can burden you with my problems.'

'Come on, what's the matter?'

'I'll tell you when you get home. How are the boys?'

'Difficult to know. They seem all right. They don't say anything, but they smashed a church window on Saturday morning, so I suppose I'm in for a lot of trouble. How did you get on in London?'

'It's too complicated to start on that. But one thing I probably ought to tell you is that I met a chap I used to know at art school and discovered I was still in love with him. I know that must seem very trivial to you at the moment. All the same, I feel I should let you know.'

'Yes. Thank you. To be honest, this is the best time because

105

at the moment I'm only able to think of Eliza, how much I used to love her. And how I let her down.'

'You were a good husband, Thomas. Don't blame yourself too much. Eliza changed a long time before you did.'

'Yes, I realise all that. I've gone over it hundreds of times in these last few days, but it doesn't make it any easier, doesn't make my guilt any less.'

'She became completely obsessed by her work.'

'She became far too ambitious, I know. But I'm convinced now that it was only because I wasn't ambitious enough. I remember how she used to badger me to put in for a promotion – Head of Department, even Headmaster – but I never felt ready for it. And she couldn't bear to try to live on a teacher's salary. And you can't blame her for that.'

'I do blame her, Thomas. At least, I blame her more than I blame you. Whatever her reasons, she cut you out of her life, so what were you to do?'

'Anything other than what I did. As soon as I met you, I just let her go her own way. I didn't try to change the direction of her life. And she obviously suspected what was happening.'

'By that time I don't think she cared what was happening. I do realise that what we did was wrong. I've been feeling pretty awful about it, too – don't think I'm trying to get out of my share of the blame. All I'm saying is that your marriage had become stale and unworkable before our affair started. Thomas, we didn't rush headlong into it, did we? We were just friends for ages, two lonely people finding comfort in our companionship. We were friends long before we became lovers. But you wouldn't be feeling as guilty, would you, if we hadn't had sex, and I can't see that that changed things all that much.'

'Don't try and excuse what I did. I was in love with you from the beginning. And that's what changed everything between Eliza and me.'

'No, it wasn't. You're not seeing this clearly. Eliza had already changed before you met me. Hold on to that. If you have to blame yourself, for God's sake don't take more than your share, because that's just being weak.'

'I am weak.'

'Well, maybe you are. But listen, weak people are always,

always much more worthwhile than strong people. Strong people are horrible and cause all the trouble in the world.'

'What's the matter, Rosamund? You may as well tell me.'

'It's something to do with Anthony's horrible first wife. Not worth bothering you about. I'll see you soon. Thomas, I hope we can still be friends.'

There was a longish pause. 'I suppose so. After a time, anyway. I'm not at all myself at the moment.'

'I can understand that, And I'm terribly sorry. Terribly sorry about everything, believe me. How is Joss?'

'He seems fine – a great help to Harry, I think. He wants me to call the baby Jim. What do you think? I can't seem to give it much thought.'

'Yes, I like it. James Woodison.'

'Not James. Jim.'

After talking to Thomas, Rosamund felt ready to tackle her own problems. She decided not to answer the solicitor's letter nor to contact Molly. It was Erica she was concerned about. She would telephone her.

'Erica, this is Rosamund. Rosamund Gilchrist.'

'Hello, dear. Yes, I'm much better again, thank you. I had a little turn on Friday, but I'm quite well again now. Your friend shouldn't have worried you about it. It was nothing serious.'

'Erica, I didn't know you'd been ill. What friend of mine are you talking about?'

'Miss Walsh. Ingrid Walsh. She came to see me about this mess I'd got myself into. I had no idea, you see, that the poems were not legally mine to publish.'

'I know nothing about the letter you got from Molly's solicitor. It was nothing to do with me. And whatever Ingrid Walsh may have told you, she called to see you because the man who was helping you with the book was her boyfriend and she was anxious to trace him.'

'Yes, she mentioned that.'

'I'd really like to see you, Erica, to talk about the book, but I can't come up to London at the moment. You see, my young son has been away and I don't want to leave him again, at least for a while. So I've been wondering whether I can persuade you to visit me. My stepmother would call for you and drive you to Paddington, and of course I'd meet you at this end. Would you like a few days in the country? It's very beautiful here at the moment.'

'Oh, I would, I really would. It's my favourite time of the year.'

'Good. When could you come? I have to attend a funeral on Wednesday. Could you come on Thursday?'

'Yes, Thursday would be fine. I shall look forward to it.'

'And the next day we'll have lunch at that country hotel you and Anthony used to stay at. He pointed it out to me several times. It looked a lovely place.'

'Oh, it was. Near Stow-on-the-Wold. It overlooked a golf course, I remember. Not that we played any golf.'

'No, I suppose Anthony would have had other things on his mind. I never imagined golf being the chief attraction, somehow.'

'The food was excellent and they had huge log fires everywhere, even in the bedrooms.'

'I'll get my stepmother to contact you – she's called Dora Harcourt, by the way. I'm really looking forward to seeing you again, Erica, and planning our next move about the book. I've been wondering whether we shouldn't write it together and share the money.'

'What a very good idea. What about young Ben though? He's very angry and put out, according to your friend.'

'I think we'll have to disregard young Ben. As well as Molly Gilchrist and her precious solicitor.'

# Chapter Thirteen

After Rosamund's return, Dora had several disturbed nights trying to work out how she could find Daniel. The only feasible idea she'd come up with during the entire weekend was to contact the Brighton Art School to find out whether they still had an address for him. She telephoned there as soon as she got into work on the Monday morning, but was informed that records were kept only for seven years.

'Lost touch with a boyfriend?' a colleague asked her.

She just had time to tell her what had happened to Rosamund before they were both caught up in the day's business.

'I've been thinking about your stepdaughter,' her colleague said as she was going off to lunch. 'What you need is a private investigator. He'll find the chap in no time.'

At first, Dora rejected the idea as sordid – connected with marital infidelity and debt-collecting – but as the afternoon wore on, had to admit that she'd come up with no alternative plan. Rosamund herself had phoned every D. Hawkins listed in the London directories.

When she arrived back at the flat that evening, she consulted the *Yellow Pages*, and from the plethora of enquiry agencies, private investigators and detective bureaux, she telephoned the first that offered free confidential advice. 'Could I make an appointment for free confidential advice?' she asked. 'Certainly. When would you like an appointment?' 'Are you the investigator?' 'Yes, that's right.' 'Good. Could I see you tomorrow morning?'

She was delighted that she was to see a woman. A man, she felt, would be too ready to decide that Daniel had simply changed his mind, and therefore not be as open to other possibilities.

She felt optimistic, almost light-hearted as she began to prepare the evening meal.

'And what are you looking so smug about?' Paul asked her when he came in.

'I'm more than usually pleased by my progress at work. And what are you looking so glum about?'

'You might not believe this, but I was thinking about poor Rosamund. She's had a pretty rotten life, hasn't she? Seems such a shame that that bloke didn't turn up the other day. It would almost certainly have turned out badly, even disastrously, but beginnings are usually very hopeful.'

'Do you remember our first meeting?' Dora asked.

'Of course. I'd understood you were a theatrical agent so I insisted on buying you a drink. And by the time I'd found out you were an estate agent, I'd fallen in love with you.'

'That's not how I remember it.'

'No?'

'No. I remember seeing you at Hoffners, thinking you were very dishy, and asking you to have dinner with me.'

'Which I accepted. Because I thought someone had said you were a theatrical agent. And also, of course, because I thought you were madly attractive.'

They smiled comfortably at each other. Dora considered telling him about the investigator, but decided against it, since the likely cost might ruin his appetite.

'Do you remember the time you had that operation on your spine?' she asked, instead.

'What about it?'

'I made rather a fuss, didn't I?'

'You certainly did.'

Paul, who had always, he said, despised women who made scenes, remembered with love and pride the loud and frequent scenes Dora had made at the hospital. 'I was ashamed of you,' he said, nuzzling her neck.

*

The next morning Dora found the address she was looking for in Clapham – a shabby double-fronted Victorian house converted into offices, went up in the antiquated lift, found the right office and knocked at the door.

'Mrs Harcourt? Come in, please,' the woman at the desk said. 'Do sit down. I'm Caroline.'

Caroline, small and blonde, hadn't felt the need to dress in a business suit of clerical grey; she wore a pale pink dress with frilly collar and full sleeves and a great deal of make-up. It was difficult to tell her age. At first Dora thought she was twenty-three or four, but later felt she might be as much as ten years older.

'I specialise in missing persons,' Caroline said in a voice which was pure stage-Cockney, even to the hint of slightly nasal gentility. 'I don't do debt-collecting or contract because my heart wouldn't be in it. But, you see, I really like finding people for people. I'm good at prying into their private lives. I've always been a very curious person, if not downright nosy, and I've got a lively imagination, so I can often put two and two together and discover the sort of things they might be doing, the sort of places where they might be hanging out. And I'm a bit psychic as well – at least that's what I like to tell myself. Now, what sort of free confidential advice were you interested in?'

'I'm going to skip that part,' Dora said. 'I've decided to employ you.'

'I don't think you'll be sorry, Mrs Harcourt. At any rate, I'll do my best.'

'I want you to find my stepdaughter's boyfriend.'

'Is she pregnant?'

'No, nothing like that. It was only a chance meeting in the Underground.'

'Oh, right.'

'Though she knew him when they were in college together, fifteen years ago. She was to have met him again the next day, but he didn't turn up. Now, my stepdaughter is a wise and mature woman of thirty-five, not one to make foolish mistakes about a person's intentions. She was convinced that he intended to turn up – in fact, that he wanted the meeting as much as she did, but he didn't show up. They hadn't exchanged addresses or telephone numbers. She has no idea how to find him, which is why I've come to you.'

'Do you have a photograph of your stepdaughter?'

'I do, as a matter of fact. But why is that useful?'

Caroline didn't answer, only thrust out a small, manicured hand for the snapshot Dora took out of her handbag and stared at it for several moments. 'Beautiful, but not streetwise,' she said at last.

'I think she's got her feet firmly on the ground.'

'And the boyfriend's name? Plus everything you can tell me about him, please. No detail too unimportant.'

'Daniel Hawkins. Artist. Unsuccessful, I think. I haven't any other details, I'm afraid.'

'No photograph, of course?'

'Sorry, no.'

'Age?'

'Two years older than Rosamund – so around thirty-seven. Oh, and she described him as thin and very shabby. She could hardly believe it because at college he'd been very self-assured and well-dressed. No – *beautifully* dressed. Not quite the same thing, perhaps.'

'Did she find out whether he was married?'

'He'd had a long-term relationship with an American, he told her. But she'd recently gone back to the States so he was on his own. Definitely not married.'

'Right. I agree with your stepdaughter that he intended to turn up. I feel she's the sort of woman a man would turn up for – at least once.'

'They were to have met outside the National Gallery, and she waited hours for him. There was no possibility that he mistook the venue – it was mentioned several times.'

'And this was last week? What day?'

'Wednesday of last week.'

'He might have been in a road accident. Excited, possibly a little late, he might have stepped into the road too hurriedly. My first job will be to contact hospital casualty departments.'

'Rosamund contacted several of the better-known art galleries in case someone had his address.'

Caroline shrugged her shoulders. 'Unsuccessful, shabby, so unlikely to be selling his pictures to galleries. Unsuccessful and shabby. Unsuccessful and shabby. Why is she so keen to find him? Need one ask!'

'Her first love, she says.'

'Unsuccessful artist, thin, shabby, thirty-seven years old, abandoned by American partner some time ago, but yet a man to love and be in love with. I'm getting a picture. I don't think I'll have much luck with hospitals but I'll give it a go – and after that something else might come through to me. Sorry, Mrs Harcourt. So many of my clients seem to want "things to come through to me," but I think you'd prefer things to occur to me in a logical way.'

'Logic, intuition, supernatural power – it's all the same to me as long as you track him down.'

'Give me your telephone number, Mrs Harcourt. I'll telephone each night to report to you. I charge for one day's work at a time, two hundred pounds plus expenses, and you employ me by the day. And I'd like one day's pay in advance, please.'

Dora wrote her a cheque, gave her work and home telephone numbers, took her card and left.

As she went down in the lift, she was surprised once again by the love she felt for Rosamund; she had many friends and social acquaintances, but the people she truly cared about, wanted to help and protect, were very few.

113

# Chapter Fourteen

Joss arrived home just before six on the Tuesday evening, Thomas dropping him off at the gate without a word or a wave.

Watching her son walking up the path, Rosamund thought he looked taller and altogether older. 'You're getting so big,' she said. 'I keep forgetting that you're almost ten. You'll soon be a teenager and then, I suppose, you'll be wanting to leave home. Have you had a good time?'

He dodged her as she tried to put her arms round him. 'No. Everyone was bad-tempered, even Thomas.'

'You said you were having a great time at the funfair.'

'The funfair wasn't too bad. The rest was crap.'

'Crap isn't a very nice word.'

'Stephen and Martin say it.'

'You can say it when you're thirteen.'

'Harry says shit – and he's only ten.'

'You can say crap and shit if you let me give you a really big hug.'

He gave her a quick, sideways look. 'OK.'

They hugged, rocking tightly together for a few moments. She suddenly thought of Thomas's boys arriving home to an empty house. She hugged Joss again, even though she could feel him straining to get away from her. He smelt of bananas and crisps and his skin was pale as milk. Why wasn't he healthy and brown like other boys?

'Stephen says you and Thomas will get married now,' he said, as soon as she released him. 'Will you?'

115

'Of course not.'

'Why?'

'Because Thomas and I are good friends, but there's a lot more than that to getting married.'

'Love and all that stuff. Yes, I know.' He was still looking severely at her. 'Were you and Eliza good friends? Did you really like her?'

What was all this about? Rosamund suddenly remembered the first time she'd met Eliza; a night before Christmas when Joss was still in nursery school. They'd called for Harry to take him to the carol concert. Stephen had answered the door and led them into their large, warm kitchen where Eliza and the boys were making mincepies. Eliza had looked relaxed and pretty that evening, in a bright red dress with a tea-cloth pinned round her waist. She'd smiled her welcome and poured Rosamund a sherry. Stephen and Martin were putting spoonfuls of mincemeat into some prepared cases, Eliza was making more pastry, while Harry was haphazardly stamping a star-shaped cutter onto the pastry already rolled out and shouting, 'I'm a star, I'm a star, I'm a star,' which, though not exactly scintillating, got a laugh each time. They'd seemed such a happy family. Rosamund shook away the tears from her eyes. She hadn't thought of that evening for years – for years she'd steadfastly thought of Eliza as a dedicated career woman – why had that memory returned now to torment her?

She'd always sensed that Eliza felt superior to the women who stayed at home, content to be wives and mothers, with perhaps poorly paid part-time jobs in the village; she'd never wondered whether she was just shy, waiting for others to make the first move.

'Were you and Eliza good friends?' Joss repeated.

'No, not really. I hardly ever saw Eliza because she worked very long hours. It was always Thomas who came up here, wasn't it, bringing Harry or fetching him. I liked Eliza well enough, but I can't say we were close friends.'

'Are you sorry she's dead?'

'Of course I am. Very sorry. What has Stephen been telling you?'

'Nothing. Can I have my tea now? Granny Woodison says

116

that young people don't have proper food these days, only junk food. And junk food makes your teeth rot and your skin get pimply and after a while you don't grow any more.'

'So what shall we have tonight?'

He gave the question a moment's serious deliberation. 'Junk food, I think. Oven chips and pot noodles.'

He was reluctant to go to bed so Rosamund let him stay up until ten. 'Come on, tell me what's worrying you,' she said at last. 'Is it the thought of the funeral tomorrow? You and I don't really have to go, you know. Thomas thought Harry would feel a little better if you were with him, but I think he's going to feel pretty rotten whether you're there or not.'

'He wet the bed last night.'

'Poor love. He must be taking it very badly.'

'Stephen and Martin called him a sucky-baby.'

Rosamund sighed. 'They're unhappy as well, you see, and it's making them cruel. That happens sometimes.'

He shot a quick glance at her. 'Stephen and Martin say that Thomas gave Eliza pills to make her die.'

'That's a really wicked thing to say. And of course it's totally, totally, untrue. You do believe me, don't you? *Joss?*'

'Yes.'

'Thomas is terribly unhappy because she's dead. You know what a kind man he is. Would Thomas hurt anyone?'

'He said they'd been watching too much television.'

'That's probably true as well.'

'I hate them. I hate them saying things like that.'

'Everyone is afraid of death, you know. Even grown-ups. Would you like me to read you a very good poem about death?'

'No, thank you. Tell me about when I was a little boy and I wouldn't let you say that Peter Rabbit's father was put in a pie.'

'Well, when you were a little boy, I used to have to say that Peter Rabbit's father had gone into Mr McGregor's garden and that Mr McGregor had caught him and put him in a cage.'

'And then?'

'And then Mrs McGregor had felt sorry for him and let him out again.'

117

'Yes, that's right. And then he went hopping away down the garden. I was silly, wasn't I? I think I'll go to bed now.'

'Good night, little rabbit.'

'Good night, little mummy.'

Rosamund and Joss didn't attend the funeral the next day, but spent the morning walking on the hills, talking about rabbits, the death of; lambs, the death of; fox-hunting, duck shooting, abattoirs, child abduction and murder. 'For God's sake, let us sit upon the ground,' Rosamund said at one point, 'and tell sad stories of the death of kings.'

'All right,' Joss said, sitting down obligingly.

Thomas rang during the evening, sounding tired but less miserable, or at least less desperate, than he had on Sunday.

'Stephen and Martin are incredibly hostile,' he said. 'If they lived in a war-zone they'd be out with guns, shooting everyone within sight.'

'How is Harry?'

'He seemed a little better today. He saw the funeral of some Irish bloke on telly last night and noticed that some of the mourners were even younger than him. And strangely enough that seemed to give him some comfort. How's Joss? I'm afraid he's been dragged into it all, hasn't he?'

'He was very fond of Eliza. But I think a psychologist might say that he's working through his grief.'

Dora had agreed to drive Erica Underhill to Paddington, but rang later that evening to say she'd managed to get a day off work and had decided to drive her all the way to the schoolhouse, hoping to arrive by about three.

She sounded rather brusque and businesslike on the phone, which left Rosamund feeling uneasy.

Dora had heard that morning from the Enquiry Agency. Caroline had reported that it had taken her only two days to trace Daniel Hawkins. At one of the hospitals where she'd been making routine enquiries, the receptionist had recognised his name; she'd managed to get his latest address and had made contact with him. 'I hate to say this, but it was what I'd imagined all along,' she said. 'One minute positive and cooperative, the next, unable to do anything but plan how to get the next fix.'

'Oh God,' Dora said. 'Do you mean . . .? Oh God. So what happened?'

'I didn't actually talk to him, Mrs Harcourt. He was lying, either asleep or unconscious, on the floor of the sitting room when I got there, but one of the others confirmed that he was Daniel Hawkins and that he was an artist and a musician as well. "A hell of a great guy," was how he described him. Yes, I've met quite a lot of those in my time.'

For once Dora was speechless.

'It's pretty terrible, isn't it?' Caroline continued. 'Yes, I hate to give people bad news and this is the worst sort.'

'At least he's not dead.'

'But he may not be too far off it either, if you want my opinion. And I know what I'm talking about because I had a cousin went that way. Lovely bloke he was, just twenty-five. If I were you – and I know it's none of my business, I just had a job to do and I've done it – but if I were you, I wouldn't pass on this news to your stepdaughter. Finding him will bring her nothing but grief, Mrs Harcourt. She looked a lovely woman and you told me she'd got a little lad, too. Isn't it better for her to remember this guy as he used to be than get involved in this no-hope situation? If she tries to help him it will take all her money, all her energy, all her youth. And most probably all for nothing.'

'Thank you. Thank you for your help,' Dora said, since some response seemed called for.

'You're offended with me now, aren't you? I spoke out of turn.'

'No, no, I'm just stunned by the news. I think you're a very kind and caring person. And I'll send you the money I owe you straight away.'

'Thank you. And if you want to talk some more, or if your stepdaughter would like to contact me, I'll be only too pleased. Here's the address, Mrs Harcourt. There's no telephone number. And if you do decide to tell her and she does decide to contact him, then the sooner the better.'

*

119

Dora left work immediately, offering no explanation or excuse. No one questioned her and she drove home in a daze, thanked God that Paul was at a rehearsal, then contacted the Drugs Helpline, who assured her that every case of heroin addiction was different, and that no case was hopeless.

'I'll have to tell Rosamund,' Dora told herself. 'I'll just have to tell her. Oh my God, why was I the person who had to involve her in this mess?'

At three the next afternoon, Dora arrived alone at the schoolhouse.

'But where's Erica?' Rosamund asked her, after they'd kissed.

'I called for her, but she didn't feel well enough to come. Oh, that isn't true. Darling, I went to see her and explained that this was not a convenient time for her to visit you and she quite understood and sent you her love and sympathy.'

Rosamund suddenly noticed how pale Dora was under her heavy make-up. 'Dora, I don't understand. What are you trying to tell me?'

They went into the kitchen and Dora broke the news to her stepdaughter and sat with her while she struggled to accept it.

'I don't believe it. I simply can't believe it.'

'It's terrible. I can't tell you how sorry I am.'

'But it was only a fortnight ago that I met him. Yes, he seemed thin and shabby, but perfectly well. He couldn't have been a drug addict. I'd have noticed something.'

'But darling, that's why he didn't meet you the next day. I'm sure he wanted to, but his mind wasn't functioning – either because he'd had heroin or because he needed it.'

'He's on heroin?'

'Yes. A known heroin addict.'

'That's why he was playing his violin in the Underground.'

'Is that how you met him? You didn't tell me that.'

'I didn't think it was important. He told me he didn't have any money or even a place of his own any more, but I didn't take much notice. I've never thought money was very important.'

She thought of his bony face, his dark eyes, the way his

smile made him look sad rather than happy; more than anything of the power he'd held over her when she was at art school. When she'd finally realised that he was going to leave without any further attempt at seeing her, it was as though she had nothing further to hope for. And what she'd done over the next years had been of no consequence.

'That's because you've always had money, darling.'

'Just enough to live on. I don't live extravagantly, you know that.'

'Perhaps you should try to forget him. You only met again by chance. You don't owe him anything.'

'I know you don't mean that, Dora, so I'll forgive you.'

'Oh Rosie, you think your love can save him, don't you?'

'Yes.' There was a moment's silence. 'I know it will be difficult,' she said afterwards, 'but I have to believe it.'

'So what are you going to do?'

Rosamund sat for a few moments rubbing her eyelids and trying to relax her shoulders. 'Well, I'm going to have to leave Joss with my mother again, take a bedsitting room near wherever Daniel lives, and try to get him to move in with me.'

'You're going to try and rescue him single-handed?'

'No, I'll take all the help I can get. But I'm going to rescue him, yes.' She opened her eyes. 'Would you like a sandwich?'

'Do you have any whisky?'

Even with a large whisky – and then another – inside her, Dora couldn't accept that Rosamund intended to plunge into a life so fraught with disappointment and pain.

Her stepdaughter looked so young and beautiful, her hair bleached by the sun and her skin lightly tanned. She looked very like Paul, but whereas disillusion and cynicism showed in his eyes and the cut of his mouth, Rosamund seemed so blithe, so pure somehow, so vulnerable.

Dora lay back on the sofa feeling old and bitter. 'You know there's a choice involved here, don't you?' she said, her voice harsh. 'Between Daniel on the one hand, and the rest of your life, including Joss, on the other. If you decide on Daniel, it'll mean you won't be able to devote anything like the same amount of love and care to—'

'I won't have that sort of talk, Dora. I intend to bring Daniel back here as soon as I can and then we'll all be happy together. At first people will have to understand that he's a sick man, but that shouldn't be too difficult, should it?'

'I don't know. I think perhaps it—'

'Please be positive about it, Dora. You're the one who's always believed in me. You were the one who told me I was wise enough and mature enough to make the right decision about my future. Dora, don't let me down. Say you're happy for me.'

'I can't.'

Rosamund's voice changed. 'Say you're happy for me!' she repeated, descending on her, putting a cushion over her face and tickling her. 'Say you're happy for me. Say it Dora, say it!'

She took away the cushion, pulled Dora up to a sitting position and kissed her rather wildly, desperate for her approval.

'I can't,' Dora said again, even more sadly. 'Playing the violin in the Underground can't be giving him anything like the money he needs, but if you turn up he'll feel saved and he'll bleed you dry.'

'Why should he think I've got money? I haven't. And if he thought I had, why didn't he turn up the other week when he promised to?'

'I don't know. But I do know that if you get together, he'll take every penny you've got. That's probably why his American girlfriend left him. You said they'd been together for several years. Well, she probably couldn't bear seeing him go from bad to worse, having to sell everything, unable even to go on painting. Rosamund, he's now living in some sort of squat.'

'Well, people do. I don't suppose they want to, but they have to. What else can people do when they can't afford anywhere to live; I can at least give him somewhere to stay and somewhere to work, can't I – offer him a new start? I'm not saying we'll get married or that we'll be perfectly and utterly happy, but at least he can come here and share this studio.'

'Oh yes, it could work if he was simply a down-and-out. If he'd just come out of prison, for instance – yes, I'd be worried, but I'd feel you had the right to try to rescue him. But heroin addiction is something completely different; it's something no one except the person involved can do anything about. I've seen horrifying programmes on the television; families desperately trying to help but failing completely.'

'I accept that I may fail completely,' Rosamund said after a moment's silence. 'But I won't accept that I can't try.'

Dora got up and helped herself to another whisky.

'Will you be all right with Granny and Brian for another week or so?' Rosamund asked Joss when he got in. 'You see, I have to go to London again.'

'Oh, not again.'

'But I'll be back very soon.'

'Will you be back for my birthday?'

'Definitely. With a very good present. Not a baby brother because you know as well as I do how much time that takes. But something very unusual and exciting. And I'll ring you every night. OK?'

'OK. Can I go now? Harry's got a new computer game.'

'What about Erica's book?' Dora asked later that night. 'I know you can't give it much thought at the moment, but I promised to let her know how you felt about it.'

Rosamund showed her the letter she'd received from Molly's solicitor, getting angry about it all over again. 'I'm certainly not going to let Molly frighten her out of publishing the book. When I talked to Erica a couple of days ago, I suggested that we should write it together, but now I'm obviously not going to have any time.'

'You own the copyright of all her poems?'

'They're technically mine, but they're really hers, aren't they, whatever anyone says. All the same I'm not against asking for a share of the money because I'm going to need it. And as soon as possible too. Perhaps Ingrid can contact Ben to get him onto it again. I can't say I liked Ben, but I don't suppose that's relevant.'

'Have you any idea what sort of money is involved?'

'Not the slightest. But Ingrid felt that even Ben's share was going to be quite considerable, otherwise he wouldn't have been so surly about losing the job. In fact, he didn't lose it, but backed out when he thought the poems couldn't be included in the book, which meant it wouldn't make the sort of money he was after.'

'If he backed out, then surely he forfeits any rights he had in the project?'

'I suppose so. Yes . . . Perhaps Ingrid would like to take it over. She's a journalist as well, though she says she's not in the same class as he is.'

'But if he's dumped her and gone off in a huff, she'd find it rather pleasing, wouldn't she, to be offered his job? And the money he was so loath to lose?'

'Dora, you've got a wicked gleam in your eye.'

'So have you, darling.'

'I'd better phone Paul,' Dora said, as they were getting ready for bed.

'What will you tell him?' Rosamund asked.

'Not very much. He doesn't care to be informed of the sad trivia of everyday life.'

# Chapter Fifteen

Dora and Rosamund arrived in Fulham soon after eleven the next day. After a quick coffee Dora went back to work, and soon afterwards Rosamund took a tube to Seven Sisters where Daniel lived. She found the area, even the actual street, but decided to get herself a bedsitting room – now called a studio flat – before doing anything else. Dora had told her that she'd need a month's rental and a roughly equal sum for a bond against damage or non-payment, so she'd already transferred all her savings into her current account so as to be able to meet the incredibly large sums her stepmother had mentioned.

Unfortunately it still didn't prove easy. She went to three letting agencies, but in all three she was informed that she couldn't rent any property without having job security. In spite of her unblushing insistence that she was not only solvent but an internationally-known artist with pictures in every famous gallery, in their eyes she was unemployed and therefore not eligible to rent even the cheapest property. 'So what do unemployed people do when they come to London?' she asked at the third agency. As though she didn't know.

She had a feeling that Ingrid would know what to do. She phoned and found her in. 'I'm trying to find somewhere to live but nobody'll have me.'

'Come round,' Ingrid said. 'We'll have some lunch and then we'll talk. I've got no work, so I'll come out with you later on, give you a reference and an employer's address and so forth. You have to lie and cheat in this jungle.'

'Of course you could stay with me,' Ingrid said as soon as

she opened the door. 'Ben hasn't been back so I'd be really pleased to have help with the rent.'

'The thing is, I've discovered Daniel's whereabouts and I'm looking for a place big enough for the two of us.'

When she told Ingrid about Daniel's predicament, her reaction was exactly as Rosamund had expected: she was throwing away her money and wasting her time and energy on someone she didn't even know properly.

'Perhaps I am,' Rosamund said wearily, 'but it's what I've decided on. I'm in love with him and I'm going to try to cure him.'

'Unfortunately love doesn't cure addiction. In fact, it often makes it worse. Junkies don't want the added guilt of letting people down. That's why they're happier with other junkies.'

'It may not work out, but I'll have tried.'

'Why haven't you been to see him? To see how he is? I'd have thought it would be the first thing you'd have wanted to do.'

'I was frightened.'

'Good. At least you're being realistic. I'll come with you when you decide to go.'

'No, I'll have to go on my own. But I thought it might be easier if I had a place to bring him back to. Obviously I can't expect him to come home with me straight away. He'll have things to sort out; I understand that. I wish I knew more about these things.'

'Ben wrote an article on drug addiction a couple of years back, did a lot of research for it. He'd help you if he was around. Or he might not. You could never tell with Ben.'

'Hasn't he been back at all?'

Ingrid sighed. 'Yes. He came when I was out, took all his things, didn't even leave me a note. That's why I went to see Erica Underhill. Thought she'd have an address for him, but she didn't. Or if she did she wasn't prepared to divulge it.'

'She probably didn't have it. He backed out of the job when he found that she didn't own the copyright of the poems and couldn't publish without the estate's permission. That's why he was furious with me. He thought I was involved, but in fact it was Molly's solicitor who'd written to her. I'd had nothing to do with it.'

Ingrid was looking at her, but her mind was on other things. 'Anyway, I think I'm getting over Ben. He's treated me pretty badly but at least I'm fully aware of it. Not that that's any guarantee of recovery.' She sighed again. 'All the same, I have the odd five minutes now when I'm not thinking about him.'

Rosamund gave this her full consideration. 'You told me that work was the answer,' she said. 'Are you working?'

'No.'

'Would you like some work? Would you like to take over Ben's job? It seems that I own the copyright of Erica's poems and I'm going to give her permission to publish them in spite of Molly. I shall ask her for a certain share of what she's likely to make, but I feel sure she'll agree. So how about it?'

'My God, that would be burning my boats, wouldn't it!'

'Well, it would serve him right. Bastard. Coming in here taking all his things away without even a by your leave or thank you for having me. What did you do? When you found out?'

'Had the locks changed.'

'Good for you. So you've burned your boats already.'

'I suppose I have. Yes. It would be sweet to think of him calling round late one night when he'd had too much to drink, and being unable to get in. Sweet.'

'But what if he rang the bell? After trying a few times?'

Ingrid thought about this. 'Oh, I'd let him in, I suppose. So it wasn't all that much use, was it? Changing the locks, I mean.'

'But perhaps it symbolised something. I remember my mother saying that she'd felt much easier and freer in her mind after throwing her wedding ring away. Getting her divorce through wasn't nearly as liberating, she said.'

'Ben didn't give me a ring to throw away. No ring of any sort. Nor any promises. And I always knew he had another girlfriend too – someone he'd known at school, I think. Whenever he went home to see his parents, he always came back very dejected. I think she might have been married.'

Ingrid sighed again. 'You see, I can't stop thinking about him. Before Ben, my self-esteem was in quite a healthy state. It

127

hasn't just shrunk, it's shrivelled up. Even at the very beginning of our relationship he could never bring himself to say anything affectionate. The first time he came back here and we had sex, the only thing that really seemed to please him was the size of my bed. He liked the bathroom too. Said it was very sexy. Sometimes I think he only wanted to move in with me because of my big bed and my sexy bathroom.' Ingrid laughed, but the effort seemed to hurt her. 'It would be just too humiliating to have him back now,' she said. And after a while, 'But I probably would. Oh, let's talk about something else, for God's sake!'

'Erica. Let's talk about Erica. Did you like her? How would you feel about writing her autobiography? Did you feel sympathetic towards her?'

'Of course I did – another who loved and lost. But I think she'd much prefer to work with Ben. She thought he was really something, I could tell that. She's the sort of woman who'll still be flirting with handsome young men on her deathbed.'

'If you'd like the job, I'm sure I could arrange it with her.'

'Ben wouldn't give it up without a struggle. Once he knew the project was on again, he'd be back, you can be sure of that. Reminding her of the bargain they'd made, of the work he'd already done, of his achievements as a journalist. He stood to make a lot of money from that job.'

'You told me you didn't know how much money was involved.'

'He didn't tell me what his share was going to be, but I think he said Erica was likely to make something like eighty or a hundred grand after the paper had taken extracts, which they'd promised to do. And I presume his share wouldn't be less than ten, fifteen per cent. I'm only guessing.'

'Something like ten thousand quid then. For two to three months' work – Erica mentioned two to three months. Wouldn't that be something to think about?'

'Supermodels get a thousand a day.'

'But they're eighteen and anorexic.'

Ingrid looked doleful. 'Do you think we've learnt anything since we were eighteen? Anything worthwhile? What are your achievements since you were eighteen?'

'Plain cooking; very plain cooking. Sewing patches on jeans. Hey, let's talk about Ben again.'

After a rather surprising lunch – coffee, slimming rolls which tasted like building material but were probably quite nourishing, and dried apricots – Ingrid took Rosamund to an agency she knew in Islington High Street. The woman behind the room-sized desk; chalk-white face, flame-coloured hair, black dresslet, didn't inspire confidence, especially when she begged them to call her Buzz, but immediately and rather proudly produced a one-roomed flat with bathroom on the landing, available for short-term let, for almost exactly twice the huge sum of money Rosamund had managed to get together.

'I'll need to think about it,' she said.

'Of course,' Buzz murmured with a very tiny smile. 'We want you to be happy, happy, happy.'

'Don't even bother to think about it,' Ingrid said when they got outside and could breathe again. 'You pay half my rent for a week plus my airfare to Italy and you can have my flat and I can have a holiday.'

'Wonderful,' Rosamund said. 'That will mean I'll still have some money left for the rest of my life. How soon can you go?'

'Will tomorrow morning be soon enough? My sheets are clean on this week and by great good fortune my food cupboard is completely cleared out except for a big jar of pearl barley which you're welcome to dip into. In a week you'll get everything sorted out and I'll come back completely cured of Ben with possibly a passionate new boyfriend who'll promise faithfully to ring me but won't.'

'A week of destiny,' Rosamund said. 'I feel faint.' And I feel totally inadequate, she thought. I dressed in a hurry this morning, my skirt feels too long and my shirt is faded and not really my colour. Everyone else here looks much younger and more dashing than I do. Why didn't I at least wash my hair last night instead of drinking too much with Dora? I've even got a touch of indigestion and my nose is probably as pink as a rabbit's.

'Do I look all right?' she asked Ingrid as she left her, but was afraid to wait for a reply. *The fair Rosamunda*, she thought, with a smile that was almost a grimace.

She got to Eversley Place where Daniel lived by five o'clock. It was a warm afternoon, the sun golden in a mild blue sky. The street was rundown, many of the houses having boarded-up windows, but they had once been rather grand flat-fronted early Victorian residences. She imagined prosperous families living in them; several children and a servant or two, she imagined small boys bowling hoops along the pavements and little girls with Kate Greenaway dresses.

She realised that she was thinking of anything rather than the prospect immediately facing her. All the same, the light was mysterious, almost an evening light though it was still afternoon. The light of a dream, Rosamund thought, and I'll soon be waking from it. She dreaded what she would find, dreaded seeing Daniel as he might be.

Someone eventually answered the door – a young girl, blonde, slightly dishevelled, a small, pale face.

'I'm a friend of Daniel Hawkins. May I see him?'

The girl smiled. 'You're Rosamund, aren't you? We've been expecting you. Caroline told us you would come.'

'How is he?'

A moment's hesitation. 'He's upstairs. Follow me. I'm Marie, by the way. I'm with Edmund. It was Edmund who saw Caroline the other day.'

Rosamund followed the girl up the dusty uncarpeted stairs to the top floor. She knocked on one of the doors which had once been painted a brave shade of deep red, but was now blistered and shabby.

'Yes. Come in.' It was Daniel's voice.

'I'll leave you,' the girl said and went back downstairs, her tread light as a child's.

Rosamund opened the door.

Daniel looked, not just thin as she'd thought the last time they'd met, but painfully thin, almost skeletal. She felt she could pick him up and carry him away. 'Rosamund,' he said, spreading out his arms for her. 'They said you'd come.' He held her tightly. She could feel his heart beating very fast.

They moved to the bed and lay there together, neither saying anything. The room had an unhealthy air though the window was slightly open. After a while Rosamund wondered whether he'd fallen asleep.

'I've come for you,' she said at last, her voice trembling a little. 'Will you come away with me?'

There was a long silence. 'I can't, Rosamunda. I've started on the bloody Methadone again and I go to therapy as well to try to keep sane. It's hell but I've done almost two days. I only started on it again because someone said you'd tracked me down.'

'Does it get easier? It must get easier, surely.'

'No. I've done it so many times, the so-called cure, but I've always given up on it after a while.'

'I've borrowed a flat in Islington, only two stops away by tube. You could still go to your therapy.'

'You can stay here with me.'

'I will if that's what you want. But if you come to my friend's flat, wouldn't that be a new start?'

'I've had too many new starts. I'm better off here where everybody knows how hard it is. How bloody impossible it is.' He looked into her eyes and stroked her hair. 'Rosie, I'm sorry. I should have told you, but I couldn't. You looked so happy.'

'I was happy, blissfully happy. But I was very unhappy the next day.'

'I honestly meant to turn up the next day, I meant to tell you then. But it got to me – what I was losing – and I stayed here instead, getting high. Don't think you can save me, Rosie, because you can't.'

'I know I can't. I know I can't do anything but be with you.'

'And how long can you be with me? How long can you stay here? You've got your own life to lead. You've got a little boy, haven't you? You can't really stay with me, can you?'

Rosamund felt her determination falter. 'I'll stay with you for week or two anyway. Have you been to therapy today?'

'Yes, but it doesn't do any good. Fucking useless, in fact. Talk, talk, talk. Motivation for the future. All the great things we're going to do when we're clean. That sort of thing. Nobody believes any of it. It's all useless.'

'What are the other people like?'

'They're just people, good and bad. Of course the public

thinks we're all crooks. Takes a lot of money, so we're all crooks, simple as that.'

'So how did you get money?'

'In the past, by selling things. Everything I possessed, in fact – my paintings, my paints, my furniture, my clothes. And all for next to nothing. These days I play the violin in various places, but I never make enough. That's why I've got to give it up.'

Daniel suddenly became restless and turned from her.

'What's the matter? Are you in pain now?'

'Yes.'

'Is there anything I can do?'

'No.' He rocked back and forth, doubled up with pain.

Rosamund caught sight of herself in a mirror; her face sharpened by anxiety, her eyes full of hurt and shock. She felt completely out of her depth. 'I'm just going to find a lavatory,' she told him. He didn't answer her, didn't look up at her, only went on rocking, sweat pouring from his face.

She found a lavatory, but so wretchedly dirty that she couldn't sit and cry there as she'd intended. She couldn't go back to Daniel either, at least not immediately, so she went downstairs hoping to find Marie, the girl who'd let her in and taken her to Daniel's room. She'd seemed kind. Perhaps she could give her some information, help, advice, courage. She certainly needed courage.

She knocked on several doors, but no one answered. There were people inside, she felt sure, but perhaps locked up in their own private griefs. She went from door to door feeling helpless and wishing she was somewhere else.

At last she found Marie alone in a small, cluttered but fairly pleasant sitting room whose French windows were open to a strip of untended garden full of discarded mattresses, pieces of carpet and a large old-fashioned pram; scarcely a blade of grass.

'Don't break your heart,' Marie said. 'He's a super bloke and you must take him as you find him.'

'But can't I help him in any way?'

'Visit him. That's about all you can do. That may help him. Or of course it may not.'

'But he doesn't seem to care that I'm with him.'

'Of course he doesn't. He's going through hell, that's why.

He's sick and in pain. Don't you know how it is? Don't you understand?'

They were both silent for a few moments. 'Would you like to see my baby?' Marie said then.

To Rosamund's surprise she was taken out to the old pram in the garden. 'Here he is. Three weeks old. Theodore.'

He was tiny, with a tiny wizened face.

'Theodore. He's lovely.' Rosamund could hardly believe that Marie was old enough to be responsible for a baby. 'Do you have everything you need for him?' she asked.

'Are you a social worker?'

'No. But I've got a little boy myself and I've still got masses of baby clothes.'

'My mum brings me things. She comes to see him twice a week.'

'Oh, good. Tell me, does Daniel's mum visit him?'

'I didn't know he had a mum. You're the first one who's visited Daniel since Annie went back to America.'

'His girlfriend?'

'Yes. Annie something. She was all right, but I don't think he ever hears from her.'

They stood looking at the sleeping baby for another few minutes. 'I'm pretty well clean myself,' Marie said. 'Anyway, I'm off smack. But you see, I wasn't on it for long so it was easier.'

'How old are you?'

She looked Rosamund up and down as though deciding what to tell her. 'Are you a social worker?' she asked again.

Rosamund declined to answer her. 'I need to get some things from the corner shop,' she said instead. 'Will you be here to let me in again in about half an hour?'

'Sure. By the way, I could do with some Pampers if you've got the cash.'

'Anything else?'

'Food. Cigarettes. Aspirin. Toilet paper. Whatever you can afford, basically.'

'Fine.'

'*Are* you a social worker?'

'I'm not sure.'

\*

133

Rosamund didn't feel up to spending the night in Eversley Place. She wouldn't mind, might even enjoy, buying stocks of food and other necessities whenever called upon to do so, but cleaning stairs and lavatories she wasn't prepared for. And though her standards were not of the highest, she wasn't prepared either for grime and dirt and no hot water for baths. 'I can only do what I can,' she told herself. 'It's wise to know one's limitations.'

Outside, the air was clean and mild, the light beneficent.

# Chapter Sixteen

Marian was under the impression that Rosamund's hurried return to London was connected with her work on Erica Underhill's book, but when Rosamund phoned her that evening, she revealed something nearer the truth.

'I'm trying to get Ingrid to take over the book, Mum, because I'm looking after a friend of mine. A man I used to know at college.'

'A *man*?' Marian said as though hearing the word for the first time.

'I think I told you something about him at the time. Daniel Hawkins. I was very much in love with him.'

'*In love*? You were *in love*?' Her mother was enormously surprised, amused rather than disapproving.

'And I still am, Mum. But he's not very well at the moment, so I'm having to look after him.'

'Good gracious, you are a dark horse, Rosamund. You keep everything hidden away.'

'There's been nothing to tell until now. I lost touch with him and didn't see him for fifteen years.'

'So what does he do?'

'He's an artist, Mum. But he's had a sort of breakdown. A lot of trouble and bad luck.'

'Oh, he would have. You've never managed to be interested in anyone who's got anything to offer you. I can't forget how devoted Dr Wilby was. Such a pleasant young man, such a good practice.' She sighed in the dramatic way Rosamund had got used to. 'Still, it's your life, dear, and you know you can depend on me to do what I can to help. How old is this man?'

'Two or three years older than me.'

Marian brightened. 'Good heavens! When you mentioned looking after him, dear, I thought he was going to be another elderly man.'

'No . . . No, he's not elderly.'

'And how long do you expect to be away?'

'I'll be back next weekend and we'll talk again.'

'Oh good. I'll hand you over to Joss, dear. He's very anxious to have a word. Joss!'

'Hello, Joss. How's school?'

'Oh Mum, you always ring when it's *Star Trek.*'

'How's Harry?'

'He's probably watching *Star Trek.*'

'Well, I must go, love. I have to watch *Star Trek.*'

'Don't be silly, Mum.'

All that evening Rosamund felt depressed and confused. Daniel seemed a different person. She realised how much he was suffering, but the most dispiriting thing was that he was so pessimistic about his chances of a cure. If he could endure ten days, he'd told her, he'd be on the first step to recovery, but then he'd added that every hour was like ten days. 'No, I won't make it,' he'd said over and over again. 'I feel so desperately ill.' And he'd told her of a friend who'd managed, after superhuman effort, to break the habit, but who still felt in danger of succumbing to it again: 'This is living in a twilight world,' he'd said, 'and being on heroin is like being in the sun.' And the sun is God, Rosamund thought.

Ingrid, packing for her unexpected holiday, was happy and excited, as though she was managing to forget Ben already. Once or twice Rosamund couldn't resist the disloyal thought that she'd like to be going to Italy with her.

Next morning she was up at eight to wave Ingrid off to Heathrow. Afterwards she telephoned Dora, giving her an optimistic account of Daniel's condition, had a large nourishing breakfast in the first café she came to, feeling it might well be the only solid comfort she'd have all day, then took the tube to Seven Sisters. The weather had suddenly become hot and sultry. Naturally, she thought, I have brought the wrong clothes, so that I shall look as well as feel out of place. Why should it be as hot as this in the middle of May?

Eversley Place looked even more rundown and desolate in the bright morning sunshine. There was no one about; people who had work to go to had already left for buses and tubes, and people with no work obviously saw no reason to be out so early. When she arrived at the house she had to stand at the door for several minutes; the bell didn't seem to be working and there was no knocker. She rapped on the door until her knuckles hurt and eventually an extremely large and inadequately dressed man opened it, frowning heavily.

'I'm Daniel's friend,' she said in a mild placatory voice. The man seemed half-asleep but let her in. 'I know my way up,' she said, walking to the foot of the stairs. She looked back, giving him a nervous smile, but he was still frowning and looking puzzled.

She walked upstairs still feeling uneasy. She knocked on Daniel's door and getting no response, walked in.

Daniel and Marie were lying together on the dirty counterpane of the narrow bed, with the baby, Theodore, in a box or a drawer on the floor near them.

'We've had a terrible time with him,' Marie said, sitting up and yawning, 'but it's probably done Danny a lot of good because he walked round with him half the night and now he's fast asleep, look, and all he's had is a couple of my sleeping pills and some valium. We'll let him sleep, OK? It'll make the day shorter for him.'

She yawned very thoroughly again and then sprang out of bed, as easily and as artlessly as a child. She was dressed in a short T-shirt and seemed to see no reason to put anything else on.

'Do you want to nurse Theodore?' she asked Rosamund with the air of one conferring a favour. 'He was fed half an hour ago. He'll soon go to sleep.'

'Thank you,' Rosamund said, taking him from her.

'He's doing very well, isn't he?' Marie asked, her tone less assured than her words.

'He seems fine. A bit damp, but otherwise fine. Have you had a health visitor round?'

'Probably,' Marie said. 'But no one lets her in, that's the trouble. Anyway, you're a social worker, aren't you?'

'No, I'm Daniel's friend.'

'Oh, I know that. But aren't you a social worker as well?'

'No, but I've got a little son myself, so I know something about babies.' Her heart gave a lurch as she remembered Joss at three weeks old. His astonishing beauty.

'Perhaps you'd like to bath him?' Marie asked. 'Only I'm too scared to. Anyway, I haven't got a baby bath. My Mum brought me a little white bowl, perhaps I'll just wash him a bit.'

'That'll be fine. With perhaps a clean vest and so on.' The whole room smelt of drains, so she couldn't tell if he needed changing, but clean, or at least cleaner little garments seemed an excellent idea.

'My room's next door. Shall we go and see what we can find?'

She sounded so like a small child that Rosamund half-expected her to put her hand in hers. In fact, she was probably not much more than a child, Rosamund thought, certainly not more than sixteen. Just six years older than Joss.

Her room was identical to Daniel's, but with a small cooker and a wash basin in a corner. There was no wardrobe or chest of drawers though, only some heaps of clothes on the floor, one of them baby clothes. Theodore started to cry again as Marie sorted through the pile. 'Everything he's got is wet or soiled,' she said, looking as though she, too, was going to cry. 'The trouble is he shits all the time.'

'Take the whole lot to the launderette,' Rosamund suggested.

'Much too expensive.'

Silently Rosamund handed her a five-pound note which she silently accepted.

'Do you want to leave Theodore with me?'

Marie gave her a beatific smile. 'Oh, please.'

138

She's a child, Rosamund told herself. She'll cram all the dirty clothes into one machine and escape to the nearest café for a coffee, a sticky doughnut and a cigarette, several cigarettes. She felt pleased to have engineered that little escape for a youngster who should be out with other youngsters, not cooped up in that terrible unhygienic and probably unhealthy house. She carried the baby back to Daniel's room which was marginally less odorous.

'Where's Marie?' Daniel asked. He was now sitting up and moving his head from side to side as though trying to discover something about his condition.

Rosamund looked at him rather severely until he stopped. Then she sat on the side of his bed, tilting Theodore towards him. 'She's gone to the launderette. The baby needs clean clothes.'

Daniel looked at him for several seconds. 'I only hope she comes back,' he said then.

Rosamund felt a chill fall on her, the air of the room become heavy with menace. 'Of course she'll come back. Why shouldn't she come back? To her baby and to . . . Edmund? Didn't you say she was with someone called Edmund?'

'Yes, but he seems to have moved on. He hasn't been around the last couple of weeks. People stay out when the weather's good. Anyway, she may come back.'

'Of course she will.' She studied his face. 'You seem a little better today.'

'And I haven't even had my dose yet. I'm usually at the chemist's at eight waiting for it. Anyway, I'll cut along there now, the pains are starting again. And I'll look out for Marie and bring her back with me. You stay here, darling, and look after Theodore.'

The endearment brought a lump to her throat. It was difficult for her to think of Daniel as the person she'd decided to fall in love with – is that what she'd done? She watched him pull on his jeans and his shirt, saw his thin legs and his pitifully thin chest.

He noticed her staring at him. 'Are you all right?' he asked her. 'Are you sorry you came?'

'Not if you want me here.'

139

'I want you here. Of course I do. Listen, I'll be back very soon.'

He seemed in pain again as he left.

As soon as he'd gone, Theodore started to cry and she had to walk about, patting him on his back to quieten him. How would she cope if Marie didn't arrive back for his next feed? The heat was becoming stifling in the small attic room and the smell was getting worse, a faint suggestion of fish and rotten vegetables. Why hadn't she gone with Daniel to the chemist's?

She put the baby on the bed, dragged a chair to the window to try to open it wider but couldn't shift it and to her horror found herself crying with frustration. She got down, picked the baby up again, waiting for someone, anyone, to come to her rescue. It didn't seem fair that people had to live in such conditions. No wonder they needed drugs to support them. She'd only been there an hour and she already felt panic spreading through her body. She'd have to insist on Daniel coming back with her to Ingrid's flat. She realised she wasn't up to spending even a part of the day at Eversley Place.

It was an hour later before Daniel returned. 'I went looking for Marie,' he said, 'but she wasn't at the launderette. But she'll come back, I'm sure.' He seemed fairly well, fairly cheerful.

'This baby will need a feed soon.'

'I know how to do it. You have to boil water and then cool it and mix three measures of milk powder with the cooled water. The bottle should be in some sterilising stuff. I think I'll be able to do it.'

They went to Marie's room together and she watched as Daniel concentrated on his task. 'Come home with me, Daniel,' she pleaded. 'I don't think I can stay here.'

He didn't answer or look in her direction until he'd mixed the feed and poured it into the bottle which, to her surprise, had been soaking in a saucepan on the stove. He handed it to her and she sat on Marie's bed waiting for it to cool.

'This is day three,' he said. 'If I make it for seven more days I'll ask you to try to get me into a clinic. They'll take me if I've done ten days. They'll know I'm serious.'

'And do you think you'll be cured afterwards?'

'I can't even think about it. There are seven days to go through first and every day gets worse, hour by hour. Anyway, could you afford the fees? I've no idea how much it would be.'

'Yes, I'll manage the fees. I'll borrow money if I have to. Can I come with you to your counselling session this afternoon, if Marie decides to come back?'

'No, it's pretty harrowing. We all have cramps or panic attacks. No one wants to talk or cooperate. You take Theodore to the park. You can leave a note for Marie.'

It took a whole hour to feed the baby. He was so small that the effort of sucking tired him so that he slept every few minutes. It was a pleasant hour though, Daniel and she sitting on Marie's bed, Daniel's hand resting companionably on her thigh.

When Daniel left, the baby was sleeping so peacefully that she couldn't bear to wake him to take him out. She'd bought a newspaper earlier and she sat and tried to read it. The room was hot and uncomfortable as ever, but she seemed to have got more used to the smell.

She heard a knock at the front door and eventually footsteps, heavy and purposeful, on the stairs. Who was it? It certainly wasn't Marie. A tap on the door. With thumping heart she got up and opened it to a black woman in nursing uniform. She breathed a sigh of relief.

'Do you want to come in? Have you come to see Theodore?'

'Where's Marie? I need to see both of them.'

'I'm looking after the baby at the moment. Marie's taken some of his clothes to the launderette.'

'Are you a relative?'

'No. A friend of someone staying here. My name's Rosamund.'

The black woman looked hard at her. Could she suspect her of being a pusher? 'Mine's Jo,' she said at last.

Jo picked Theodore up from his bed in a drawer and examined him. 'Is she looking after him properly?' she asked. 'He's awfully thin. I've warned her that we'll have to take him into care if we ever find that she's neglecting him.'

141

'She seems to be coping,' Rosamund said, but without much conviction.

'She struggled hard to get off the heroin – that took some guts – but whether she'll stay off is another matter. When will she be back?'

'I told her I'd be here for the rest of the day.'

'I'll call in again when I can . . . Where's his bottle?'

'Over there in the sterilising solution.'

That seemed to have been the right answer.

'Do you think she'll manage to look after him properly in this house?'

'I don't know,' Rosamund said, her voice trembling a little.

Her hesitancy seemed to resolve the health visitor's doubts. 'I think she will,' she said. 'She's quite mature for sixteen, and if you can look in to keep an eye on her from time to time it'll be a great help.'

'What about her mother? She told me her mother visits her and buys things for the baby.'

'Oh yes, her mother's a very nice person. I've known her mother for years – Iris. Only of course she's an alcoholic and she's got little ones of her own. But oh yes, Marie will shape up, I'm sure. She and her mother, they do their best, fair play.'

Rosamund felt a rush of love for a woman able to be so tolerant and calm when she herself felt so intolerant and angry.

Daniel returned at four, going straight to lie on his bed and turning his face to the wall.

'Don't you dare go to sleep,' Rosamund told him in a quiet but rather brutal voice. 'Marie still hasn't come back and you've got to look after Theodore while I go out to buy him some clothes and nappies and some more milk powder.'

Daniel struggled to sit up. 'Fair enough,' he said. 'I'll give him another feed when he wakes up, shall I?'

'That's up to you. He's not my responsibility.'

'How long will you be?'

'I don't know.'

She'd only gone as far as the front door when Marie arrived

back. 'I'm sorry I was a long time,' she said, giving her a radiant smile. 'But you see, I knew Theodore would be fine with you.'

It was as much as Rosamund could do not to shake her.

'You can't fucking take this, can you?' Daniel said when she got back with the shopping. 'You were exactly the same in college. Too fucking middle-class. Too good for me. Too good for everyone. Too good for everyday life. For God's sake, just go, will you, and leave me alone.'

'I'm not too good for everyday life. This isn't everyday life, this is squalor. I want to help you, but you won't help yourself.'

'What the hell do you think I'm doing? I'm bloody well going through hell trying to help myself. And you can't even bear to stay the night here.'

'You've never asked me to stay the night here. Marie seemed to be with you last night.'

'She's lonely too, you know. She's only a kid and she's on her own. You don't know anything about life, do you? Real life? Being frightened and hungry? Being desperately cold with nothing to put in the meter? Being hungry with absolutely no money to buy food?'

'I've never known that sort of hardship, no. But I've often been very lonely and unhappy. Money doesn't shield you from those things. I know about those things. And they're bad enough.'

'I don't even know what you're doing here.'

'Don't you?' Rosamund felt her blood rising. 'Well, I'll tell you. I was in love with you, deeply in love with you, when I was nineteen, and I've never really been in love with anyone else. Pathetic, isn't it? I got pregnant by accident and married someone old enough to be my father and I've been on my own for almost ten years, with just about enough money to live on. I paint because I feel the need to do something, but as you may remember, I'm not all that good. Whereas you were bloody brilliant and you've thrown it all away and you'll probably never paint again because you feel you're living real life in this place.'

'I'm in this bloody place because I can't afford anything else.

Why don't you bloody listen?' Daniel threw himself down on his bed. 'Why don't you go?' he asked in a different voice.

Rosamund's voice changed too. 'Do you want me to?' she asked quietly.

'No.' He held out his arms for her and they lay down together without further words. Then he undressed her and she undressed him and they kissed each other, very tenderly at first and then more and more passionately, their hands hot on each other's bodies. Until Daniel finally broke away from her and cried. And she comforted him and told him there was plenty of time, plenty of time, my love, my darling, and held him until he went to sleep. She sat in his room all night, dozing in short snatches and watching his restless sleep. When he woke, he was again fretful and in pain, seeming to have forgotten their brief truce.

The following evening, feeling a desperate need for a bath and a bed, Rosamund returned to Ingrid's flat, and before settling to sleep phoned her mother for news of Joss.

'I'm so glad you rang, dear. I was at the schoolhouse this morning looking for socks, the phone rang and of course I answered it thinking it might be Brian, but it was Mrs Gilchrist, dear, who seemed in a fine old temper.'

'Don't worry, Mum. She's probably annoyed that I haven't written to reply to some demands she was making. I'll give her a ring tomorrow. It's too late now, she'll probably be in bed.'

Rosamund felt too benighted by real problems to be much concerned with Molly's petty grievances.

'But when I explained that I was your mother, dear, she told me to tell you that she could do you a great deal of harm, and would, if you didn't agree to suppress the poems. I think that's what she said.'

'Good heavens, the woman's mad. You see, Mum, she got her solicitor to get in touch with Erica Underhill to warn her off publication. But she had no right to do it because the copyright of the poems are mine. And I want the book to go ahead because I want a share of the money.'

'Of course you do, dear. I'm sure you're completely in the

right. But what about this harm she can do you? That's what I'm worried about.'

'She can't do me any harm, Mum. Don't give it another thought. Perhaps she intended to leave Joss something in her will, but I hardly think so. How is he?'

'He's fine, dear. Brian and I had to take him to see Jim after school this afternoon. Jim. The new baby, dear. Yes, he's home now. I don't think Granny could cope with him, but at least she's paying for a trained Norland nanny to look after him for a twelvemonth. Yes. But not at all the sort of person you'd think of as a Norland nanny – you know, brogues and tweeds and so on. No, in fact the sort of person you'd think of as Swedish au pair. Or even Swedish tart. She was in the briefest of brief bikinis when we arrived and Jim was completely naked, lying on a rug and completely naked.'

'And how was Thomas?'

'Oh, Thomas was fully clothed, dear, and very kindly made us a cup of tea.'

That night Rosamund dreamed that Marie had abandoned her baby and that Jo, the health visitor, had agreed to let her have him. She'd had to smuggle him away in a taxi before any one else – Marie's mother? Edmund? – had arrived to claim him, and in the taxi she realised that she hadn't stopped to feed him; he seemed to be shrinking even as she nursed him and fixing his large sad eyes on her as though accusing her of neglect. She'd beaten on the glass separating her from the driver, but he'd taken no notice, though she was sure he could hear her. And where was he hurrying off with them? To her horror she realised that she'd given him no address. And, oh God, he seemed to be driving her onto the Shuttle. And all the time, she was beating on the glass and crying and hugging the little baby to her breast to try to keep him warm, to keep him alive.

She woke sweating and weak with relief to discover that she was safely in bed and not guilty of kidnap or neglect. She put the light on and kept it on for several minutes, looking about her at Ingrid's pretty bedroom and longing to be at home with Joss. She corrected herself. 'With Joss and Daniel, I mean,' she said.

# Chapter Seventeen

'Can't I come with you?' Marie asked, when Rosamund told her she intended visiting a friend that afternoon while Daniel was at his counselling session. 'I don't like being here by myself.'

'Don't you know the people downstairs?'

'Yes, but I don't like them. They don't talk to me.'

Rosamund had only come across one other tenant, the large, frowning man who'd let her in the previous day, though she'd several times been to the communal kitchen on the ground floor. 'How many people are there in the house?' she asked.

'I don't know. Quite a lot. Edmund and Daniel had these two rooms first of all and me and my friend, Kim, had the room downstairs with the doors to the garden.' Marie's voice hardened. 'Only Kim left when I moved in with Edmund.'

'And don't you see her now?'

Rosamund had a long wait before Marie answered. 'She came back Christmas-time, but she wasn't well. Daniel got the ambulance. Daniel went up the road and phoned for the ambulance.'

Rosamund was aware from Marie's reluctance to continue that things had gone badly, very badly. All the same she couldn't resist another question. 'And what happened to her?'

'Oh, she died,' Marie said in a shockingly bright voice. 'Silly cow. All her own fault. On heroin and only fifteen with all her life in front of her.'

'Is that what people said?'

'Yes.'

'Most people are ignorant and stupid,' Rosamund said. 'But I bet Jo didn't say that.'

'Jo? Jo Watson? How do you know Jo?'

'She came here to see Theodore when I was looking after him. I thought she seemed a good sort. She seemed to like you a lot. You and your mum.'

Marie's face relaxed. 'Yes. Jo was brought up in care herself, so she understood about Kim.'

'Kim was brought up in a Home?'

'Only she ran away at fourteen.'

'Didn't she have a mother?'

'Don't know. Didn't ever ask her. Didn't think it was my business to ask her.'

'You're quite right. And I won't ask you anything else.'

'I don't mind. I don't mind talking about Kim because she was my friend, my best friend.'

'Tell me a bit more about her then.'

'Not much to tell. She had curly brown hair and it gave her a lot of grief because she thought it made her look like a kid and she wanted long straight hair. She had a brilliant laugh. She even laughed that night she came back here. When I told her I was up the creek.'

'Don't cry. I didn't mean to upset you.'

'It's OK. I don't mind talking to you. You seem like a lady at first, but deep down you're not.'

'And deep down you seem the sort of person who could be a sort of person like Jo.'

'Don't be daft.'

'Tomorrow afternoon we'll go up West and go shopping in Oxford Street.'

'With what?'

'I've still got a bit of money left. But I've got to go on my own this afternoon. It's to do with my work.'

'You said you was going to see a friend.'

'A very old lady. And to do with my work.'

Marie sat for a while looking at Theodore who was sleeping sweetly in his drawer under a Mickey Mouse blanket. 'What I really want is a buggy, a second-hand buggy. I've put a pound fifty down on it. Out of that fiver you gave me for the launderette.'

'How much is it?'

'A lot.'

'How much?'

'Twenty-five quid.' She looked up at Rosamund. 'But it's in good nick. I tested the brakes and that. And it folds up ever so easy. I could take it on buses, go to see my mum, go anywhere.'

'We'll go and see it tomorrow. You stay in today, then you'll be here when Daniel comes back. He likes to see Theodore.'

'He likes to see me as well.'

Erica seemed more frail than Rosamund had remembered, but was in high spirits – due, she said, to the excellent weather. She was dressed in a pale grey silk dress, a white chiffon scarf round her neck. Rosamund felt an awed admiration for her; she was old with wrinkles, loose skin, hooded eyes, but her expression had remained young and eager and this was what you noticed.

Rosamund apologised for postponing the arrangements made for her visit to Gloucestershire, but Erica assured her that she was happy to think of it as a future treat. 'I like to anticipate,' she said, 'don't you? Don't you think that looking forward to something is often the best part? When Anthony used to telephone in the morning to say he'd be coming round that evening, I'd spend a lovely day waiting for him. Whatever work I was doing, my mind was attuned to his arrival. Even preparing a meal for him was full of a quite extreme pleasure. I often think of those days, that joy.'

'And you see,' she continued, when they were seated at the window of the elegant dark red sitting room, 'writing one's autobiography is a very pleasant occupation because one is made to think of the past instead of the future.'

'You've started on it?'

'Not the actual writing, no, but I've been busy thinking back and making notes. Of course at my age one's always thinking of the past, but now it's in a structured way, so that one feels more like a writer, even an historian, and less like a maudlin old woman.'

Rosamund started to tell her that she was at the moment

149

unable to undertake the actual writing, but found that Dora had already explained the position to her.

'My dear, I quite understand. If this young man is important to you, he must come first. I know young women these days like to feel that they owe as much loyalty to other women as to the men in their lives, but that's quite alien to my way of thinking. I would always put a man first and I would always expect my girlfriends – not that I had many girlfriends – to do the same. Don't you agree with me?'

'I'm not sure. Anyway, at the moment Daniel, the man in question, has to come first because he's had a breakdown and needs all my attention. I haven't many girlfriends either, though I'm very fond of Ingrid, the girl who called here to see you.'

'Ah yes, Ben's girlfriend. Or is that over? She seemed to think it might be over. He hadn't left her his address, I think.'

'Yes, it's probably over. And since he doesn't seem interested in carrying on with the book now, I thought you might be willing to let Ingrid take it on. She's a journalist as well – that's how I got to know her. She came to the schoolhouse to do an article about me, about my painting.'

'I liked Ingrid well enough, but I think I'd be able to talk more freely to Ben.'

'I don't think he's to be trusted, though. He gave up this job as soon as he thought he wasn't going to get enough money from it, which seems pretty rotten. And he's been pretty rotten to Ingrid as well.'

Erica seemed reluctant to let Ben slip out of her life. He had brought her expensive flowers from Harrods; dusky black tulips the last time he'd come, saying they'd remind her of passion, get her in the right mood. All the same . . . 'Well, I'm ready to settle for Ingrid if you're ready to give me permission to use the poems.'

'Oh, I am. And I was hoping perhaps you'd suggest paying me a certain amount as well.'

'I'd already thought of that. We'll have a contract drawn up. Ben's agent was going to see to that, now we'll have to think of someone else. I wish I had some champagne to celebrate our agreement. Haven't had any champagne for ages.' Erica was sure Ben would have brought champagne. 'When will Ingrid be able to start? I'm longing to get going. I really do need some money before next winter.'

'She's coming back from a holiday in Italy on Saturday and she'll ring you. She's anxious to start too.'

'Where in Italy was she making for?'

'I'm not sure. Her air ticket was to Pisa.'

'I lived in Italy for several years. It was just before I met Anthony.'

Erica seemed suddenly tired so that Rosamund offered to make some tea. She'd bought a cherry cake at the corner shop.

She was pleased to find the kitchen tidier and cleaner than before, which seemed a positive sign. There were even some dark tulips on the windowsill, dead now, their stems arched almost double so that they looked like curtseying ballerinas, but all the same, evidence that Erica felt she had something to live for, had hope for the future. She put the kettle on, placed cups and saucers on a tray and carried it into the sitting room.

Erica had her spectacles on and was reading a letter. After a few seconds she passed it to Rosamund. It was from Anthony, the address somewhere in Provence.

'*Oh dearest, I can't sleep, can't eat, can't exist without you. My life with M is a travesty of marriage, I have nothing to give her. I know she understands this, because she is far from stupid, yet chooses not to, refuses to question me, refuses to recognise my anguish at being away from you. She has taken this house for a month. How long can I stay here? Oh waste of moon, waste of night, darkness and stars. Dearest, you have all my love.*'

Rosamund sat perfectly still, hardly breathing, reliving the tragedy of those three people. After a while she realised that tears were running down her cheeks, so she blew her nose, poured out the tea, cut the cherry cake, passed the plate to Erica and took a few sips of her scalding tea.

'I don't know what that was all about,' she said. 'It just shows how worked up I am, I suppose. Oh, why do things go so wrong for us all?'

Erica said nothing, only sat patiently waiting for her to continue.

So Rosamund sniffed again and told her about Daniel

who'd been the great love of her student days, how she'd met him again and how she was now trying to help him. 'Not for his sake, of course, but for mine. In the hope that he'll be able to fill the emptiness in my life.'

'When I married Roger,' Erica said, 'that was after the abortion when I felt so abandoned, I found I'd filled one emptiness and created another. Being married to the wrong person isn't the answer. Most of the people I used to know seemed to be unhappily married, but they thought, as I did, that it was better than being alone. I now think being alone is the second-best option.'

Rosamund thought about that as she munched her piece of cake. 'I suppose it might be, but I think I've been alone too long. It's something I've tried and found wanting.'

'Anyway,' Erica said, 'you're embarked on a very exciting project. You might be giving Daniel a new start in life. And even if it is, as you say, mostly for your sake, he'll certainly reap the benefit. And if he's got great talent, as you seem to think, he might be even greater after this ordeal he's going through.'

'Or perhaps he'll always feel hungry and deprived for what's missing from his life.'

'I had to give up smoking three years ago because of my chest and I found it hell. And giving up heroin is of course far, far worse. I don't suppose he believes in prayer, does he?'

'Why, do you?'

'No. But I still prayed. A priest at the hospital – yes, I had bronchitis very badly and had to go to St Thomas's – had given me a special prayer written down on a card, and I used to recite it quite often. The words were very beautiful, I thought. Something about sinners and the grace of God.' She sighed. 'The repetition seems to calm you down,' she said.

'Do you ever go to church?'

'Yes. I like to go on a fine summer morning. Especially when I haven't been anywhere else all week. Well, for one thing it's the only chance I get to wear a hat and I have several pretty hats. And there's coffee and biscuits afterwards in the vestry and always someone fairly interesting to talk to. You meet quite a nice type of person in St Mark's.'

Old people seemed to be so lonely, Rosamund thought. And yet she'd prefer to battle on alone like Erica than be cooped up in an old people's home. Cooped up; old people crowded together like chickens.

'I wonder if you'd like a young companion to live with you? To do your shopping and so on?'

'Oh, I don't think so, Rosamund, thank you. I have my home-help twice a week and I like to go to bed early. Why? Did you have anyone in mind?'

'No, not really. But there's a young girl called Marie Brenner who lives in the same house as Daniel, and I suddenly wondered if you might have her here. But on second thoughts I don't think either of you would be too happy with the arrangement. She's got a baby so there'd be a fair bit of noise, and anyway her boyfriend may come back to her. I suddenly thought of her because she wanted to come with me to visit you today.'

'She could come to visit me, by all means. I could give her a cup of tea or even a little lunch. Does she like baked beans on toast? That's what I usually have for lunch. Sometimes an egg.'

'Her baby's called Theodore. He's almost a month old and rather small and he cries a lot. Her life has been quite hard, I think, though her mother helps her as much as she can. I'll probably never see her again after this week, but I know I won't be able to stop thinking about her. Anyway, I'll tell her she can visit you. She may turn up. I think you'd like her. You're the same type. Both of you brave and gutsy.'

But Erica had switched her attention to happier times. Her eyes, still turned towards Rosamund, no longer saw her. 'I remember a country wedding Anthony took me to,' she said, her voice remote and dreamy. 'I don't know how he'd been able to take me instead of Molly. It was the marriage of a young poet who perhaps didn't know him personally but only as an older poet who'd helped and encouraged him. Anyway, it was by far the nicest wedding I've ever been to. It was late June and we walked to the village church along a narrow path fringed with ferns and tall grasses. And the reception was in

153

the garden of the bride's cottage, quite daring because it could have rained – but didn't. And we sat at long tables borrowed from the village hall with white cloths and bowls of wild flowers; dog roses and honeysuckle and red campion. And we had delicious home-baked bread and cold ham and cheeses and patés and crisp lettuce and watercress and big Victorian jugs of beer and cider with gooseberry crumble and thick yellow cream to follow. And then someone played the violin and the children danced and no one made speeches and I think everyone there was happy.'

'How lovely,' Rosamund said, waiting for the dénouement. Had the rains come? Had someone embarrassed Anthony by referring to Erica as his wife? Had they quarrelled? Missed the train back to London? What?

But there was nothing more. Erica's head had slipped back against the wing of her armchair and she was asleep.

And Rosamund suddenly understood that for Erica, that day had become theirs; a celebration of their union, hers and Anthony's; that cloudless June day when they'd been in perfect harmony, holding hands, looking at each other knowing that they were as happy as two people could ever be. And the children had danced and someone had played the violin. Life in a day, Rosamund thought. And realised it was a phrase from one of Anthony's poems.

She took the tray back to the kitchen, washed the cups and saucers, put the remains of the cake away, picked up her bag and let herself out.

When she got back to Eversley Place, she found Daniel worse than she'd ever seen him; he couldn't seem to stop shaking, couldn't stop groaning. She did her best to comfort him. 'Listen, you're halfway through now. You're winning. You're doing very well.' But her words sounded glib and foolish, even to herself.

She tried again. 'Is it pain or nausea?' she asked him in a very gentle voice. She felt another surge of love for him.

He didn't answer, just sat slumped in his chair, breathing heavily, his head almost touching his chest.

'Both,' he said after a minute or two. 'Both, and much more

as well. Oh God, it's like your blood curdling in your veins and you're breathing poison gas. Like being wounded in the trenches and the stretcher-bearers passing you by.' He tried to smile, as though admitting to being melodramatic.

'But the Methadone helps?' she asked, desperate for some reassurance.

'You couldn't go through it without that,' he said. 'Not unless they put you in a strait-jacket and left you to scream.'

'And what about the clinic, if you get that far? You'll still get Methadone there?'

'Yes. Only they give you smaller and smaller doses and gradually try to get you off it. Oh, God knows how they try to do it. Don't let's think of it. Anyway, it won't work in my case.'

'It won't work if you're determined it won't. You must try to be more positive, Daniel.'

'Christ, you sound exactly like a bloody social worker. No wonder Marie is frightened of you.'

'Is she? Is she really?'

'No, of course she isn't. Don't fucking listen to me when I'm like this. Don't take everything so fucking seriously, for God's sake.'

He started moaning again, rocking back and forth in his chair. She tried holding his hands, then wiping his forehead and chest with a cold wet cloth, but he couldn't bear her to touch him, and after about half an hour, begged her to leave.

'I love you,' she said as she left him. But he couldn't or wouldn't respond.

She tapped on Marie's door and found her sitting on her bed painting her nails.

'I got this stuff in Merstow Street market this afternoon,' she said. 'Only thirty-five pence. It's called Dark Passion. Do you like it?' She held out her small hand in a graceful curve.

Rosamund inspected the bitten fingernails, now dark and shiny as blackberry jam. 'Lovely. The smell's lovely too.' It was a pungent, healthy smell.

Theodore was asleep, his breathing hardly moving the little sheet that covered him.

'I'm leaving now,' Rosamund said, rather sadly.

'Yeh, I'm keeping out of his way, too. No one can help him when he's like this.'

# Chapter Eighteen

After phoning and visiting several centres and getting refer-
ences from the therapists running the counselling sessions he'd
attended, Rosamund managed to get Daniel into a private
rehabilitation centre in Richmond.

He was nervous and withdrawn when they arrived, object-
ing to the rules, though they were few, the too-genteel decor;
pale grey and white, and the hushed, hospital atmosphere. She
stayed with him as long as she could, hoping his mood would
lighten, but finally had to tear herself away to catch the last
train home, and though he kissed her as she left, he refused to
smile. She was very distressed on the journey home, wondering
what the outcome would be. That day he'd been even more
pessimistic than usual about his chances of recovery.

'I'm not too sure about him coming to live with us,' Joss had
told her on the phone. 'I may like him, but then again I may
not.'

'I think you will. Anyway, he's only coming as a lodger.
Only for a few weeks, probably. If you like, you can come with
me to visit him at the clinic, but you must remember that he's
been seriously ill so that he's rather quiet and reserved at the
moment.'

'There's a Daniel in my school who's a pain in the bum.'

The next day was Joss's birthday, and as she'd been in London
for over a week, Rosamund knew she'd have to make a great
effort to be in party mood; Daniel and his problems had to be
pushed to the very back of her mind.

She'd bought Joss a four-man ridge tent – PVC windows, corded steel uprights and ridge poles, guylines, pegs and carry case – and intended to set it up in the garden that afternoon before he came home from school. When she heard the car drawing up outside, she thought it would be her mother and Brian coming to help and supervise, and she rushed to the door.

It was Molly Gilchrist in a long black car driven by an elderly and rather stern-looking man with grey suit and grey hair.

'I thought it was time we had a talk,' she said, getting out of the car very slowly and regally, her hand on her primrose yellow hat. 'This is Ambrose Lockhart, my solicitor. Ambrose, Mrs Rosamund Gilchrist.'

'I'm sorry I haven't been in touch with you,' Rosamund murmured. 'I meant to, but I've been away looking after a sick friend. I only came home yesterday. Do come in.'

Molly walked into the studio like someone in a dream, like someone intent on noticing nothing of the house where her late husband had once lived. Ambrose Lockhart helped her into an armchair.

'Would you like some home-made lemonade or some tea?' Rosamund asked.

'Tea, please.'

'Tea, please,' echoed Mr Lockhart.

Rosamund went to the kitchen to put the kettle on and took some deep breaths before returning.

'I'm sorry, but I didn't feel I could refuse Erica Underhill permission to publish the poems. I suppose that's what you've come about.'

Molly inclined her head a fraction. 'Yes.'

'As I told you, I think she really needs the money. And as the copyrights are mine, I felt it was my decision.'

'Shall we have tea before we discuss the matter?' Mr Lockhart asked. 'Mrs Gilchrist is far from well.' He got up from his chair and went to stand close to her as though to protect her from Rosamund.

'Of course. The kettle won't take long.'

Molly was sitting up very straight, her eyes closed. She

looked, indeed, far from well. Rosamund tried to feel sorry for her, but failed. She's too much the avenging angel, she told herself.

She made tea, laid out a tray and carried it into the studio. 'It's my son's birthday today,' she said brightly, noticing them glancing at the cards on the windowsill.

Neither Molly nor Mr Lockhart made any response, only sipped their tea and looked at each other gravely.

Molly declined a second cup and sat up even straighter in her chair. 'I'm determined that Underhill shall not publish Anthony's poems,' she said then, 'nor benefit from them.'

'The copyrights are mine,' Rosamund said again, but with less conviction than before.

There was another silence. Mr Lockhart cleared his throat as though to speak, but before he did so another car drew up and, 'Rosamund!' a voice sang out. 'Rosamund, dear, where shall I put the bicycle?'

'It's my mother,' Rosamund told her guests.

Marian, a little flushed from her exertions and her birthday excitement, wheeled the be-ribboned pink and silver bicycle into the studio. 'How lovely to meet you,' she said on being introduced to Molly and Mr Lockhart. 'Have you come up for the birthday party? How very nice. Yes, the bicycle is from my husband and me. It's what is called a mountain bicycle. Hideously expensive, but Joshua's little friend had one for his birthday, so we thought he should have one too. Is it all right to leave it here, Rosamund? Against this stack of paintings? Right. I've got a strawberry pavlova in the car. I'm afraid I ordered the birthday cake from Wimpole's this year, dear. He wanted a spaceship, Mrs Gilchrist, and that was totally beyond my capabilities, I'm afraid. I'm a good plain cook, I admit that, but spaceships are another matter entirely.'

Molly stood up as though to rise above Marian's chatter, followed a second later by Mr Lockhart. 'Are you aware, Mrs Spiers, that your daughter has decided to side with her late husband's mistress rather than with me?'

Marian looked deeply shocked that Molly should bring up such sordid matters on the occasion of a joyous family celebration. 'I'm sure my daughter has her reasons,' she said, her voice loud, clear and icy.

Molly looked through her. 'And if she persists in flaunting my wishes, I shall have to inform the Press that she tricked my late husband into marrying her. That he was not the father of her child.'

'Why ever would you want to do that?' Rosamund asked her.

'I wouldn't want to do it. But I certainly *shall* do it if you allow that woman to publish those wretched poems.'

'In other words, you're blackmailing me?'

'Not at all,' Mr Lockhart said, his voice mild as milk. 'Mrs Gilchrist is most anxious to settle this matter amicably. But her son has certain rights and is not prepared to forfeit those rights to someone who is on a collision course with his mother.'

'Her son?' Marian wondered aloud. 'What rights can her son expect in all this?' For a time her head seemed numbed by the effort she was making to understand the solicitor's matter-of-fact assertions. What possible connection did Molly's son have with Joss? What rights could he have? Good Heavens, she thought at last. Good heavens.

'We must go,' Molly said, her voice dripping with malice. 'We've obviously come at an inopportune time. Most unfortunate. But I'm sure you'll agree with me, Mrs Gilchrist, that it's in your interest to get in touch with me at your earliest convenience.'

'Thank you for the tea,' Mr Lockhart murmured as they left.

Bewildered but still undaunted, Marian sat down. 'What an unpleasant woman,' she said. 'And that ridiculous hat. What could she have been thinking of? And did you notice her shoes? She could hardly walk in them . . . You really should have told me, dear,' she said then. 'You should have let me know.'

'I didn't think it mattered. Anthony knew. I didn't deceive Anthony.'

'And his son Alex, Anthony and Molly's son, is Joshua's real father?'

'That's right.'

'Did Anthony know that?'

'Not at first. At first I simply told him I was pregnant. In fact I intended having an abortion at that time, and wanted him to give me – or lend me – the money for it. But he wouldn't hear of an abortion. And then Alex followed me here and eventually told Anthony it was his baby. Anthony was furious, shocked and furious, and threatened to tell Alex's wife unless he promised to give up all claims to the baby. Which he did readily enough. But now that he and Selena are divorced, I suppose he thinks it's safe for him to break his promise.'

'You had a love affair with Alex, dear?' Marian asked rather timidly.

'No, Mum. Whatever it was, there was precious little love in it. Alex had met me here, decided I was Anthony's mistress, which I wasn't, and I suppose concluded that I was anybody's. You know, one of these promiscuous Bohemian types that men dream about. And having decided that, he made some excuse to call at my flat in Liverpool and refused to change his mind.'

'What a dreadful man. But I must say Anthony seems to have behaved very well towards you.'

'Anthony seemed more than happy with the arrangement. He didn't get on with Alex, but he liked Selena and wanted the marriage to last. Also, he was a bit in love with me, you know. Or at least, liked me quite a lot.'

'You should have told me, dear. I would have been much more understanding for one thing. So would your father.'

'Paul? He doesn't really trouble himself about me.'

'He never troubled himself about me, either. It's a good thing he's got Dora to pander to him. She's coming down this evening, dear, I hope that's all right. She'll be here about seven. She rang me because she couldn't get in touch with you. She's bringing Joss a microwave oven – you know how he loves mine – and some M & S frozen meals. Isn't it sad to think that that awful woman, that Molly whatsit, is his other Granny? Isn't it a good thing he's got Dora?'

Rosamund let Marian take over making tea; the sandwiches and the sausage rolls, and went back to the garden to set up the tent. It was getting hotter and more sultry by the minute,

161

and as she puzzled her way through the instructions she felt sick with worry. For herself, she didn't much mind what Molly chose to reveal to the Press or to anyone else, but how would it affect Joss, to be informed that his real father was alive and anxious to get to know him? Not that she could believe that Alex, with two estranged children from his own marriage, would much relish an active share in Joss's upbringing, but that would be the fiction they'd be putting about.

Alex seemed to have all Anthony's faults, his infidelity and lack of purpose, without any of his strength and sensitivity. She knew that things were going very badly for him, that Selena had divorced him, that he'd had a complete nervous breakdown – during which he'd probably confessed to Molly about being Joss's father – and that he was drinking heavily and had lost his job. He'd been left nothing in Anthony's will, so was no doubt wholly dependent on his mother even for the maintenance he had to pay his children. And as he was a mean-spirited man with a definite grudge against her, he'd do whatever his mother put him up to. And how could she, Rosamund, bear the responsibility of letting him trouble Joss in any way?

If she explained the position to Erica, she'd surely understand that she had to put her ten-year-old son first? And then Molly would be satisfied and the threat of Alex's interference in her life would be called off. That was her obvious plan of action, she thought as she struggled with the first tent poles.

But why should she, *how* could she let Erica down? She felt close to her, almost as though they were related. And Erica had been let down too many times already. Joss was only just ten, but very mature for his age, and would understand how she'd had to mislead him. And surely he'd be able to tolerate Alex's occasional presence? Might even be pleased to discover that his father was alive and not dead?

On the other hand . . . 'Mum, that's a super tent, but you've got it all wrong. Let me and Harry do it.'

'It's not all wrong. Don't be mean. I've been at it for ages. Following all these terrible instructions in German, French, Arabic and Japanese. I want to finish it myself. *Please.* You two go in and have some lemonade and see what Granny's got for you.'

They ignored her and got the tent up in less than two minutes, without once consulting the three pages of minutely-printed instructions.

'There!' Joss hugged her, nearly knocking her off her feet. 'Can we sleep in it tonight? Can we sleep in it every night for the rest of the summer? Hello, Gran. You should have been out here helping Mum. I bet you'd know the difference between the fly sheet and the ground sheet.'

'Don't be unkind to your mother, dear. She's got a lot on her mind at the moment. Harry, how is Jim? I do hope Mary-Louise hasn't got him out in this heat.'

'She puts sun-block on him, Mrs Spiers.'

'And he needs a vest, shirt and knickers and a sun-hat as well. You tell her that, will you, dear? Oh, she seems very foolhardy. I saw her striding about the village this morning, nothing on her feet but nail-varnish.'

'She's put nail-varnish on Harry as well,' Joss said. 'Miss Adams wasn't half mad in PE. Show her, Harry.'

Harry took off his socks and sandals and displayed beautiful pink-tipped feet.

Marian tutted in dismay.

'She put pink nail varnish on Dad's toenails as well,' Harry said defensively.

Marian tutted again.

And Rosamund turned away to hide a sudden spasm of anger. Was she jealous of Mary-Louise, she wondered. 'Are they coming up later?' she asked then.

'I don't know,' Harry said. 'Shall I phone them? Mary-Louise might like to come. Dad could look after Jim.'

'I'd rather have Jim,' Joss said. 'I bet he'd like it in the tent. He never cries when I'm looking after him. Mary-Louise is a spoil-sport always wanting to put him to bed so that she can watch telly. I'll phone and ask Thomas and Jim over. It's *my* birthday.'

'All right, dear,' Marian said. 'And Martin and Stephen can come too if they promise not to fight. I'm sure Mary-Louise can find plenty to do while they're away.'

But Joss came straight back, the phone-call forgotten, and

stood by the door looking shy, almost sheepish. 'Granny, is that bike for me?'

'Do you mean the pink and silver one, dear? The one with red ribbons on the handlebars?'

'Yes. That one.'

Marian held out her arms and Joss hurled himself into them and submitted to being hugged and kissed.

The birthday was happy and successful, though it lasted too long, as birthdays will. It was eleven before Joss and Harry were bedded down in the tent, half-past before Marian and Brian finally left.

'Thomas seemed a nice chap. I liked him,' Dora said as they were having a last drink.

'I like him too, very much, though he's changed a lot since Eliza's death. He was always so easy-going and understanding. He's become bitter now and rather sarcastic. Not as good-tempered towards the children, either. He was absolutely furious with Martin at one point tonight, quite white with anger.'

'I should think Martin is going through a particularly difficult phase.'

'He's always been difficult, ever since I've known him, but Thomas is usually very patient.'

'He must be having a hard time.'

'Of course he is. He feels terribly guilty, for one thing, and now he seems to blame me for it. He hardly said a word to me all evening, did you notice?'

'I certainly noticed that he didn't seem very happy when you were talking about Daniel. Had you mentioned him before?'

'Oh yes. I told him exactly what had happened as soon as I got back from London that first time. I'm hoping he and Daniel will be friends.'

'I don't think they will.'

'Oh Dora, life is so impossibly difficult. Daniel is trying desperately hard to get off heroin, I admire him so much for it, but there doesn't seem much of the Daniel I knew left.'

'He's not himself. He's casting off one skin and hasn't yet grown another. You'll have to be patient, darling.'

164

'I'm quite prepared to be patient. But what if . . . what if . . .'

'What if he's not the person you've dreamed of all these years? Is that what you mean?'

'Something like that, yes.'

'Well, when he's fully recovered you'll have plenty of time to get to know him properly. You haven't made any commitment to him, have you? If he's not the right person you'll find that out.'

'But Dora, if he's not the right person, then nothing in my life makes any sort of sense.'

'I don't think romantic love ever makes too much sense, darling. But perhaps all the anguish we suffer for it makes us appreciate getting over it.'

'That's very cynical, Dora. And very sad.'

'Not sad. I only meant that the best was yet to come.'

'You mean mature love? Companionship and slippers by the fire?'

'And suppers in bed, expensive wines and the newest videos. Trips abroad in some degree of comfort. Restaurant meals and concerts. Not too bad, darling.'

'Not too bad,' Rosamund agreed. Not too bad . . . But not what she wanted.

# Chapter Nineteen

The next morning found Rosamund again trying to decide between the two alternatives Molly had presented to her. Her sympathies were with Erica who had loved and lost, but she couldn't forget the almost demonic look on Molly's face as she'd said, 'I'm determined that Underhill shall not publish Anthony's poems nor benefit from them.' What was she plotting?

On their previous meeting Rosamund had thought that Molly's antagonism towards Erica was beginning to soften. When she'd mentioned her poverty, the lack of heating in her unmodernised, inconvenient flat, she'd seemed almost concerned. Had something happened since? Was it something to do with Alex? Alex was probably desperate for money, but how would he benefit from the suppression of Erica's book? Unless he was trying to cut in with a book of his own, his father as hero, stepping in to save his son's marriage by making an honest woman of the girl his son had made pregnant?

She felt a sweat break out over her body. Anthony was considered a major poet, some said the most original voice of the twentieth century after Eliot and Yeats, and now, less than ten years after his death, publishers, serious newspapers and presumably the public seemed much more interested in the complexities and irregularities of his life than in his life's work.

At least Erica had eighteen very beautiful poems to contribute, poems which Anthony himself had wanted published, though not for another ten years. Whereas anything Alex had to add would be less than the truth. Anthony had married her because he loved her, or at least loved her company, loved having her with him. It wasn't to save Alex's marriage, not even primarily for that. And they'd been happy together. That's what people didn't want to believe. When she was pregnant he'd looked after her so tenderly, shopped and cooked for her, though she was young and healthy and perfectly able to manage everything for herself. He had really cherished her, as in the marriage service. She became tearful, remembering all his kindness to her.

And she'd always told Joss about her happiness with Anthony, how good he'd been to her, so it would be really painful to have to tell him that he was not actually his father. How would it affect him?

During the lunch-hour she phoned the school where Thomas taught. 'Thomas? Can you call round after school?'

There was a long pause. 'I can't come immediately after school, but I'll come as soon as I can. What's the matter?'

'Oh Thomas, I've got something on my mind which I want your advice about. Why can't you come straight after school?'

Another pause. 'Because I have to get back to take over from Mary-Louise. Jim's quite difficult in the afternoon and she's at the end of her tether by four-thirty.'

'I thought she was supposed to be a trained nanny.'

'Well, she is. But she's only twenty-four. Very young to have sole care of a three-month-old baby. And I don't want to lose her.'

'You won't lose her, don't worry. She does nothing much but lie about in the sun all day, according to my mother.'

'Rosamund, what's the matter with you? You don't seem yourself today.'

'I don't like to think of this girl twisting you round her little finger.'

'Every woman in my life seems to do that.'

'Oh, she's one of the women in your life now, is she?'

'Well, she's in my life at the moment. And, yes, she's certainly a woman.'

'Oh, certainly.'

'Listen, I'll come up as soon as I can. I enjoyed the party yesterday, by the way.'

*

168

It was another hot day, the hills heavy with the weight of summer. Dora had left at seven, and after Rosamund had got Harry and Joss off to school, she'd done very little but brood.

She was having her lunch – bread and cheese – on the patio when she heard someone trying to get in through the side-gate, which she kept bolted.

It was Mary-Louise with Jim in a sling on her back. 'Rosamund? I was walking up the hill so I thought I'd call. I thought it was time we met.'

Mary-Louise was the last person Rosamund wanted to see – she already felt hostile towards her – but she tried not to show it. 'Would you like some bread and cheese? Some cider?'

'No, thank you. I've already eaten. I'd like some water, though, if that's all right.'

'Of course.'

Mary-Louise was even more attractive than Rosamund had expected. Fair hair tied back in a ponytail, pale brown eyes, a golden tan, long legs. She unstrapped the baby and laid him on the grass. He started to whimper but she said, 'No, Jim. Go to sleep, please.' At which he immediately stopped crying and closed his eyes. Was this the person who needed Thomas's help at four-thirty every day?

Rosamund fetched her a half-pint tankard of water which she drank in one long swallow.

'How are you settling down with the Woodisons?'

'We're getting used to one another.'

'Are you finding Stephen and Martin difficult?'

'Of course. Teenagers are always difficult and they've had a traumatic time.'

She didn't seem to want to say anything else. Her eyes were cool and dismissive. She sat upright in the garden chair, her enormously long legs thrust straight out in front of her.

'Harry is a sweet boy,' Rosamund said, somehow feeling a need to keep the conversation going.

'No, Harry's not sweet. Not at all.' She frowned at some unsweet memory of Harry.

Rosamund sat back in her chair and closed her eyes. She decided not to attempt any further small talk. Mary-Louise

169

seemed neither to want nor merit it. She had taken off her T-shirt and was now sunbathing, and would obviously sit there, languid and topless, until she decided to move on. Rosamund tried to calm down, made herself think of waves breaking against rocks; it sometimes helped. Am I jealous? she asked herself. Is that why I'm feeling so irritated by this girl? She made herself think of rock pools and sea gulls and quiet seas.

She was almost asleep when Mary-Louise next spoke. 'I've been reading Eliza's diary,' she said.

Rosamund was so taken aback that she failed to say anything. How bizarre to confess to reading another person's diary. She couldn't absolutely swear that she herself wouldn't have, if she'd come across it, but she'd certainly have kept quiet about it. Did that make it better or worse?

'She mentioned your affair with Thomas.'

Rosamund ground her teeth in another effort to remain calm. 'I don't want to hear whatever it is you've come here to tell me,' she said quietly. 'And perhaps you should go now. You've had a drink and a rest.'

'She wrote that she'd had it out with you, but that you'd refused to give him up.'

Rosamund wanted to shriek out her denial of this account, but managed to go on breathing evenly and saying nothing. She sat watching the cumulus clouds on the horizon, their shifting opalescent shapes. A beautiful summer sky.

'Unfortunately Martin has read it as well. It was in his room that I found it.'

'Please go now. If I were you I should discuss all this with Thomas.' She looked at Jim who was practising little smiles as he slept.

'I have discussed it with Thomas.'

'Then why are you bothering me about it?'

Mary-Louise seemed to give this question due consideration. 'I was annoyed that you didn't ask me to your party last night.'

Rosamund couldn't help but admire the honesty of that admission. It was so childish and well . . . even likeable. She almost smiled.

170

'I need to work now,' she said, trying to soften her earlier peremptory request that she should leave.

'What work do you do?'

'I paint.'

'An artist! No one told me. Can I see some of your paintings?'

Again the childlike response which left Rosamund totally bemused. Perhaps the girl was not so much malicious as simple-minded.

'Another time,' she said. 'I'll show them to you another time.' When I'm feeling less misjudged and tormented, she thought.

Mary-Louise put her T-shirt back on, packed Jim into the sling and hoisted him onto her back. Again he started to cry, but again stopped when commanded to do so.

And Rosamund, still disturbed and enraged by the encounter, marched into the studio, pulled out a large sheet of paper and some charcoal and tried to work out her anger on a drawing; a drawing of a tall, bare-legged young woman striding up a hill, a pack on her back. She worked for almost two hours and then stood back, her hand to her mouth, astonished to find that it was good, very good, the best thing she'd done in years. She had a moment's exquisite pleasure. She'd forgotten how wonderful success felt. A bit like sex; getting it right.

She thought about Thomas; how he'd always seemed afraid to be too passionate, to let himself go. Was it because he was always conscious of being a married man, and not wanting to involve her too fully? He was a kind, thoughtful man. She hoped he wouldn't be ensnared by Mary-Louise, her childlike ways and her long legs.

She was suddenly furious again, remembering what Eliza had written in her diary. Was she already planning suicide when she wrote it, and wanting to leave behind as much trouble as possible? Or had her mind really flipped, so that all her fervent promises to give Thomas up had meant nothing to her?

Why had she cared so much about losing her lousy job? Was it the money that mattered so much or the prestige of being

171

the only woman director in the company? Had she had so little satisfaction in her life that those things had become all-important? She'd had a good-natured handsome husband who loved her. Wasn't that something to chalk up? Three babies before going back to work. Hadn't she felt any joy or fulfilment at being a mother? Rosamund hadn't known her well, but she'd always seemed proud of her sons, had always dressed them in clothes which, if a little too fashionable, seemed lovingly chosen. They'd had expensive gifts lavished on them and yet were relatively unspoilt. She'd had children to be proud of, but she'd wanted out.

And Martin, having read certain extracts from her diary, written either out of spite or in mental torment, thought she, Rosamund, was responsible for his mother's suicide.

Well, perhaps blaming her made it easier for him to accept it. Rosamund found that she didn't care too much what Martin and Stephen thought of her. Just so long as they didn't infect Joss with their attitude.

The garden was beautiful. For a time she watched a butterfly, a meadow brown, dancing its way over the pinks. The temperature was in the high seventies again. Perhaps things didn't matter quite as much as they seemed to.

When Thomas called by, soon after five, he apologised for Mary-Louise's visit. 'I meant to warn you yesterday about the diary turning up, but I didn't manage to speak to you alone. She doesn't truly believe the things Eliza wrote. I told her what had really happened and she seemed to accept it. I can't think what made her come up here today.'

'It was because I didn't invite her to the party yesterday.'

They looked at each other carefully. 'Is she a bit unhinged?' Rosamund asked. 'Or is she in love with you?'

'Don't be silly.'

'It's not silly. Why shouldn't she be? But just be careful, that's all. She strikes me as a bit dangerous. Beautiful but dangerous.'

'Dangerous? I'll bear it in mind. Is that what you wanted to see me about?'

'No, I phoned you before she arrived. Mary-Louise is yet

another problem. And that bloody diary. And Martin. But it was something else I rang about.' She told him then about Molly's visit, about her threat concerning Alex. 'You knew that Alex was Joss's father, didn't you? I'd already told you that.'

'Yes. And I remember advising you then to tell Joss the truth. And the sooner the better. I thought even then that Alex might break his promise to leave you alone.'

'Well, I should have listened to you. I certainly don't know what to do now. I hate the thought of letting Erica down. She seems to have had a pretty rotten life, and though she says she wants to publish her memoirs for the money she'll get – and I admit she's hard up – I think that deep down there's a much more important reason. She was Anthony's mistress for several years, I honestly believe the love of his life, so if she publishes the poems, claims them for herself, she'll achieve a certain immortality, won't she? Do you think I'm being too romantic? Erica is old, she doesn't strike me as very strong, she could die at any moment, and I think she should have this boost to her ego, this fulfilment.'

'You're absolutely right. So that's it – you haven't any choice. You can't deny her the right to her immortality because Molly's blackmailing you. You must disregard Molly.'

'Oh Thomas, it's not as easy as that. By bending over backwards to be fair to Erica, I may be damaging Joss. Don't you see that?'

'Joss has got you, love, so he'll manage to weather whatever else happens to him. Yes, Alex seems a pretty worthless type, but he can't be all bad. He was probably very jealous of his father. Sons whose fathers are successful and famous have a pretty hard time trying to catch up. Perhaps he seduced you to get back at his father.'

'Oh, thanks. I thought it might have been because . . .'

'And even if Molly insists that he becomes involved in Joss's life, he probably won't have enough interest or energy to make a nuisance of himself. You said he was an idler and a waster.'

'He certainly didn't work at his marriage. And Molly told me he doesn't often see his other children. She said it was because their mother had taken them to live in France, but that may be only an excuse.'

'If I were you, I should tell Joss about Alex tonight – I'll take Harry home with me. Tell him you decided to wait till he was ten before telling him so that he'd be old enough to understand. That way he'll be on your side and won't start off feeling deceived and injured.'

'Tonight? Are you sure?'

'Quite sure. It would be disastrous if he heard it from Molly. Or from Alex himself.'

'Tonight? Oh God, I only hope you're right.'

'Yes, we do sex education. Yes, we've done it all. Penis and vagina and so on. I can draw pictures for you if you want.'

'That wasn't exactly what I had in mind, though.'

'And Stephen and Martin have told us more things. About having a hard-on and wet dreams.'

'Yes, well, I'm glad you know all about it. But I wanted to talk about sex in a much more personal way. You see, when I was young there was a man who was very keen to have sex with me. His name was Alex. Well, we did have sex together, and as you know women have these eggs inside them . . .'

'In their womb.'

'Yes. And an egg I had in my womb got fertilised. But we'd been very foolish. Because this man called Alex was already married.'

'Oh sugar!' Joss smote his forehead in sympathy. 'So you had to have an operation?'

'No. I didn't really want an operations – they're called abortions, by the way – so . . .'

'They don't seem all that popular, do they? Miss Adams doesn't think they're a very good idea. Condoms are a much better idea she says. But I suppose they didn't have condoms in the old days.'

'Anyway, I didn't much want an abortion. So I went to see this very nice older man I knew who suggested that I should marry him instead, that he would look after me and love me. And I did and was very happy. And that was Anthony.'

'My father?'

'Anthony was your father in every way except that one way which was to do with sperm and so on.'

'Anthony wasn't my sperm father?'

'No. That was the man who was already married. Of course it was very foolish of me to have had sex with that married man.'

'Was it Thomas?'

'No, his name was Alex. I told you.'

'Right.'

'Now to make things even more complicated – and this is why I needed to wait until you were old enough to understand properly – this man called Alex was Anthony's son. But he promised Anthony faithfully that he'd keep right out of our lives from then on. And not interfere with the baby in any way.'

'And that baby was me?'

'Yes.'

'Did Anthony love me?'

'He was besotted about you. As I was.'

'You were both besotted about me?'

'Absolutely. We couldn't stop looking at you. And every time you cried, we cried too.'

'I'm besotted about Jim.'

'Jim's lovely. But you – you were lovely as an angel.'

'Mum, that's silly. You've never even seen an angel. Perhaps they don't even exist.'

'Anyway, to get back to our story, this Alex has chosen to forget his promise to leave us alone, and wants to come to see you from time to time.'

'Oh.'

'How do you feel about that?'

'I don't think I want to see him. I shall tell him off for breaking his promise. Anyway, everyone thinks Anthony is my father.'

'He is really. But Alex feels he wants a little share of you.'

'I shall talk to him like Granny talks to the paper-boy, polite but very chilly. "And please forgive poor little Willy for saying his prayers in bed. It's chilly." Do you remember that, Mum?'

'So you don't think you'll be too worried about having to meet Alex?'

'Is he coming to live with us?'

'Heavens, no. I'm not at all fond of him.'

'Well, there's lots of children in my school with an extra father. I don't mind seeing him the odd Sunday afternoon. What car has he got?'

# Chapter Twenty

The next day Rosamund felt relief flow through her body like champagne bubbles. She hadn't realised how much of a burden keeping Joss in the dark about his father had been. Now that she'd told him about Alex, however little had sunk in, at least it was out in the open and she felt almost ready to forgive herself for the whole sad episode.

She expected Joss to bring up the subject again over breakfast, but the only thing on his mind then was his games kit.

'You *never* wash my things. I wish I lived with Granny.'

'If I was perfect you'd have to be perfect too, and you'd find it an awful strain.'

'No, I wouldn't. Anyway I only want my games kit washed.'

'Then remind me about it as soon as you've used it, not in the morning just before you need it again.'

'I hate it when you shout at me.'

'Then don't shout at *me*. Listen, I'll dry-clean it for you.

'How?'

'I'll take it outside and scrape the mud off. You finish your toast.'

She dropped him off at school and then waited for Thomas who was driving up with Harry.

'Thanks for your help, Thomas. You were quite right. I explained things to him and now I feel so much better. Something's decided now. Quite a lot, in fact.'

'Good. I feel better this morning too, it must be the weather. Stephen and Martin are behaving abominably, I'm way behind with my marking and my A-level results are going to be atrocious, but damn it, I'm coping. I haven't got over Eliza's death, but I feel I will sometime.'

They waved to each other and drove off in different directions.

Rosamund felt so full of hope and excitement that she knew she couldn't settle to the housework and gardening she'd planned to do that day. Her whole life seemed to have opened out in front of her. Her drawing of Mary-Louise had proved to her that she did have a future as an artist. She'd looked at all her early paintings and realised that they were full of promise. Her failure had been owing to a lack of confidence after Anthony's death; she'd carried on painting the same old subjects feeling it was all she was capable of, repeating herself without developing her talents in any way. Now she planned to move in a totally different direction, figure-drawing first, then naturalistic studies of men and women against backgrounds of luxuriant colour; Brian working in his garden, his gardening clothes immaculate, his dahlias in serried ranks, the sky behind cloudless and acid blue; Paul in theatrical pose, vanity and world-weariness on his features, a backdrop of velvet curtains in royal purple; Marian and Dora sitting side by side on a squashy tomato-red sofa, the colour behind them intense but rather dark; Joss with frown and cricket bat in front of a tracery of the tenderest summer leaves; she could visualise them all and couldn't wait to begin.

She did some shopping in the village – fresh peas, asparagus, little round red radishes, bright green and white spring onions. That day she bought only things that were beautiful; she was an artist and might try a still-life later on. Every shop she went into was full of people she wanted to paint; plump women whose faces were soft and ripe as plums, thin men with weathered brown faces and winter-white arms, pre-school children, Botticelli angels with freckled faces and pink noses.

She passed the newsagent's window and saw a display of the new *Country Homes* magazine. 'Local Artist wins London Acclaim' a poster announced – in Marian's spiky lettering which she'd recognise anywhere. She'd get her to add another.

'Sale of Pictures. No Offer Refused.' She'd need space for her new work.

'I'm going to start on some life-drawing, Mum,' she told Marian when she dropped in on her for coffee. 'You're absolutely right. What I need now is to concentrate on my work.'

'Is that what I said, dear?'

'Yes. And thank you for doing the poster in Mrs Johnson's window, too. I do hope Joss sees it.'

'Brian will take him along there after school to get some strawberry ice-cream . . . Have you decided what to do about Molly?'

'Yes. I shall refuse to do what she wants but in the friendliest possible way. I'm going to take Joss up to London with me next month and we'll visit her. I've already told him about Alex and he seemed to take it in his stride, so she can't threaten me about that.'

'Will you stay with Dora, dear?'

'No, with Ingrid. Take a sleeping bag for Joss.'

'You'll do the rounds, though?'

'Of course. Daniel first, then Erica. And Dora and Molly on the Sunday. Ingrid says she and Erica are getting on really well with the book. All she has to do is try to keep up with the flow of reminiscences. I couldn't bear to take that away from Erica, all that pleasure and satisfaction.'

'You're quite right, dear. Molly can look after herself. She seemed a real old battle-axe. I'm not going to feel sorry for Molly and neither must you. Anyway, she's got Joss as compensation and I only hope she appreciates him and leaves him lots and lots of money in her will. How is Daniel?'

'I don't know. He said he'd try to phone me this week, but he hasn't so far. I hope he'll be reasonably well when I take Joss to visit him.'

'What exactly is he suffering from, dear?'

'Heroin addiction.'

'Heroin addiction! Oh Rosamund, I think you go around looking for trouble.'

'But he's in a rehabilitation clinic, Mum. So with luck he'll get over it. You remember Marie, the girl I spoke to you about? The one with the little baby called Theodore? Well, she was on heroin and she managed to come off it. It is possible. And Daniel seems very determined. At least, most of the time.'

'Well, dear, I hope you know what you're doing.'

'Today, I honestly feel as though I do. Of course, it may only be the weather . . . Hello, Brian. Finished the shopping?'

'Just about. It's taken much longer than usual because everyone's been stopping me to comment on my brilliant step-daughter. What it is to be related to the famous, eh Marian? Mrs Langsdale wants to buy one of your paintings, Rosamund, for the lounge in the George. And she could display a dozen or so, she says, in the dining room. She won't be taking any commision either, because Marian and I are amongst her regulars. How about that?'

'Brian, you're wonderful. Bring her up to see them before she changes her mind. Bring her up to tea. I've got some birthday cake left.'

'Have you any idea what to charge her, dear?'

'No, but I'm sure Brian will manage to work something out.'

Some weeks later Rosamund called at the Woodisons' house and found Mary-Louise in the front garden trying to force some mushy pale green substance past Jim's clamped lips. She stood for a while watching the struggle.

'Another obstinate one,' Mary-Louise said at last. 'At four months old he's supposed to start on puréed apple.' Her voice was shrill.

'Would you like to model for me? Life-drawing?'

'How much?'

'Three quid an hour.'

'Four.'

'Three-fifty.'

'When?'

'Any time you like. As soon as possible.'

'I'll give you a bell.'

'Right. Bye, Jim – I think you won that round. Bye, Mary-Louise.'

*

180

By this time Rosamund was looking forward to working from a model, but in the meantime started on another waist-length self-portrait.

My face isn't bad, she told herself. I think I'm better-looking than when I was twenty, my bones are more in evidence, I'm much leaner. I was certainly plump as a child. No wonder my mother despaired of me. She'd have liked her daughter to take after her, small-featured and slim, a perfect size ten, whereas I took after my father, much too tall for a girl, large nose and mouth, and overweight as well. I'm sure she didn't mean to make me feel inferior, but she did. 'Oh, not another cake, dear. Think of those hips.' I wasn't clever or amusing or smart, and I had no self-confidence. No wonder she wanted to send me off to art school. She couldn't be doing with me.

She dotes on Joss, but she never doted on me. I think she's fonder of me now than she's ever been. She's quite proud of my achievements, meagre though they are, but most of all I produced the perfect grandchild for her and Brian to cherish and adore.

I think my self-esteem was at an all-time low in my first year at art school. When Daniel used to say I was beautiful, I thought he was being either kind or sarcastic. I felt he rejected me, but in fact I suppose I rejected him. I was unable to accept him as a lover because I felt he wasn't taking me seriously enough. For God's sake, what did 1 expect from him? That he should propose marriage to me, when I was twenty and he twenty-three? Yes, I suppose I did want some high-seriousness, some definite commitment, though I can't understand why, because I'd seen what early marriage had done to my parents.

That's not a bad face. Not a bad likeness either. Not bad.

My breasts are OK, too. Though of course it's taken me years to accept that. For years I thought they were too big, too floppy, too pink. I longed for small breasts with small brown nipples. Life-drawing at art school should have made me tolerant of all shapes and sizes but it didn't. The really sad thing is that I would have been much more ready to have had an affair with Daniel if I hadn't been ashamed of my body.

I was still a virgin when I left art school. Ingrid wouldn't believe me. She had sex at fifteen. She probably had all the confidence in the world, as well as small, pert breasts with brown nipples. I'd like to do a drawing of Ingrid. And of Erica, come to think of it. Perhaps for the jacket of her book.

My arms are nice; soft and shapely. I love arms. I love elbows. Thomas used to comment on the way I was always caressing his elbows, hardly conscious of it, just circling one and then the other with the curve of my hand, enjoying the intimacy of bone and skin. Thomas had – has – a lovely body, not spectacularly male – wide shoulders, narrow hips – but strong-looking and flat-bellied. Very hairy, too, a great surprise to me the first time I saw him naked, because I'd thought of hairy men as the Italian-type extroverts who wear fancy suits and medallions. Whereas Thomas wears tweed jackets and corduroy trousers and lace-up shoes. I'd like to do a drawing of him in the nude, but I don't think he'd want me to. He's rather shy.

We shouldn't have had an affair, I realise that now. I think he always felt guilty about it; he's a nicer person than I am. I didn't worry about it too much. I was convinced that Eliza had cut him out of her life, and I was right about that. She didn't want him until she'd lost everything else.

And I did want him. He was warm and loving, and even if I only saw him alone for an hour in the week it was enough to comfort my loneliness.

I've never tried to do a drawing of Thomas, though I did one of his mother a couple of years back. He'd brought her up to visit me here, she saw the drawings I'd done of Joss and asked me whether I'd do a quick sketch of her. She's a large domineering woman in her seventies and I suddenly realised that I'd like to do a pastel of her, treating her like a piece of landscape. She had that enduring look about her; her suit was a heathery tweed, her skin downy, almost fleecy, her hair slate-coloured and her eyes a watery blue like the early-morning sky. So I did a line drawing and coloured it in with tiny feathery strokes of pastel, one shade over the other as I do for hills. I thought she'd hate it, I'd made her look really ancient, all veins and wrinkles, but she liked it and insisted on buying it. 'You've really got her character,' Thomas said. Perhaps I'm better than I think.

I shouldn't be thinking of you, Thomas. Whatever we had is over. Perhaps you're having sex with Mary-Louise now. What's this about her painting your toenails? Sounds very intimate to me.

Why should I care anyway? I'm in love with my first love. And in the brief moment when we met again after fifteen years, he was in love with me. And now? Well, now he's in some sort of hell-state when he can't talk to anyone, can't think of anyone, doesn't want anyone, doesn't want to touch anyone. He may get through it. He may not. He told me in a lucid moment that he'd started on heroin because he just couldn't take the world without it. 'All that shit,' he said. Well, the world won't get better; will he get better at accepting it as it is? Will I be able to help him accept it? Will he ever live here with me?

The phone.

'Thomas! I was thinking about you. What do you want?'

'I've had a phone-call from Mary-Louise. She's in a right state. Wants me to come home, but I can't – I've got classes all afternoon. Can you possibly go down to sort her out?'

'Sort her out? What the hell's wrong with her?'

'She couldn't tell me. She seemed quite hysterical. Jim's OK, though. I got that much out of her.'

'I saw her a couple of hours ago and she was fine. Having a bit of a battle with your youngest son over some apple purée, but otherwise fine.'

'Something must have happened since.'

'All right. I suppose I'll have to leave my work and go . . . Of course I'll go, Thomas. Of course I will.'

'Thanks, love. I'm available for a few minutes at three-forty. Give me a ring then if you need me. I've got chess club after school, so I won't be back till gone five.'

'What's the matter, Mary-Louise?'

'My boyfriend phoned.'

'Oh God, what?'

'He says he's got another girlfriend. I must go to see him.'

'Will it be worth it? Mightn't it make things worse? Where does he live?'

'Oxford. I've got to see him. He won't be able to dump me when he sees me again. Can you have Jim? And can you run me to the station? I've got to go now. I must catch him before he leaves work. There's a train at three-ten. Please, Rosamund. I'll do anything for you. I said I'd model for you. I'll do it for nothing. As often as you want.'

'I'll run you to the station, but we'll have to hurry. Where's Jim?'

'Ready in his car seat. My bag's packed.'

'When will you be back?'

'I'll ring Thomas and let him know.'

They made the station with seconds to spare. And then Rosamund was left with Jim, wide-awake and looking hungry.

'Right, Jim. Babies love being in cars, don't they, so I'm going to take you on a nice slow tour of the Cotswolds till your Daddy comes home from school. I'll just fill up with petrol while you're in a good mood and then we'll be off.'

Petrol and then a quick phone-call. 'Miss Adams, will you please tell Joss to go home with Harry today bacause I shan't be there until about five. Thank you so much.'

Another blissfully warm summer's day. After her successful self-portrait, Rosamund felt elated as though all, or almost all, was right with the world. The sun, shining through the open window of the car, seemed to enfold her in a sensual glow. When Jim was fast asleep, not even stirring, she stopped the car and listened to the birds and the silence.

If only her present optimism could last, the belief in beauty, the hope of success. She wished she could pray, wished she believed in prayer.

Thomas came to fetch Jim soon after five and took him home to feed him without even stopping for a cup of tea.

'You can send the boys up here if you'd like to,' Rosamund told him. 'Joss can make them a meal in his microwave and you can concentrate on Jim. His last feed was at one, so no wonder he's irritable. I've been singing to him but it's not what he wants. Do you know how much formula he's supposed to have?'

'Of course I do. Thanks for having him, love. I'll ring when I hear something from Mary-Louise. I hope she won't be away long.'

'Why didn't you tell me she had a boyfriend?'

'You didn't ask. Why shouldn't she have a boyfriend?'

Rosamund went back to her drawing but somehow wasn't as pleased with it as she'd been before. She decided to start again. 'This time I must try not to flatter myself,' she told herself. 'Truth. Truth is what I'm after.'

She'd hardly started on the new drawing when the phone rang again.

'Joss is not here, Rosamund. I thought I ought to let you know. Apparently he and Harry fell out about something during the afternoon and they left school separately. I suppose Joss must have gone to your mother's. I'd offer to fetch him but Jim's crying hard now.'

'It's all right. Mum will bring him back. She'll probably give him his tea first.'

She rang Marian but there was no reply so she concluded they were on their way back. She returned to her drawing and was immediately absorbed in it.

At half-past five she rang Marian again. This time she was in. But no, she hadn't seen Joss. It wasn't their day for having him. She and Brian had been out shopping since three. Wherever was he? They'd go to the school to see if he was hanging about there. There could be a cricket match on, but surely he would have mentioned it.

Rosamund said she'd go to the Woodisons' to get what information she could from Harry. Perhaps Joss had gone to Whitemore School to look out for Stephen and Martin who didn't finish till four-thirty. Possibly he was still with Stephen and Martin. She told herself she wasn't worried but her mouth felt dry.

Harry was cagey. 'I don't know where he went and I don't care.'

'What did you quarrel about?'

'I can't remember.'

'I bet it was something about Jim.'

'No, it wasn't. It was about Thomas. He said Thomas was his father. He said you said so. And I said he jolly well wasn't.'

'He and I did have a talk about his father, but he obviously got it wrong. Thomas isn't his father.'

'That's what I said.'

'You were right. So now will you help me find him?'

'I suppose so.'

Stephen and Martin were watching television. No, they hadn't seen him.

'Will you go out on your bikes, please, to look for him?'

'Isn't he at his Granny's?' Stephen asked.

'No, I phoned there.'

'Oh, he's all right. He's hanging about somewhere to give you a fright.'

'Stephen, you're old enough to know that there are men about who could harm him. I'm getting really worried and his Granny will be frantic. Please help me look for him. Harry can come with me in the car. If we all go in different directions we'll find him sooner . . . Thomas, should I ring the police? It's six o'clock and he came out of school at a quarter to four.'

'Yes. Phone this minute. As soon as I've changed Jim's nappy I'll put him in the car seat and join the search. He may have gone up Barrow Hill. He could just be fed-up with Harry and striking out somewhere on his own. Stephen, will you go up Barrow Hill?'

'It's not my fault,' Harry said.

'Of course not.'

'We'll get someone to drive round looking for him,' the policeman said.

Oh God, they're taking it seriously, Rosamund thought.

Seven o'clock. Rosamund and Marian hugged each other wordlessly as though already comforting each other. Brian insisted that they should have tea and biscuits if nothing else. He poured out yet more cups of tea.

They phoned Miss Adams who said it had been a perfectly

normal day and that Joss had been completely unperturbed by the message that he was to go home with Harry. She'd known nothing of their quarrel. No, he hadn't been in trouble with anyone.

At eight o'clock Brian collected some volunteers from the George to make door-to-door enquiries; someone must surely have seen him. Some boys from Stephen and Martin's school started racing about to search the children's playground, the churchyard, the caravan park, the field by the river.

Stephen came back from Barrow Hill saying he'd been all the way to the top, calling and calling.

No one had anything to report. Martin, in a bad mood and uncooperative as usual, was sent to the schoolhouse to await a possible phone-call.

By nine o'clock two policemen had come out from Admington. Had Joss ever gone missing before? Was he in trouble with anyone? Had they spoken to all his friends? Had any strangers been seen in the village? Anyone hanging around the school gates? They left to contact the Headmistress. At ten Thomas took Harry and Jim home, but promised to get a colleague to babysit so that he could come back. To do what? There didn't seem anything more that anyone could do but wait. The whole village had been searched.

'Do you think Molly could have had anything to do with this?' Rosamund asked her mother, the words tearing at her throat.

'Oh darling, it's been on my mind from the beginning, but I didn't want to add to your worries. I can't forget that venomous look on her face when she left the schoolhouse on Joss's birthday. And I know we've all preached and preached about not taking a lift from strangers, but what if she'd sent Alex to pick him up outside the school and he'd said, "Hello, Joss. I'm your Dad." How could a dear friendly little boy resist that?'

'Mum, I don't think Alex would be prepared to do anything as ruthless as that.'

'But you told me he was in his mother's power. And she'd stop at nothing, I'm sure. I don't think she'd harm Joss, dear, but she seems really determined to harm you.'

'How would Alex recognise Joss? He's never seen him,

neither has Molly. Oh, I'm sure this is a red herring, but perhaps I should phone her to see how she reacts.'

'I think you should, dear. Be very upset and contrite. Offer her whatever she wants. Those poems, dear, oh let her have them. What do you think, Brian?'

'I'd certainly like to think it was his grandmother behind this, Marian, and not some evil-minded pervert.'

'Brian, stop it. Phone Molly, Rosamund, for God's sake. Or would you like me to tackle her?'

'No, I'll do it.'

'Miss Drew, may I speak to Mrs Gilchrist? It's Rosamund Gilchrist.'

'I'm afraid Mrs Gilchrist is in bed and most probably asleep. She's had rather a bad day so I dare not disturb her. Can I help?'

'Is Alex Gilchrist available, please?'

'I'll see if he's in. Hold on, please . . . I'm afraid he's still out, Mrs Gilchrist.'

'No, he's not. I heard you talking to him. Please tell him that I shall go on ringing till he comes to the phone. It's a matter of great urgency.'

'What is it, Rosamund? I'm not very well, I'm afraid, and not entirely sober either.'

'Alex, my son is missing and I'm going through hell. Please tell me if your mother had anything to do with it.'

'My mother? Are you mad? Of course she had nothing to do with it. Do you think she's some sort of monster? I'm shocked that you felt you needed to ring. She may be ruthless but she's not cruel. I'm really shocked.'

'For God's sake, try to understand how I'm feeling for once. My son is missing! We've looked everywhere, done everything. And now my stepfather is beginning to suspect that some wretched pervert may have lured him away. It happens, for God's sake, it happens. And I'm too frightened to think about it.'

A moment's silence. 'I wish I could help you, I really do. My mother had nothing to do with it though. That's all I can say.'

*

188

'They know nothing, Mum.'

'Don't say anything else, Brian. Don't even think it. It doesn't help. The police are searching for him and they've circulated his description to other areas. They can't do more. *We* can't do more.'

Rosamund drove back to the schoolhouse, somehow feeling the need to be there. She was light-headed with anxiety. There'd been no phone-call. Martin left as soon as she got back. She had nothing to say to him, simply watched him hurrying towards his bike and vaulting onto it.

She stood by the open door looking down at the valley. It was beginning to get dark, a few white stars piercing the violet-blue sky. Her heart felt pierced, too. If only she knew Joss was safe and well, she would ask for nothing more. The air was cool and scented, but the exaltation of the morning, the drowsy happiness of the afternoon seemed a mockery and pitiful.

The phone rang. Thomas. 'We know where he is, love. We're just going to fetch him. Hold on. Phone your mother. Tell her we know where he is. Tell her he's safe.'

Safe. Numb with shock and relief, Rosamund rang Marian who failed to say a word, only passed the receiver to Brian who said he'd felt sure he was safe all along, and then abruptly put the phone down.

Rosamund went back to stand outside. Tears streamed down her face. 'Oh, God. Oh, God. Oh, God.' Her voice didn't sound like hers. Where was he? When would Thomas bring him home?

Marian and Brian drove up. 'Where is he? When will he be home?'

'I don't know. But I know Thomas is doing all he can. He didn't have time to talk. He's safe. That's all that matters. He's safe.'

'We've brought some brandy, dear. Let's go in and have a stiff drink.'

Brian put his arm round Rosamund and squeezed her. He looked old and haggard; in the twilight the lines on his face were deep and blue.

Half an hour passed. No further news from Thomas. No further news. They were too overwrought to talk to one another. Even Marian, who could never bear to be idle, sat quietly with her hands in her lap.

Another car, and this time it was Thomas. He burst in, hugged Rosamund and then Marian, shook Brian's hand and went on shaking it. 'He's all right. He's in the cottage hospital. They're keeping him in tonight, but he's all right. You can go along to peep at him if you want to, but I promised Sister you wouldn't wake him.'

Still unable to say a word, Rosamund followed Thomas to his car.

'We won't come to the hospital, dear,' Marian said. 'Now that we know he's safe and well, we'll wait till tomorrow morning.' She and Brian got into their car and followed Thomas down the hill.

'Mrs Jordan is with my lot,' Thomas said. And then: 'I'm afraid it was all Martin's doing.'

# Chapter Twenty-One

He was awake, very small and pale in the white bed.

'Mum, I've got six stitches.' He held out his arm, the soft, tender, inner part and showed it to her. Six little black stitches in a straight line and some deep-yellow medication. 'But Mum, they won't even put a bandage on it.'

'It'll heal better without,' Thomas said, since Rosamund seemed far beyond saying anything. He hoped she wasn't going to faint. 'Sit down,' he told her. 'For God's sake, sit down.'

'Martin forgot about me,' Joss said.

'He's going to be punished,' Thomas said grimly. 'He's going to be punished, I can assure you of that.'

'He gave me a ride on the bar of his new bike, though. And I did ask to go with him . . . Mum, can I have a kitten?'

'Yes,' Rosamund said, her voice gentle, but a little hoarse.

'Why don't you ask her for a tiger, man, or a lion? She's not going to refuse you anything tonight.'

A nurse came up to them, very young but reassuringly solid in her heavy black shoes. 'I'm afraid I must ask you to go,' she said. 'He must sleep or Dr Clifford won't let him out in the morning.'

Rosamund bent to kiss him. 'You got hold of a bottle of teething-drops when you were a baby and drank it all. I didn't think anything in life could be worse than that.'

'It was Mary-Louise who put me onto it,' Thomas said when they were back in the car. 'She rang to say she'll be home on the first train tomorrow, and just before she put the phone down, asked if Martin had been to feed the cats. Apparently he'd forgotten yesterday until quite late. "Don't ring off, Mary-Louise," I said. "I know nothing about him feeding any cats. Whose cats are they?" '

'She couldn't tell me much except that his friend Andrew was in Majorca with his parents and that Martin had been paid to feed the cats every day after school. She thought the cleaning woman was doing it in the morning.

' "What's all this about feeding Andrew's cats?" I asked Martin. "I've already done it," he said with that shut, sulky look which is almost permanent with him these days. But the way he spoke and immediately looked away alerted me that this was something different. "Where does Andrew live?" I asked. "Right outside the village. I don't know what the lane's called. Towards Admington." "Take me there." "When? After school tomorrow?" "Now. This minute." "Joss is there," he said.

'The only thing I can say in his defence is that he seemed relieved to be found out. I think things had gone much further than he'd intended.'

'He took Joss there on the bar of his bike?'

'Yes. He saw Joss outside Marian's house and offered him a lift.'

'How strange that no one saw them. Brian went round all the new houses.'

'Incredible, I know. Anyway he told Joss where he was going and apparently he wanted to go with him. The house is about half a mile down this lane and quite isolated – it would be, wouldn't it? Martin unlocked the back door and they went through to the kitchen where Joss discovered that one of the cats had four kittens, just old enough to climb out of the basket to play. After opening a tin of cat food and putting down some water, Martin went up to Andrew's bedroom to look at something, then wanted to leave. And according to him, Joss begged to stay a while longer, so he said he'd leave him there for a time. And – again according to him – that was the first moment he'd thought of shutting him up there. Anyway, that's what he did. Christ knows why.'

192

'To punish me,' Rosamund said sadly. 'He can't have believed you when you told him I wasn't responsible for Eliza's death. He hates me, I know. And in a way you can't blame him. I wonder how long he intended to leave Joss there? All night?'

'He won't tell me that. Perhaps he doesn't know.'

'Poor little mite. You'd think he could have got out, though. Wasn't there a phone?'

'A phone point, but they must have disconnected it and put it away. Probably thought the cleaning woman – or Martin – would use it. And the house was completely burglar-proof, everywhere double-locked. Joss finally smashed a tiny window in the pantry and tried to squeeze out. Which is how he ripped his arm open.'

'I want to be sick.'

'No, you don't. Take a deep breath. I haven't got time to stop. I've got to run Mrs Jordan home and you still have to talk to Marian and Brian.'

'I'd better come with you, hadn't I, to babysit?'

'No, they'll be all right for twenty minutes. Stephen is almost fifteen. And I don't particularly want you to have to face Martin tonight.'

'He'll probably have a harder time facing me.'

'I hope so. I hope he isn't completely without remorse. What am I going to do with him, Rosie?'

'There isn't an answer to that. He's suffering too.'

'I said I was going to take his bike away from him, but I don't suppose I will. Eliza bought it for him and it would only make him more angry and intractable. I may ask the Head to have a word with him, pointing out what might have happened. I've said enough, but hearing it from someone else could have more effect.'

'Joss could have cut an artery. Could have bled to death.'

'Anyway, he didn't. Thank heavens.'

'Thank heavens,' Rosamund echoed fervently. 'Thank heavens. Whatever that means.'

'Good night, love. Sleep well.'

'I won't sleep a wink.'

'Do you want to come home with me, then? I'll stay awake with you.'

193

'It's all right, love. I'm just being melodramatic, I suppose. Thanks, Thomas.'

'He was punishing me,' Rosamund said when she was telling Marian about Martin. 'And perhaps it was fair.'

'I'm not going to go on talking to you, dear, if you're in that silly mood. Punishment indeed! It's Martin who needs punishment, it seems to me.'

'He thinks I'm the cause of his mother's suicide.'

'His father should have put him right, then, about that.'

'He did try, but Martin is a stern judge. And, oh Mum, my conscience troubles me.'

'You were both very lonely people.'

'I know that. At the time it seemed something tender and comforting and relatively unimportant. But everything you do can have repercussions which don't bear thinking about. The only thing I remember from my O-level Science is that frightening law: Every action has an equal and opposite reaction. Too dreadful to think about.'

'Then don't think about it. Go to bed, dear, and have a good sleep. You've had a terrible ordeal – well, we all have – but it's ended happily. Brian and I will be up to see him tomorrow. And I daresay we'll buy him a few odds and ends to keep him occupied till he gets back to school. So go to bed, dear, and no more talk of a guilty conscience, I beg you.'

Rosamund was allowed to fetch Joss at ten the next morning.

He was subdued at first, trying to work out whether Martin had really intended him harm. 'He was a bit cross because 1 wanted to play with the kittens instead of coming home, but I thought he'd come back after having his tea. The kittens are so sweet, Mum, black and fluffy with blue eyes and they kept climbing right over my shoulders and down my back and peeing in my shoes. And I played with them for ages and ages. But then I started to feel hungry and I couldn't open any of the doors or windows to get out and I got rather frightened. I turned lights off and on as a signal but I don't think anyone noticed because it was still light outside. And I did worry about you waiting for me, honestly Mum, but I couldn't do anything about it. I looked all over for a phone but there wasn't one. I found biscuits and chocolate though, and a full bottle of coke, so that was all right for a while, but when it was nine o'clock I decided to break the pantry window and climb out. But I fell against a jagged piece of glass and had to get myself down to wash the blood off.'

'Oh darling, was there a lot of blood?'

'Gallons. I got a tea-cloth and put it round my arm and went to lie on the sofa to watch television, but the blood came through and made me feel sick. But after a while Thomas came, so then it was all right. I don't know why Martin was being spiteful to me except Thomas says he's spiteful to everyone since Eliza died. But it wasn't my fault, was it?'

'I don't think he meant to be spiteful to you, darling, but to me. You see, he blames me for Eliza's death.'

'I know. He thinks Eliza was jealous because you and Thomas were friends, but I think people *should* be friends with people.'

'Thomas loved Eliza very much, but she was always busy with her very important job, and didn't realise it.'

'I miss Eliza. She was cross sometimes, but sometimes she was good fun.'

'Thomas misses her too.'

'I know. Sometimes he's very sad and won't talk to anyone, not even me . . . Mum, can we go down and choose a kitten as soon as Andrew Newman comes home from holiday? Oh Mum, they growl and spit and arch their little backs pretending to be fighting. They're really fierce. Can we go on Sunday?'

'Of course, darling. We want the best one, don't we?'

'I did try to clean the blood from the sofa, Mum, but I only seemed to make it worse.'

'No more talk of blood, please, Joss. Granny's got some special stain remover. I'm sure Brian will manage to get it off.'

'Mum, wouldn't it be terrible if I'd bled to death?'

Rosamund didn't answer. Simply put her hands over her ears.

Martin came up on his bicycle after school. Rosamund watched him walking towards the door, his face clenched as a fist.

'I'm to apologise to you,' he said.

'Is that it?'

Even more curtly, 'I'm sorry.'

'Do you want to come in?'

'No. No thanks.'

'I think you should apologise to Joss too. He had to have six stitches in his arm and a night in hospital. He's in the garden.'

'Thomas only said I was to apologise to you.'

'Well, you have. Do you feel any better for it?'

'Not really.'

'You think I deserved it? All that worry? That anguish?'

'I suppose so. Yes.'

'So there's not much point in saying any more, is there? You can tell Thomas that I accepted your apology in the same spirit as you offered it.'

'I don't understand that.'

'It doesn't matter. We don't understand each other. Given time, things may improve. I hope so.'

'I'm going to leave home as soon as I'm sixteen. And that's all because of you.'

'You've got almost three years to think that over. I hope you change your mind.'

He looked at her bleakly, his eyes narrowing. 'I have to go now.'

At that moment Joss came through from the kitchen. 'Hi, Martin,' he said. 'Come and have a look at the model aircraft Granny brought me. I've got stuck on it, but I bet you could finish it. Where's Harry?'

'At home. He's coming up after tea.'

They went round the house to the garden and Rosamund, at the kitchen window, stared out at them in amazement. They were squatting down on the ground immediately immersed in their task, poring over the instruction sheet, passing pieces of balsa wood and glue to each other, as though no other world existed, as though the previous day had never happened.

# Chapter Twenty-Two

Rosamund had to postpone her plans for the weekend in London, but since the next week was the beginning of Joss's summer holiday, they were able to go on Tuesday afternoon after the stitches had been taken out.

She knew she had suffered far more than Joss. For him the ordeal had been tinged with excitement; it had been an adventure, frightening at times as adventures often are, but afterwards something to boast about. Whereas for her it had been a premonition of disaster, and try as she might, she couldn't dismiss the idea that the long, terrifying evening had been a just punishment. She had made free not only with someone's husband, but also with someone's father. She'd been able to justify it at the time, but realised that she hadn't given it enough thought.

It would have been easier to excuse if she'd been in the grip of a deep passion, but she and Thomas had become lovers almost by chance; because they were both lonely, because it had been easy to manage, because it had seemed relatively uncomplicated. She'd readily accepted that his real life was with his wife and sons; she was only a little extra, she'd known that, but had never let the idea worry her because she knew Thomas valued her as both friend and lover. But yet there were sinister consequences, an endlessly spreading network of results waiting to happen. If she hadn't felt so distressed at having to give Thomas up, would she have been so determined to find another way of life; a man, a relationship, a baby? Would meeting Daniel in the Underground have had the same impact on her? She shivered in the July sunshine, putting out her hand to touch the sunwarmed stones of the house to steady herself. Somewhere she'd taken a wrong turning, she knew it.

Though she hadn't managed to appease her conscience, she felt happier in Ingrid's company. Joss was tired after the journey, and after a late supper, settled down in his sleeping-bag without even watching the video Ingrid had brought for him.

'So you're back with Ben,' Rosamund said. 'I'm very disappointed.'

'Or perhaps he's back with me,' Ingrid murmured. 'Anyway, you knew it was on the cards.'

'So changing the locks proved an unnecessary expense?'

'Well, I think it may have impressed him. Oh Rosamund, don't try to be superior. You know what it's like.'

'I'm honestly not sure that I do. I'm honestly not sure that I could love someone who's quite so ruthless and self-centred as Ben.'

'Yes, you could. When you're in love you make all sorts of allowances. I saw this programme on Channel Four. I forget what it was called, but it was about women being absolutely saintly to the most ghastly men. It's an undeniable part of our nature, Rosamund.'

'No, it's not. That's Victorian thinking. Women had to be forgiving and saintly then, because they hadn't the means or the independence to fight back. Anyway, you promised me you'd find someone else in Italy.'

'I did. And he was absolutely gorgeous. Francesco. About twenty-five, very handsome, very ardent. But after a couple of days I found out he'd got a gorgeous wife who was about nineteen and a gorgeous baby as well. So when I arrived back here, Ben seemed relatively straightforward, fairly decent. And he came to Erica's the first day I was there and was so helpful. He gave me all the notes he'd made and promised to edit the finished typescript with me as well.'

'What's he hoping to get out of it?'

'He said he realised what a bastard he'd been and wanted to make up for it. And he has made up for it, Rosamund . . . Oh

198

Rosamund, I'm pregnant and we're getting married next month.'

Rosamund sat back in her chair, trying to appear calm. 'You said you didn't want a baby,' she said at last. 'Oh God, it was me that wanted a baby, not you.'

'I know. Life's crap, isn't it? All I ever wanted was a career. But all the same, I do seem to be extraordinarily happy. My bloody hormones, I suppose. I keep on making little trips to Mothercare to look at first-size vests. Ben's the same. And Erica. Erica's going to be godmother. She's never been a godmother. We keep on making lists of names . . . You must give Ben another chance, you know, Rosie. You saw him at his worst. He was really horrible when you were here, but it was partly my fault. I was so furious with him that morning that I told him you and I had been lovers. And he was jealous as hell.'

Rosamund sighed again. 'That's all very well, but why had he stayed out all night, until after three, when he was supposed to be back for a meal?'

'I forgot to ask him that. But since I've forgiven him, I think it's only fair that you should too.'

'I suppose I'll have to, otherwise I probably won't get to see the baby. And I love babies.'

It was Ingrid's turn to sigh. 'I only hope I shall. Ben wants three . . . How's Daniel?'

'I'm seeing him tomorrow. He's still sweating it out at the clinic, which is something, I suppose. I mean, it shows he's serious about getting free of heroin, but I've no idea how serious he is about me. He may come to live with me – I mean, may come to share my house – but I doubt if it'll turn out to be much more. He was in love with me for about half an hour when we met in the tube, but since then he's become more and more distant. When I phone him, he says how grateful he feels towards me, but no more than that. I don't know what will happen.'

'Do you still feel the same about him?'

There was a long silence. 'I don't know what I feel about anything,' she said at last. 'It's been a strange episode altogether. My life seems to have changed completely since

199

you came up to do that article and told me about Erica's poems. Do you think the book will make it all worthwhile? All the upheaval?'

'Well, Erica is certainly enjoying it and that's something. She's getting a chance to relive her great days – and getting a lot of attention from her publishers too. And she was due for some compensation, wasn't she? She seems to have suffered enough, losing her baby, losing Anthony and so on. But to be absolutely honest, Ben doesn't think the poems are going to make much of an impact. They'll create a stir for a few weeks, then the shock-waves will die out and everyone will realise that a great poet's erotic poems are not so very different from anyone else's.'

'When I read them I thought they were pretty wonderful.'

'They're good, of course, but trivial compared to his serious body of work.'

'That's according to Ben.'

'And I agree with him.'

'I'm not so sure. I'd certainly feel very proud if even one of them had been written to me. I used to beg Anthony for a poem, but I never got one. A little verse occasionally to make me laugh, but that was all.'

'You're feeling sorry for yourself, aren't you?'

'Not really. I'm worried about a great many things, but I don't think self-pity comes into it. As a matter of fact I've had quite a burst of confidence about my work. I've started on something different and I'm excited about it. Your coming to see me had a lot to do with that, too, because it made me assess where I was at. And suddenly I found myself doing something different, something better.'

'Oh, Rosie, I'm so pleased. Did you see my article, by the way?'

'Yes, you did me proud. Thanks. As a result of your article, Ingrid, I now have nine large paintings in the dining room of the pub in the village. How's that for fame?'

'Ben and I must come to see them. We'll take you out to dinner and sit there surrounded by beauty.'

They smiled at each other.

'I thought I might do a pastel of Erica tomorrow. A three-quarter profile against the crimson walls of her sitting room, with those huge copper earrings that make her look so primitive and powerful. What do you think? And if it's any good, I thought it might make a jacket for the book. What's it to be called?'

'We can't decide. The publishers want *Mistress and Muse*, but Ben thinks it should simply be *Erica*.'

'I think *The Reckoning* would be a good title. One of Anthony's best poems and written at the end of their relationship. It's been on my mind a great deal lately.

> *The dread of winter's dawn,*
> *The sour light and the keening wind*
> *The hand on the shoulder.'*

'Why should that have been on your mind? What hand on the shoulder are you dreading?'

'Conscience, I suppose. Guilt.'

'Oh, don't start on that again. It wasn't your fault. Now, I have a very comfortable little theory about guilt: the man is always to blame. Keep that in mind.'

'I don't think that's true about Thomas, though. But anyway, I feel Erica should have the final say about the title. I'll ask her when I see her tomorrow afternoon. I've got to take Joss to see Molly in the morning – think of me – but I'll meet you at Erica's afterwards.'

'No, I'm taking a couple of days off. I'm very sick in the morning and dead tired in the afternoon.'

'And hungry and bad-tempered in the evening. Oh Ingrid, you are lucky. I do envy you. And it was me who wanted a baby, not you.'

Molly's bed was covered by a white open-work linen bedspread and her pillowslips were bordered with lace. She had her eyes tightly closed. She looked old, frail and ill, but not too ill, Rosamund was pleased to note, for discreetly applied make-up and carefully arranged upswept hair.

'Is this my grandmother?' Joss asked, wonder in his voice. He'd obviously expected his new grandmother to be another version of Marian, youthful and slim and eager to entertain him. This one was even older than Granny Woodison and had the same bossy face.

'Ssh! We'll wait till she wakes up. You sit there by the bed and I'll sit at the window.'

Joss made an effort to whisper. 'How long are we going to wait? I think I'd rather be watching *Holiday Roundabout*.'

'She's looking forward to seeing you, Joss.'

Another tremendous whisper, 'She's left it a jolly long time.'

Before Rosamund could reply, Lorna Drew came nudging into the room carrying a large oval tray. 'Wake up, Molly,' she said in a loud, cheerful voice. 'You asked Mrs Gilchrist to bring her son to see you and here he is.'

She put the tray down on the bedside table and smiled, first at Rosamund then at Joss. See how well I deal with this difficult old lady, her smile seemed to say.

Molly opened her eyes as Lorna helped her up to a sitting position. 'I wasn't asleep,' she said.

'Oh good,' Joss said. 'I hoped you weren't going to sleep all through our visit. Would you like to see my wounds?'

Without waiting for a reply, he thrust the inside of his arm to a position a few inches from her eyes and breathed at her. 'I had to have six stitches. Dr Clifford said I was *fairly* brave. Well, it was my first time in hospital and the smell wasn't very nice.'

Lorna Drew poured out a coffee for Rosamund and took it over to her. 'Would you like milk or barley water?' she asked Joss.

'Coke, please. But if you haven't any, I'll have coffee and biscuits. What are you having, Grandmother?'

'I'll have coffee, too.'

'My grandmother will have coffee,' he told Lorna.

'I'm your Aunt Lorna,' she said, unwilling that Joss should take her for a nurse or an attendant. She squared her shoulders and smiled at him in a proprietary way.

'You're not his aunt. You're his second cousin once removed.'

Lorna seemed to shrink. 'His father always called me Aunt Lorna.'

'I think I shall call you Great-Aunt Lorna because I haven't

202

a great-aunt and Harry's got a Great-Aunt Priscilla. Harry is my best friend, Grandmother. It was his brother, Martin, who locked me into the house I had to break out of. When you come to stay with us you'll meet them. There's also Stephen, Jim and Thomas.'

'I'm not very likely to visit you, Joshua, I'm afraid.'

'Why not? I expect you think you're too old, but I bet you're not so old as Dorcas Armitage who Granny takes meals-on-wheels to. She's ninety-nine. How old are you, Grandmother?'

'I don't discuss my age with anyone except my doctor.'

'Why is that? I'm exactly ten years one month and nine days. I expect you didn't know it was my birthday last month? – June the tenth. Quite an easy date to remember . . . Isn't my father here? When is his birthday, by the way?'

'Your father will be visiting you very soon.'

'Have you got a photograph of him? I expect he's quite old, too. This is very good coffee, Great-Aunt Lorna. Nicer than the one we have. We have instant, you know. Mum, aren't you having one of these biscuits? They're rather interesting. A bit like eating sugary spiders' webs.'

Joss couldn't help noticing the way his grandmother was ignoring Rosamund and made a bid to rectify it. 'Grandmother, do you like the way my mother has her hair? Her friend, Ingrid, has been telling her to have a fringe and a bob, but I like it long and mussed-up. What do you think?'

Molly turned her head and fixed Rosamund with a steely glance. 'It's very nice either way,' she told Joss, her voice revealing a massive indifference.

'I think we ought to go now. Your grandmother is tired,' Rosamund said.

Joss sprang to his feet. 'I do hope you'll be better soon, Grandmother,' he said. 'And I really don't think you're too old to visit us. And if you do, I'll make you a meal in my microwave. You too, Great-Aunt Lorna. And you can see my new mountain bike and my four-man tent. And I'm soon having a black kitten, by the way.'

'This is for you. And this is for your mother,' Molly told him, handing him two thick white envelopes. 'I'm very pleased to have met you.' She turned to Rosamund, giving her another long, cool look. 'Thank you for bringing him to visit me,' she murmured, before lying back on her pillows and closing her eyes again.

'No kiss for me?' Lorna asked Joss at the front door. She was herself again; put-upon but forgiving, oppressed but unbowed.

He shot out his hand. 'Goodbye, Great-Aunt. Thank you for the coffee.'

'Mrs Gilchrist is not seriously ill, is she?' Rosamund asked.

Lorna Drew shrugged her large capable shoulders. 'Who knows! She certainly doesn't like losing a battle.'

'Shall we open our letters?' Joss asked his mother some time later when they were sitting in the tube. They'd hardly spoken on their long walk to the station.

'Yes, I suppose we'd better. Though I don't think mine is going to be very pleasant.'

'What's this?' Joss asked, handing her a large sheet of thick paper.

'It's a family tree. Look, *Anthony Gilchrist m. Marjorie Spencer* at the top. That means Anthony married Marjorie, your grandmother, who's called Molly. And the vertical line from them leads to Alexander, who is Alex, their son and your father. And he married Selena Jennings and on the next line are their children, Jeremy and Harriet, who are your half-brother and sister. And the broken line from Alexander leads to you, Joshua.'

'What a lot of new relations. A grandmother, a great-aunt, a father and a half-brother and sister.' He had another look inside the envelope. 'No fiver, though. I was expecting at least a fiver. Mum, what would we do if Grandmother left us a million pounds?'

Rosamund opened her letter. A thick white envelope lined with green tissue, one large sheet of paper. A message which looked as though it was written in Indian ink. '*For Joshua's sake, I forgive you. M.J. Gilchrist.*' She stared at it for a long time.

They had lunch with her father and Dora. A lovely summer

lunch; cold salmon with avocado mousse and a salad of oranges, watercress and black olives. ('Please may I have some tomato ketchup?' Joss asked.)

In the afternoon Paul and Dora had volunteered to take Joss to see the fire-eaters in Covent Garden while Rosamund visited Erica.

'I'm still sorry you opted out of the book,' Dora said. 'You'd have had such sympathy. You'd have done it marvellously, darling.'

'All the same, I think Ingrid's getting on very well. Erica has found all the details she needs, dates and so on, and her memory is wonderful. She could have been a writer herself, she brings scenes to life so vividly. When I was with her last she told me about a country wedding she and Anthony had been to forty years ago. And I've thought about it ever since.'

'Oh, darling,' Dora said when Joss had gone to watch television. 'I do hope you'll find Daniel improved. Apparently there's a very good success rate. Once a person is determined to give it up, a cure is definitely on the cards.'

'All the same, forty per cent of those cured have a relapse,' Paul said. 'Let's not get carried away.'

'Paul, you're such a pessimist.'

'Anyway, people aren't getting married these days. And Rosamund's surely old enough to be over wedding fever.'

'She's exactly the same age as I was when I married you. And I don't remember hearing you say that to me. You certainly seemed as feverish as I was.'

'I can't help thinking that you were very, very lucky,' Paul said.

Erica looked almost as old and ill as Molly. Ingrid had talked of her being happy and in high spirits, so that Rosamund had expected to find her rejuvenated, but she was melancholy and in pain.

'It's come too late,' she said, 'my little share of fame and fortune. If I make it to next winter, I'll be in a nursing home, not a hotel in Florida.'

'Everybody is entitled to bad days,' Rosamund replied. 'I

205

was terribly depressed a few days ago, but now I'm ready for more. You'll be better again when Ingrid's back.'

'She's a good, cheerful girl, but she can't work miracles. I've got a weak heart and crippling arthritis, and today I'm suffering from both.'

'Don't you have anything to take?'

'Of course I have something to take. Like all healthy people you think pills and potions cure you. But all they do is confuse you and postpone your suffering.' She sat up straighter in her chair. 'Tell me about Anthony's death,' she said.

Rosamund swallowed hard. It was the last thing she'd expected. She struggled to keep her voice steady. 'He was ill for almost six months. Joss was still a baby and my mother came to look after him so that I could nurse Anthony at home. He hated hospitals, as you probably remember.'

'Did he talk about me?' Erica's voice trembled.

Rosamund paused, but decided on the truth. 'Often when he was well, but not during his illness. At the end he talked only about his childhood, about his parents and his nanny. Sometimes he didn't seem to know who I was. He'd smile very sweetly at me from time to time, but I don't think he recognised me. I'd hold his hand and stroke it and he'd look at me kindly but quite blankly.'

'I've been thinking so much about him lately.'

Rosamund thought about him too; the bony, intelligent face, sharp blue eyes, slow sensuous smile, his kindness. And some other characteristic too; something childlike and dangerous. 'Writing the book has brought him back to you,' she said.

'Yes. And I've been wondering again whether these poems he wrote for me will harm his reputation.'

'They won't, Erica. He wanted them published after twenty years. All we're doing is bringing that forward. Even Molly seems reconciled to it by this time.'

'All the same, I've decided to postpone publication until the date he suggested. I've had my say, recalled my small part in his life, even mentioning that terrible abortion that shattered both of us. And in due course you can have it published. Ingrid and Ben will be disappointed by the delay; they've worked hard on it, but I've been able to leave their baby a little something in my will. Anyway, that's my decision. The book – and his poems – will remain in the publishers' hands until the time he mentioned.'

Rosamund realised that her mind was quite made up, that she intended to forgo the ready money and the longed-for luxuries which she'd surely deserved. 'What will survive of us is love,' she said softly.

On the way back in the tube, she still felt awed by Erica's love and forgiveness. Anthony's love had wavered after the trauma of the abortion, Molly's had never been much more than pride and possessiveness, but Erica seemed to have asked nothing and given everything. In the crush of people around her, Rosamund felt she was celebrating something rich and rare.

'You'll never guess what happened at Erica's,' she said when she got back to Dora and Paul's flat.

'You'll never guess what happened here,' countered Dora.

'Alex,' Joss said. 'Alex came.'

Rosamund and Dora stared at each other carefully, their eyes expressionless. 'My father,' Joss explained, disappointed at Rosamund's lack of response. 'He was very nice, a bit old, but very nice. He's coming again when I'm sixteen, but till then he's not too sure about visiting because he's got to be in France a lot of the time. He said to give you his best wishes.'

Rosamund remained silent, so Joss turned back to his chess game with Paul, casting off a father as readily as he'd taken on a grandmother and a great-aunt.

Dora led Rosamund into the kitchen. 'He phoned to ask if he could call. I told him you wouldn't be here and he said that might be for the best.'

'Lorna asked for your telephone number this morning. I wondered why she wanted it.'

'He was very apologetic about letting his mother blackmail you, but says he's completely in her power. He looked really old and sad; told us he'd had a nervous breakdown and lost his job. Nicely dressed, but with that sort of sloping figure you see on shuffling old men. There was something about him which made me feel very uneasy, perhaps because of what you'd told me about him. Oh Rosamund, I hope you don't mind that I let him come here without consulting you. He didn't have any time alone with Joss – in fact, didn't seem to want it. I chatted to him for a while, babbled on about nothing, you know how I do, and then gave him a cup of tea and a piece of chocolate cake. But Paul was rather rude to him, I'm afraid.'

# Chapter Twenty-Three

Afterwards Rosamund remembered how apprehensive she'd felt before seeing Daniel that morning. She'd phoned the clinic the previous night but the nurse on duty had failed to bring him to the phone, which had often happened at the beginning of his stay, but not during the last two or three weeks. In itself that seemed a small thing; it was indeed possible that he'd gone for a stroll in the grounds as the nurse had suggested, but without the reassurance that he was coping with the treatment, that he was looking forward to seeing her, she felt a surge of unease which led to a restless night full of short, tormented dreams in which both Joss and Daniel seemed lost to her. By six o'clock she was sitting up in bed, determined not to fall asleep again and longing to hear the first sounds of Dora getting up for work.

She hadn't seen Daniel for almost six weeks. The doctor in charge had advised her not to visit him nor to phone more than once a week, insisting that he had to go through it on his own, that she could do nothing for him – indeed, might hinder his progress. But she was now afraid he might think she'd purposely neglected him during those long, painful, empty days.

She got up as soon as she heard Dora leave the flat. By that time the heat was already intense, the sky a blinding blue. She had a shower and washed her hair, and after much indecision, wore a new white dress, short and simple, and white sandals.

'You look like a bride,' Joss told her when she came into the kitchen where he was already having breakfast.

'No, you don't,' Paul said, seeing the startled look in her eyes. 'You look quite ordinary. Someone off to play tennis or to the gymnasium.'

She smiled at both of them, hurried over her scalding coffee and left the flat before either of them could think of any other pleasantries.

Buses and tubes were stufty and crowded, and the half-mile walk to the clinic seemed endless; walking on hot, dusty city streets was very different from walking along tree-shaded country roads. Her head ached from tension and lack of sleep and the back of her eyes smarted. Two months ago she'd been eager to move to London, but now, whatever came of the meeting with Daniel, she realised she'd be very reluctant to leave the schoolhouse. She found herself sighing. What was the matter with her? Was it some premonition of disaster? Was she going to find that Daniel had had a relapse? Some serious illness? She sighed again; she couldn't seem to pull herself together.

She tried to turn her thoughts to Erica; her unwavering loyalty to a man who had been unable to respond to her when she'd really needed him. 'My valiant heart' he'd called her in one of his last poems. And Erica was still valiant. The image of her disordered kitchen came to her; she was clearly not capable of managing alone any longer, but when she'd suggested that someone might come to live with her, she'd been adamantly against the idea, preferring discomfort, pain, danger, to the loss of dignity. Courage, it seemed to Rosamund, was the chiefest virtue. Courage, she told herself. She had the strongest feeling that she was going to need it.

The Cedars had once been a stately Edwardian residence, set in splendid isolation, but overlooking the main road to London. She could imagine a rich city gentleman with his family and retainers moving into the newly-built mansion with all its most modern features. Now though, it was very definitely a clinic or nursing home, far too big and impractical for even the richest family. It had white walls and a green-tiled roof, large curving windows, a round conservatory on one side and a turret on the other. Rosamund walked up the drive, her heart beating painfully against her ribs. She certainly wasn't expecting any fairy-tale ending. 'If he's well, or even fairly well, I won't ask anything more,' she told herself. The black and white tiles of the porch were suddenly making a kaleidoscope of patterns in her head. It was the hottest day of the hot summer. She hoped she wasn't going to faint.

The nurse who answered the bell was the one she'd met when she and Daniel had arrived. 'He's doing very well,' she said, smiling carefully. 'I'll take you to his room. He's with the psychologist at the moment but he'll be finished by eleven.' She opened the door of a light, pleasant room on the first floor, a large semi-circular window in one corner, a tiny kitchen annexe in the other. 'Help yourself to tea or coffee. There's milk in the fridge and possibly some biscuits in that tin.'

'Thank you.'

'He's doing very well,' the nurse repeated with the same closed expression.

Rosamund went to stand by the window and opened it wide, looking out at the large sloping garden and further away the sprawl of Richmond and Sheen. Had she imagined the embarrassed edge to the nurse's words? 'He's doing very well, but . . .'

'I'm not expecting a miracle,' she told herself.

As she turned from the window, she caught sight of some drawings on the table. He's drawing again, she thought. That's wonderful. He'd told her he'd done no work for almost a year. And now he'd started drawing again. Just as she had.

She moved over to the table. The drawings were exquisite, that was her first reaction. The second was surprise, even shock; they were all nude studies of Marie. Not a titillating Venus, though, but a sad little Magdalene. Beautiful. She looked at them with awe.

'Darling,' Daniel said a few minutes later. 'How lovely to see you.' He came over and hugged her, holding her close for a moment or two.

'Lovely to see *you*. You look marvellous, much younger. How do you feel?'

'Pretty grim, to tell you the truth. It's awful not to be able to shut things off. To have to face everything again. All of it. Life.'

'Is it so bad?'

'It's hell. But I'm sticking it out now. And so grateful to you that I'm able to. She needs me so much, Rosie.'

Rosamund felt as though she was tapping about her with a white stick. 'Marie?' she asked.

'Edmund didn't even turn up for the funeral. He must have known about it. Everyone knew. Everyone was on the lookout for him.'

'The funeral?' But even before she'd asked the question she knew the answer. 'Theodore,' she said, her voice trembling.

She sat on a chair, putting her hands over her heart to steady it. She felt a pain spreading through her chest. Some weeks before she'd dreamed she was being shot by a firing squad; it seemed the same sensation of burning heat.

'I wrote to you,' Daniel said. 'I thought you might have come. I was hoping you'd come. There was only her and me and her mother.'

It was then she started to cry; huge painful sobs raking through her chest. 'Theodore,' she said again, remembering too vividly his blue-veined eyelids, his careworn face, his little clawing hands.

'I didn't get a letter. I haven't had any letter from you. I would have come, of course. Oh God. Oh poor, poor Marie. Oh God.'

'You mustn't take it quite so badly, Rosamund. They discovered he had a congenital heart disease and it got worse very rapidly. He was in hospital for two days and then just stopped breathing. He had every care.'

Rosamund cried until she was weak from crying, her eyes red and swollen, her throat burning. 'Were you with her?' she asked at last.

'No, but she came here afterwards and they let her stay with me till the funeral. And she's got no one else, Rosamund, no one to look after her, so I'll have to be with her for a while. You understand, don't you?'

'Of course.' Rosamund struggled to accept the implication of what he was telling her; the full implication.

212

'And not just to be kind to her. But because I'm . . . because I'm . . . I'm very fond of her, Rosamund, feel right with her somehow, feel we belong together.'

'Yes. Yes, I see. I understand . . . Where will you live?'

'At Eversley Place until I can find something better. I'm going to start painting again. I think I'll be able to now.'

'I'm sure you will.' Rosamund dragged air into her lungs like someone rescued from drowning. 'I'm sure you will. You have enormous talent, Daniel.' Talking about work seemed strangely comforting. 'I've been doing some figure-drawing myself, a new direction for me, and I thought mine were pretty good till I saw yours. Yours are superb. No, I'm not just being kind. If someone had shown me this and told me it was a Modigliani, I'd have been quite ready to believe it. It's so delicate, the line so precise, so true.'

'That's the best I've done for a long time. I'd like you to have that one, Rosamund.'

'I'd love it. Thank you. I'll treasure it. And now, I'm sure you know what I'm going to say. Please go on working, Daniel. Please try to face life now, however hard it is.'

'I'll try. After all, you may not be around to rescue me a second time.'

They were silent for a moment or two, each aware of the other's pain.

'You and Marie must visit me,' Rosamund said at last.

'I'd like that. I'd like to see your work.'

'I've got nothing worth showing you at the moment. All the same, I've restarted after a long sterile period, and that's something. But I suppose I only carry on because I've got no other talent, no other commitment. Oh, I'll probably manage to exhibit here and there, sell a few things and become, you know, a jobbing artist.'

'That's all any of us can hope for.'

Rosamund turned on him angrily. 'Don't patronise me. You and I are not in the same league, never have been, and you know it. You'll become an important artist, Daniel Hawkins, and I'll boast about having known you.'

'In six months' time I may be a junkie again.'

'No, you won't. You'll have Marie to think about now. A life to build.'

213

'If I ever do make anything of my life, I'll owe it to you.'

'What I did was for my own rotten ends. Because I wanted you.'

'Did you? Why?'

Rosamund's chest heaved once more. 'Why? Because of what you meant to me, of course.'

'Fifteen years ago?'

She sniffed and blew her nose. 'If you prefer it that way.'

'Oh Rosamund, am I letting you down? Are you very disappointed about what's happened? Will you be unhappy?'

'I don't know. I honestly don't know. I'm so terribly unhappy about Theodore, I can't feel much more than that at the moment. But I'll try to be happy about you because I care about you. I truly care.'

'Please don't cry again.'

'I'm trying not to.'

But after the hard bitter sobbing, the tears now slipping down her face and neck seemed soothing, almost a balm. 'Make me a cup of tea,' she said at last.

'Of course.'

They sat side by side at the little table, Rosamund still holding her drawing. 'I'm wondering if Marie posted the letter,' Daniel said. 'Perhaps she didn't want you at the funeral, worried that you'd come between us. She's very unsure of herself.'

'I suppose she is. But in another way she's very . . . gallant. I liked her a lot, admired her a lot.'

'She's twenty years younger than I am, but she looked after me for months. Even while Edmund was around, I seemed her first priority.'

'"He's a super bloke and you must take him as you find him." That's what she told me about you. I've thought of that so many times.'

'Please don't cry.'

'Joss couldn't say *cry* when he was little. He used to say *fry*. And when I'd say, "Don't cry," he'd say, "I'm not frying," and used to get angry because it always made me smile.'

'There! It's almost made you smile again.'

Rosamund thought of the long terrible evening when Joss had disappeared. His safety had been the only thing she'd

214

cared about. Joss was safe. She suddenly needed to see him again. To take him home. She got to her feet.

'If I ever manage to sell some decent paintings, I'll repay you,' Daniel said. 'I'll never forget how good you've been to me. It was a huge outlay.'

'Money! It wasn't even mine, it was my late husband's. Take it as a gift from him. He'd have liked you to have it. When are you leaving this place?'

'My six weeks aren't up till Saturday, but I've decided to go today. Two days early. I've seen various people and they think I've done well.'

'You have.'

'We'll see. I can't promise anything.'

They held each other tightly for another moment and then Rosamund left, walking down the gracious staircase, through the wide-open front door onto the carefully manicured lawns. Her face was red and blotchy, dry as leather in the hot sun.

On the way home in the train Joss wondered about becoming an actor like Paul rather than a poet like Anthony, wanted to know which was likely to be more lucrative.

'Some actors make a great deal of money,' Rosamund said, 'but most make next to nothing. And most poets have to take another job to make ends meet.'

'Really? I think I may be a doctor then. Dr Clifford was really cool and seemed to be in charge and I like being in charge. Also, he has a dark green Mercedes and Paul has rather an old Renault Five. You're not listening to me, Mum, are you? Don't you like the idea of me being a doctor? Don't you like Dr Clifford? Why didn't we stay to see Dora? I didn't say goodbye to Dora before she went to work. Why did you decide to come back this afternoon? I thought we were going to see Ingrid again tomorrow. I was going to watch that video she brought me . . . Mum?'

'Joss, I've got a headache, love.'

'Is that why your eyes are funny? Is that why you're wearing sun-glasses?'

'I had rather a disappointing morning,' Rosamund said half an hour later when they'd almost reached Admington station.

215

'Daniel doesn't think he can come to stay with us after all. He has other plans, it seems.'

Joss was quiet for a minute or two. 'We don't seem to be very lucky, do we?' he said then. 'Alex too busy to come to see me, and now Daniel has other plans. Never mind, Mum, we're all right as we are, aren't we?'

'Don't try to comfort me, Thomas. I feel really desolate. Oh, he was such a sad, sickly little baby. I even had this dream that he was dying. A dreadful nightmare that I'd stolen him away in a taxi and could see him dying in my arms. And even after that I neglected him. I've only written to Marie once since I've been back and I meant to send her at least a little money every week. I feel hideously guilty.'

'Come on. I can understand it must be hell to have to accept a baby's death, but this is self-pity. You helped all you could when you were there, bought things for him, nursed him. You bought him a buggy, I remember.'

'A really shabby, second-hand one. Oh, I should have kept in touch with her, gone to see her from time to time. Her health visitor said it would be a great help.'

'Of course it would. Every poor young mother in her position could do with some help – a lot of help. But you had problems of your own and you can't expect to be able to help everyone. Oh, it's very easy to indulge in an orgy of recriminations. That's what I did: if only I'd done this, hadn't done that. But finally you'll have to accept, as I did, that the worst has happened and that all you can do is try to pick up the pieces. God, Rosamund, if Daniel is able to help Marie, even on a temporary basis, that's all due to you. He certainly wouldn't have been any help to her in the state he was in when you met him. And how much did it cost you to get him into that rehab place?'

'I did that for *me* though, Thomas. I can't count that. I didn't know Marie was going to benefit from it, did I?'

'Well, that's what happened.'

'Yes, that's what happened,' Rosamund agreed, rather grimly.

Thomas flinched. 'Of course I realise you must be very upset about Daniel, too. You told me how much he meant to you. How much he'd meant to you ever since college.'

'When we met again, it all came back, all that violent adolescent love. But I don't know, lately it seemed more and more like a dream. All the same, something is missing now.'

'Of course it is. I understand that.'

'I do feel an ache in my heart. Or somewhere.'

They looked at each other sadly.

'Try not to blame yourself,' Thomas continued. 'You did everything you could. You didn't back out when you found he was on heroin. Most people would have. You helped and encouraged him and then managed to get him into a clinic. That was a great achievement . . and whatever you say, it must have cost you a packet.'

'Let's just say that Joss and I won't be able to have a holiday in Tuscany this year. Or anywhere else.'

There was a brief pause.

'You can come caravanning with us. We'd love to have you. And Joss's tent as well. So much better than ours.'

'With Mary-Louise?'

'And her boyfriend. Why not? Plenty of room. The four lads could sleep in the tent, Mary-Louise and Oliver could have the double bed in the bedroom and you and I could have the single beds in the living room.'

'With Jim?'

'With Jim. Yes. He's got to be somewhere, poor lamb.'

'I don't think so, Thomas. To be quite honest, I can't think of anything much worse. Peeling potatoes for hours every day.'

'Mary-Louise is going to do the cooking.'

'I bet she is! No, it would be me doing the cooking and looking after Jim, you taking the boys to adventure playgrounds and water racing and rock climbing, while Mary-Louise and her boyfriend lie about in the sun being young and carefree.'

'Apart from all that, mightn't it be rather nice? Sunsets and so on?'

'I don't think so, Thomas, thank you.'

'Think about it, love. It might be OK.'

She thought about it. There was a sudden dazzle in her eyes, tears or love; possibly a little of each. 'Perhaps next year,' she said. 'When Mary-Louise has left, there'll be more room in the caravan.'

She met his eyes. 'And perhaps next year, Stephen and Martin will have begun to forgive me and I'll have begun to forgive myself.' Tears sprang to her eyes again and when Thomas came over to her and held her, she relaxed against him. 'Perhaps next year,' she said softly.